WHY DO HUMANS WORSHIP GODS?

Library of Congress Control Number:		2021917153
ISBN:	Hardcover	978-1-6641-9071-9
	Softcover	978-1-6641-9070-2
	eBook	978-1-6641-9069-6

Print information available on the last page.

Rev. date: 09/08/2021

To order additional copies of this book, contact:
Xlibris
844-714-8691
www.Xlibris.com
Orders@Xlibris.com
831916

CONTENTS

FREE PREVIEW

Religion has been the arbiter that has defined our perception of everything in the universe ever since humans acquired the ability to think. This was necessarily so because our ability to prove, or at least to logically rationalize what we imagined, was still infantile. Science was not in existence at that time. Our primordial minds imagined that everything happened because a god commanded it to happen, and that the gods had the mental and physical attributes of human beings, but were infinitely more powerful. Then science gradually made its way into the human experience and found that there is a natural law that governs the existence of everything. The only problem is that this natural law is completely neutral to human sensibilities, it does not respond to what humans wish or pray for.

This primordial mindset is static, it does not change as new knowledge is acquired. Because of this mindset, the Roman Catholic Church, which was the de facto ruler of what used to be the Roman Empire, convicted Galileo Galilei, and sentenced him to house arrest for the rest of his life for daring to write that the Earth is not the center of the universe. This same mindset is denying Darwinian evolution and is impeding research into the mutation and treatment of pathogens. This same mindset is denying that human activities are increasing the average temperature of the earth which is causing devastating climate changes. This mindset is generally anti-science because the proponents are generally pro-religion.

To contemplate what role God plays in this scheme of things, one will first have to define his or her concept of God. Some people believe that God is an anthropomorphic being, that is, God has human attributes, even though these attributes are infinitely more powerful than the human attributes. It is believed that he can listen to and empathize with our prayers and other individual emotional situations. It is believed that he can punish us for doing something wrong or reward us for doing something right. Bear in mind that "right and wrong" is an arbitrary concept. What is right in one culture may not be right in another culture. This mindset empowers some group of people to fight and kill in the name of religion, and to believe that it is justifiable to commit atrocities and claim that they are doing it in the name of God.

It is scary for anyone to be subservient to the doctrine of a deity that can only be experienced by blind faith in what an ancient guru postulated, or an ancient Pope decreed; where people believe something even though it is totally illogical, just because an old guru or an old pope said so; where the only backup one has to determine what is true from what is fake is his or her own imperfect mind. It is obvious to any free thinker that this failure to logically evaluate situations makes it easier for despots, cult leaders, and conspiracy theorists to control our lives.

On the other hand, there are those who believe strongly that God (or whatever you name your divine deity) is one and the same as Mother Nature, that there are natural, physical, not supernatural, forces that cause rain to fall or flowers to bloom, lightning to flash and thunder to blast, that cause people to get sick and die or recover from illness. They may believe strongly that these forces are the forces that dictate the laws of physics and chemistry. They know that they are yet to learn what these mysterious forces are. They know that they are yet to understand what caused life to happen, but they also know that to imagine how it happened and then assume that what they imagine is reality, is borderline insanity. They believe that love and hate, bigotry and tolerance, passion and passivity, anger and happiness are the consequences of their actions, their culture, and their genetics, not a curse or blessing from God.

identified that are said to cause this predestination to worship a god.

It is quite logical to believe that humans and other animals have evolved a behavioral mechanism, whereby the members of each species bond together for mutual coexistence and protection, and this bonding evolved into a clan-and-clan-leader syndrome. It is less logical to believe that God endows humans with a gene or genes to ensure that humans worship other gods other than himself. Assuming that there is only one universal god, why would he allow such a diversification of religious beliefs and practices, instead of a universal belief that personifies and favors him? It is hard to make the case that humans are exercising the right that God gives them to act on their own free will since this is forbidden by God himself in his Commandments: "Thou shalt have no other gods before Me." This is the word of God, decreed in his Commandments. If he is the God of the entire universe, this commandment has to be accepted as a universal decree to all mankind. Logic dictates that this decree cannot exist along with the idea that God gives humans the freedom to do as they please. It is like God saying, "Thou shalt have no other god besides me, but you can worship any other god if you so desire."

Given that diverse religious beliefs and practices have caused more grief, death, and destruction than any other factor in the human experience, how can anyone logically conclude that this human attribute to worship a god, with all its randomness, is a mandate from God? Even though God mandates in his Commandments that humans shall worship no other god, every culture has their own form of religion with their own form of god. It is claimed that God gives humans the ability and the option to choose whatever they want to do, even if it means death and destruction to others. Ask how they know that this is a concession from God, and you will get a litany of evasive answers.

A study of religious practices in the Western culture will reveal an ambivalent attitude of believers toward religion. We believe, we pray, we preach, that God is our supreme protector, provider, deliverer, healer, comforter, and friend, yet in practice, all this protection from God is largely illusionary. It cannot be demonstrated in any controlled and verifiable way that these claims are authentic. Controlled studies and peer reviews to demonstrate the veracity of these claims are not done, mainly because it would reveal that these claims are not verifiable. The supposed authenticity has to be accepted by faith, no verifiable review by any independent observer. The claims are mainly based on unverified personal experiences that may appear real to the person involved but in the real world may be just an illusion. Because the human species has evolved to be or was created to be so much more intellectually astute than other living beings, we owe it to ourselves and to future generations to fact-check, double-check, and double-blind-check the belief systems and ideologies that we indulge in.

It is inevitable that humans are motivated to pray for guidance and assistance from a higher power when we feel the need to do so. Gratitude and empathy will manifest themselves spontaneously even when we try to hide these emotions. Usually, these expressions are beyond the control of human beings. Added to this is the innate tendency to commune with other members of our clan to reassure and support one another. Given all this interplay of emotions, it is not surprising that prayers and other religious rituals have become an integral part of our society. Prayers and religion on a whole help manifest that so-called god gene in human beings to commune with one another and call upon a higher power for protection and solace.

What has also become a part of our social behavior is the tendency to believe that God can and will answer prayers that we ask of him. Even if it is obvious that our prayers were not answered, we convince ourselves that they were answered, but we were just not able to understand God's inexplicable methods of operation. "God works in mysterious ways," we say.

The following story illustrates this phenomenon.

Way back when, in the days of the cold war between the United States and the Soviet Union, I read an article in the *Reader's Digest* about the Soviet authorities' effort to wean children from Christianity and brainwash them into atheism. Here, I will try to recall the essence of that article. Normally, in the Russian schools, students were provided with lunch every day. One particular day the teachers told the students that the school would not provide lunch that day; if they pray to God and ask him to provide lunch, he will deliver it to them. When the students got hungry and sad, the teachers came back and told them, "We have some good news for you: God will provide lunch for you all. All you have to do is pray." The students were skeptical. They were still hungry and depressed, no trace of that juvenile bliss on their faces. The teachers further told them, "All you have to do is close your eyes tight for ten minutes, make sure you do not peep, pray to God, and he will deliver the lunch right to your desk."

The students closed their eyes and prayed for ten minutes. When they opened their eyes, lo and behold, there were lunches on their desks. They were delighted for the food, they ate well, and their faces were once again lit up with that juvenile bliss.

The teachers came back and asked, "You prayed to God to give you food today. Did he deliver for you?" The students were unanimous in their belief that it was not God who delivered the food. They told the teachers that they were sure the school provided the food.

The interesting takeaway from this article, though, is the author's passionate contempt for the Soviets. "How dare them try to brainwash the students that God did not provide the food?" At that time, I agreed with the author that the Soviets had no right to try to influence the beliefs of the children. More recently, I have been able to step aside from the systemic bias that permeates most cultures and ask myself, "On which side did the truth lie, on the Soviets or the side of the author of the article?" We can go to great length to say that God provided the sunlight, the water, and other ingredients to grow the crops and nurture the animals that provided the meat, then provided the strength to the humans to harvest the crops and slaughter the animals, then provided the money to pay for the food and the strength for people to cook and serve the food; but where do we stop rationalizing our ideology? Instead, we should be doing some fact-checking.

Let us assume for a moment that what those Russian teachers did was not a prank. What if they had genuinely decided not to feed those students and allowed them to go hungry? Would God have made some food materialize for them to eat? Would he have sent someone to provide food for them? Most people would rule out the idea of God making food materialize before the students, but they would readily endorse the idea that God would send someone to feed them. The problem with the latter proposition is that anyone who would give food to the students or in whichever way they were provided with food would be construed as God using his agents to provide food for them. It is hard to understand why God would use agents when he could just make things materialize wherever and whenever he wishes.

The salient factor, however, is that in situations where there is no other intervention except for the will of God, people suffered and died from hunger as well as other calamities. We do not have to look far; just recall those ghastly photographs of people who were reduced to mere skin and bones that emerged from Nazi concentration camps at the end of World War 2 and the mass of skin and bones representing people who starved to death. We can also fast-forward to our present time and watch on TV people starving to death in Yemen and other places. Our loving and caring God did nothing to stop the carnage. Yes, we can indulge ourselves in all the machinations to delude ourselves that God is protecting and sustaining us, we can concoct rationales for anything we want, but does our adventure into our fantasy world represent what is happening in the real world?

This is how religion is often practiced in our culture. We were told as children and practice as adults that God provides us with everything we need. In the case of the students with their school lunch, the students knew all along that their lunches came from the school. By the time they became teenagers, they learned to be able to switch seamlessly from the real, material world, where people work for what they need, to the religious world, where God is credited with giving people everything they need and also what they would like to have.

Somehow we know that God is not providing our sustenance; otherwise, why do we bother to go to work? Most of us have to buy, beg, borrow, or steal the things we need; else, we would die from wants after a horrible period of emaciation. This is no imaginary scenario; hundreds of people in various parts of the world die every day from lack of essential things such as food. What is our rationale for thinking that God is providing for us abundantly and allowing others in other societies to become emaciated and die of wants?

Why do humans become possessed with this bipolar personality where we go so easily from the imaginary domain of the religious world to the world of reality or even operate in both worlds at the same time? We get up in the mornings and thank God for giving us the sustenance without which we dare not survive, for providing our daily bread and everything else we need; then we put on our clothes and head for work in spite of snow, rain, bigotry, occupational or road hazard because we know that if we don't, we will end up sleeping under a bridge, begging for handouts if we live in a society that is benevolent and has the resources to give. In some other societies, we may simply die from wants. We probably will not be thanking God at that point, but if we do not want to get there, we should better not sit back and wait on God to provide us with our daily bread.

There is a consensus of opinion that the ambivalence between religious practices and life in the real world has a lot to do with two things: First, the human species is in a transitional phase from a world where scientific knowledge played no role in life because science did not exist, to one where most of what we do is a construct of scientific knowledge. In our primitive life, we assumed that everything that happened was caused by the will of God. If someone caught a fish, it was God who made it happen. If the fish got away, God did not want that person to catch that particular fish for a particular reason. If that person fell over and broke his neck while trying to catch the fish, it was God who called him home to be with him in heaven. If another tribe attacked and killed him, it was a sign from God that he was straying from God's commandments. There was no other perspective through which to view life except through the will of God, even though that god may have been one carved from stone or one that was totally imaginary. Later in our social evolution, other perspectives started to open up. We started to acquire and use scientific knowledge. We started to realize that things can, and do happen naturally without divine intervention.

Second, while the human brain was increasing in capacity, it was acquiring elements of control other than the primitive "fight or flight" mechanism. At some point, we developed a sophisticated language system to communicate with other humans and to communicate with ourselves; we now have a sense of reasoning. We also have neurotransmitters that convert our good thoughts into healing functions in our bodies and bad thoughts into harmful functions. We can pray and the chemicals in our bodies may be reconfigured to produce effects that are aligned with our prayers; therefore, our prayers are answered. However, there are a few caveats to contend with; we may not get all the healing we pray for because of physical limitations and unknown factors. It has never been demonstrated that our prayers can cause healing in someone or something who is not aware that you are praying for them. Most of the time our bodies heal themselves naturally, whether we pray or not, but we give the credit to prayer or medicine. There are myriads of natural limitations or obstruction that may be working against the natural process of healing. Our medication may be doing more harm than good. What we eat or drink may be poisoning us or may not be providing the proper nutrients. We may not be getting enough exercise to allow our lymphatic system, our muscles and our mind to function efficiently. Our problems may be psychosomatic or autoimmune. One or more organs in our bodies may have been too damaged to be repairable. There may be incurable or unrecognized sources of infection in our bodies.

A cousin of ours got inflicted with one of those rare diseases with a long name and tongue-twisting pronunciation. She was very ill, and in spite of medication, doctors believed that her chance of surviving was slim. The medication was not helping. In this age of social media, hundreds of people sincerely prayed every day for her recovery. To the joy and relief of everyone, she recovered. What a joy and celebration! God delivered! Everyone was singing praises to God for his kind mercies. Computers and phones ran hot with text messages and emails giving glory to God for the miracle. Several months later, the illness came back. The previous prayer vigils were repeated. Medication was also repeated, the prayer groups went back to work, they prayed and prayed, but this time around, there was no recovery. Our cousin died within another few months. Everyone was distraught; we had hoped that there would be another miracle. God did not hear our prayers this time around.

It is a frequent occurrence that in spite of the prayers offered for loved ones, they may die anyway or not be healed. No matter how often it happens, people will continue to believe that God will interrupt or reverse the course of physical processes and impose divine intervention to answer their prayers. Prayer may or may not cause our bodies to increase or decrease hormones and neurotransmitters that it naturally produces to effect a healing process, but it has never been demonstrated in any controlled trials or tests that God or any other deity has abrogated the laws of physics to facilitate the prayers of anyone. Prayer can affect the production of chemicals in the body, which leads to physiological or mental healing, but a divine intervention from God has never been demonstrated in any scientifically verifiable way. We cannot hide from facts by inventing excuses and rationales. If our prayers are not answered, it is not that "God works in mysterious ways, his wonders to perform. He plants his footsteps on the sea, he rides upon the storm," as the hymn implores us. It is not that our minds are too feeble to comprehend God's work; it is just that our prayers were not answered, and we do not know why.

The following story illustrates a scenario that reminds me of the way we relate to God in our day-to-day behavior. I watched a TV commercial in which a boy was playing baseball with himself. With a ball in one hand and a bat in the other, he said, "Now watch the greatest batsman in the world." he exclaimed. He threw the ball vertically in the air and took a great swing at it as it fell. He did not connect; the ball fell harmlessly to the ground. He made a second throw and took a second swing. He missed again. "Okay," he said, "watch this now." For the third time, he threw the ball in the air, and for the third time, he swung and missed. "See, you just saw the greatest pitcher in the world."

Compare this amateur ball player with the other experiences I had. At meetings that I usually attend, the first order of business is to thank God for providing us with food, shelter, and good health. We ask his blessings and guidance to allow us to get to the meeting safely and to get back home safely. Prayers are offered for God to bless everything we do, everything we eat, to give us good health and cure all our ailments. On one occasion, one of our members did not show up. We learned later that he was in an accident and was in hospital. The members of our group responded with supplications to God to allow no further harm to come to him and prayers of gratitude that he did not die in the accident. Although he was seriously injured, God spared his life. Nobody asked, why didn't God answer our prayers to keep him safe and prevent the accident? Is there a reason why the Lord did not protect our friend? Is there something we should be doing differently? Many people are often killed in accidents after they and their friends prayed to God for their safety, yet we never ask any questions why our prayers were not answered. We avoided asking these questions, but we hastened to switch the narrative to give God thanks that the poor man was not killed, even though he was seriously injured. It is not unlikely that you could have heard things like "God is testing his faith" or even that "God is punishing him for something he did wrong." If he had died, the narrative would have been that his time had come, or that God knows best, or that it was God's will, or that he is in a better place now, in heaven.

We can smile and then forgive the youthful ballplayer in his childish fantasy to switch the narrative from the batsman to the pitcher, but shouldn't we be asking ourselves if it is not just as childish to switch the narrative because our prayers were not answered? Within the blink of an eye, we changed our narrative from expecting God to protect and keep our friend safe to be thanking God for saving his life, even though God did not protect him as we had prayed. In fact, he was seriously ill in hospital contrary to what we had prayed for. Like the youthful ballplayer, we can seamlessly switch our narrative even between positions that are 180 degrees opposite from each other.

It is not logical to believe that if we sincerely pray to God, he will answer our prayers and at the same time believe that God knows best and will ultimately do whatever is best for us. We pray for something specific with the assurance that God is omnipotent and has the ability to answer all our prayers, yet when our prayers are not answered, we just shrug it off and say, "It was God's will, nothing we can do about it." Given our human nature, it is inevitable that we will pray and hope for the best, but when things do not turn out the way we had hoped, we should be realistic and realize that it is not helpful to change our narrative to say that God intended it to be that way. If it were God's will after the fact, it was God's will before the fact.

Humans have an innate desire to be involved in communal activities, and the involvement itself can have positive feedback that induces us to have even more involvement. There are people who do not have the affinity for religion, but they glorify sports, politics, or a cult. Some people embrace all three institutions. These institutions provide a completeness and fulfillment of their psyche without which they would feel very empty. Participation in these institutions and their rituals is the glue that holds the institutions together. At religious gatherings, we have prayers, hymns, and chanting to stoke the passion of the believers. Without these institutions and their rituals, there would not be a focal point that serves as a force multiplier for the believers. Without these institutions and their rituals, humans would be lonely and miserable, drifting from one calamity to another. Be aware that many so-called successful and wealthy people do fall into the category of miserable individuals drifting from one calamity to another. This is why they sometimes turn to drugs or commit suicide. Sometimes cults are cloaked in the clothing of religion.

The passion we have to do some things or participate in some kind of activities sometimes overwhelm our sense of logical reasoning. A lot of us believe stories without questions because we revere the person who told them to us or because it is in the Bible. An example of this behavior is given in this summary of the story of Job from the Bible:

Job was a wealthy man with a large family and extensive properties with livestock. He was "blameless" and "upright" in the sight of God. One day Satan appears before God in heaven. God boasted to Satan about Job's goodness, but Satan argued that Job was only good because God had blessed him abundantly. Satan challenged God that if given permission to test Job, he would relent and curse God. God took the bet; he allowed Satan to test Job severely.

In one day, Job received messages that his livestock, servants, and ten children all died because of marauding invaders or natural catastrophes. Job ripped his clothes and shaved his head in mourning, but he still praised God in his prayers. Satan appeared in heaven again, and God granted him another chance to test Job. This time Job was afflicted with horrible sores. His wife encouraged him to curse God and to give up and die. Job's friends tried to convince him that his faith in God was baseless. Job tried to contact God for answers, but God did not respond, yet Job kept his faith in God. For this, God restored his riches several folds.

This story is a wonderful source of inspiration for people who are going through difficult times, but did God really cause Job's children to be killed and his possessions taken away just to prove to Satan that Job was faithful? Most Christians believe and are inspired by this biblical story, but is it a story based on facts, or is it a Hebrew folklore? Did Satan, whatever that is, literally visit God in his palatial abode (heaven) and negotiate with God to inflict Job with the deaths of his children and servants, the destruction of his possessions, and sores over his body? Would the God that we choose to worship make a bet with Satan that completely destroyed his faithful servant, just short of killing him, just to prove to Satan how faithful this servant was? Is God likely to do the same thing to any of us? Can we believe this story and at the same time believe that God is a merciful and loving God? I put this question to someone, and his response was, "God works in mysterious ways." The story of Job is a very popular one in the Judeo-Christian culture, but it is difficult to believe that people actually take this story literally.

Some people will use the inspirational part of the story and be ambivalent about taking it literally. Others will swear that everything in the Bible is true because it is the word of God. It is, however, a historical fact that different books of the Bible existed at different times in the course of history. The books of the Bible as we know it were selected from other writings and put together by the authority of Pope Damasus I at the Council of Rome in the year 382. After this first canonization, it went through several alterations before it got to what is now called the King James Version. Now the King James Version has evolved into several other versions.

One school of thought is that humans have created a God to fit a human stereotype of emotional needs. He has all the attributes of human beings (anthropomorphic), but these attributes are elevated to an infinite degree of potency. We believe that he can talk to us, love us, hate us, empathize with us, grant favors to us, provide all our needs, punish us, protect us from harm, punish others on our behalf, bless us, and comfort us when we are suffering. We ask these favors and mercies without any rational evaluation whether God answers these prayers or not.

Some prayers may be "answered" or "not answered" in strict accordance with the laws of physics, where these prayers invoke emotional changes in hormones or other chemical substances that our bodies produce. Some people will insist that their prayers are answered even though the results are not apparent.

Our bodies have enormous abilities to heal themselves. If we generally have a positive mental attitude, do not live a sedentary lifestyle, do not over-expose ourselves to medications and other drugs, eat healthy and exercise often, our bodies are usually resourceful enough to heal themselves of most damages or illnesses caused by foreign pathogens or physical injuries. Autoimmune diseases and inherited genetic diseases such as sickle cell anemia are generally an exception to this rule.

It has been demonstrated that this healing power is modulated by the vast array of hormones and neurotransmitters that our bodies produce, which, in turn, are modulated by our emotions.

Thus, prayer works! We can be healed by praying for healing and having a positive attitude in our general undertakings. What has not been demonstrated, however, is that this healing power of prayer can be transmitted telepathically to another person to heal them without the other person knowing that someone is praying for them. It is even less likely that someone's prayer can have an effect on nonhuman organisms or any nonliving things.

No one has ever demonstrated in any properly-controlled study that this has ever happened.

It is understandable why every culture on earth has some kind of religious experience. There was an epoch in our existence when we became intelligent enough to ask ourselves, "How did we get here, what is our purpose here, where did we come from, and where do we go from here?" It appears that only human beings among all living things have developed enough intellectually to ponder these questions. Only human beings seem to be able to make that leap to engage our minds, not only in the here and now of material concepts, but also to conjure a picture of what might have happened in the distant past or to extrapolate what will happen in the distant future. Animals may be able to do this instinctively on a limited basis but not as a conscious process.

In the beginning, humans also pondered that if it were another intelligent being (God) that made us come into existence, then it was logical to deduce that he, she, it, or they also made everything else. As if to enhance and solidify this period of mental exploration that early humans were having, they also experienced devastating floods, hurricanes, volcanoes, tornadoes, earthquakes, and other natural disasters. They experienced dangerous lightning and earsplitting blasts of thunder. "This must be a god with a violent temper!" they must have pondered. They must not do anything to make this great god angry.

Modern man has not departed from this prototype. Reflect on the lines of the hymn *How Great Thou Art* by Carl Boberg.

{O Lord my God, When I in awesome wonder, Consider all the worlds Thy hands have made. I see the stars, I hear the rolling thunder, Thy power throughout the universe displayed. Then sings my soul, my Savior God, to Thee, how great Thou art, how great Thou art.}

Humans from ancient times revere and are terrified by the power of the god they worship. They envision God as a benevolent but sometimes unconscionable parent. If you cross the line, you will be severely punished, even by death. Sometimes sacrifices may be offered to appease this deity.

It was also quite daunting to deal with the possibility that when we die, that would be the end of our existence, so we conjure up, imagine, invent, or envision by divine revelation, an afterlife. This mortal body must just be a vessel that houses an immortal spirit or soul. According to which religion you belong, or which sect of your particular religion, when you die, this spirit is reincarnated in another body, or goes directly to hell or heaven, or goes to purgatory, where your sins have to be expiated before you can go on to heaven.

According to some believers, there will be a "judgement day," when everyone, dead and alive (the quick and the dead), hundreds of trillions of souls, will be judged by God, and the decision will be made whether you live with God and the heavenly hosts in eternal paradise, or you will be cast into hell, where you will burn in fire and will be tormented forever; you cannot die.

On that judgment day, it is said that there will be a "rapture," where all people who are righteous in the sight of God will be whisked off miraculously to heaven. The thousands of people who will be in an airplane at this time could suddenly lose their pilot, along with other passengers, if they are caught up in the rapture.

I have never heard it discussed if these airplanes would simply crash. It probably would not matter since those lost souls would just join the cauldron of fire, which it is believed that earth would have become. Neither have I heard it discussed what would happen to the animals and other organisms. Since they have no concept of right and wrong, would they all be raptured into heaven, or would they all join the ranks of the tormented on earth?

If God will be having this rapture, there would be no need for a judgement to separate the righteous from the unrighteous since the rapture would have already made that separation, but logic is usually irrelevant in discussion of this nature. If reincarnation is true, and the same spirit occupies various bodies at different periods, there will be infinitely more bodies than spirits. Which body will a particular spirit occupy on judgement day, or will the same spirit be duplicated in each body it occupies? Can God judge the bodies that have no spirit? Here again, logic does not apply. Believers will invent an answer anyway.

It is interesting to evaluate the process by which humans accept the information they regard as true. If an entity exists that could process all the information that human beings have processed, what process would this entity use to evaluate what is rational from what is baseless? How different would be the information that this entity call "the truth and the facts", as compared to what humans believe to be "the truth and the facts"?

Religious beliefs and rituals can invoke very strong reactions and strong allegiance in humans. This strong reaction and allegiance to religious activities has helped promote the idea of a special gene in the human genome that promotes the worship of God (or gods). On every place on planet Earth that humans reside, you can find us worshipping something. There are two notable predispositions that humans have: the first is to have some kind of allegiance to a higher authority; the second is emotional feedback that causes more emotional feedback, which drives that particular emotion out of control if it is not mitigated. (In control systems jargon, we call this dilemma *reset wind-up*.) This can be observed in religious rituals where believers "get onto the spirit" and "speak in tongues." It can happen in a group setting or an individual setting.

This allegiance to a higher authority is not limited to religious activities. It seems that we humans will latch onto whatever we can identify as a higher authority. Gang and cult leaders come to mind in this context. The proliferation of smartphones and the applications that drive the chats and text messages make it quite easy to use the electronic media to organize gang and cult activities. What used to be called conspiracy theories can now be manipulated in the electronic media by cunning and nefarious actors, operating behind the scenes, manipulating, and organizing unsuspecting people into devious cults or gangs. With the help of the aforementioned emotional feedback, this can have dangerous consequences.

Other activities that seem to bring out strong allegiance are politics, sports, and social activities. It would behoove social organizers to make sure that they are way out in front of those who are manipulating the electronic media for nefarious purposes.

Recently, I had a conversation with a friend of mine who was lamenting a spate of criminal activities in a particular community. This community has steadily been deteriorating into lawlessness for several decades. We talked about the good old days and how much violence has taken over the community. I remarked that I was almost tempted to say that only God can help this community now, but I do not believe God has anything to do with it. I was admonished by her that I am losing my faith in God. She later sent me a lengthy video making the case that this lawlessness was happening because people have turned away from God and that God is the entity that can fix this problem. She expounded that God gave the people the choice to do good or evil. This gave me cause for some serious thoughts. My thoughts were that if God, with all his awesome power, does not interfere even in cases where people are being killed, then what is his function or purpose? On the other hand, if the people are the ones who have to come together to bring change to the society, then why pray to God and depend on him to bring about change? It is the duty of citizens to come together and make laws to govern their society in a way that is good for the society at large. So why bother with the pretense that if the governance is good, it is God that made it so; if the governance is poor, God is the entity that can fix it, but he will not because he gave humans the mandate to act on their own free will?

Some weeks after this discussion with my friend, a government officer gave a public address on the crime situation in the community. In part, this is what he said: "Only God can help us overcome this problem. We need divine intervention." He implored his listeners to pray to God for deliverance from the crime wave. Apparently, God was not listening. The crime situation has not abated.

Previous to his address to the public, this government officer was introduced to a plan that has a very good chance of mitigating the crime in the community. It basically involves a cell phone application activated by electronic surveillance and a neighborhood watch system coordinated by the police. This plan was very cost effective and had the potential to be very effective generally. He ignored the plan, he called for prayers; still, the level of criminal activities has not abated. Results are not the main objective in this case; optics is more important. People tend not to look at the statistical trend that the crime rate is increasing; the politician was more interested in identifying himself with the religious bias of the people.

When I was growing up in Jamaica, religion had a very strong influence then and still does now. It was recorded by the *Guinness Book of World Records* (now *Guinness World Records)* that Jamaica had the highest density of churches per capita in the world. As children, we were required to say our prayers when we got up in the mornings. At primary school, before schoolwork started, we had to sing a devotional hymn, such as *Inspirer and Hearer of Prayer.* Before dismissal for lunch break, we had to sing *For health and strength and daily food, we praise thy name, O Lord.* After assembling after the lunch break, we had to sing another verse of praise to the Lord. Before dismissal for the day, we sang another hymn, such as *Lord, dismiss us with thy blessings, fill our hearts with joy and peace.* Back home, before we went to bed, we had to say a prayer, such as *Our Father who art in heaven.* Even our national anthem itself is a prayer to God: *Eternal Father, bless our land. Guard us with thy mighty hand.*

This religious ritual did not seem onerous to us at that time. Looking back now, I can see a blessing and a curse. The British colonial system used religion to subjugate the population. On the other hand, a society without religion or some other socially-cohesive force to keep it together is likely to become a population of selfish, tribal, inhumane, and heartless people.

One of my grandfathers was a Presbyterian deacon, and the other was a Church of God deacon. My siblings and I would go to whatever church we felt like attending. We did not have any bias in favor of one church or the other. There was a difference in the type of sermon we expected to hear. At the Presbyterian church, the sermons were well scripted. The preacher read his sermon in a monotone, hardly raising his voice beyond the level of a conversation. Service started on time and ended on time. This was the church for the elite (elite being relative because our community was not endowed with materially-wealthy people).

The Church of God was a different story. It was the church where a lot of emotions were expressed. You could hear the preacher from a country mile away; this was without any electronic amplification. His sermons were unscripted, impromptu, and usually invoked a lot of "amen" and "hallelujah." The preacher and the songs also invoked a lot of emotional responses. In the midst of the hallelujahs, people would "get into the spirit" and start to "speak in tongues."

Getting into the spirit is an interesting phenomenon. The subjects get very animated, almost unable to control themselves. In some cases, they have to be restrained. When this happens, it is said that they are filled with the "holy ghost." This physical agitation is usually accompanied by "speaking in tongues," which are hysterical verbal expressions that do not equate to any known language. Believers claim that the animated and verbal agitation is the "holy ghost" manifesting in them. People who do not subscribe to this explanation counter with the assertion that this phenomenon is a result of an overproduction of adrenaline or similar hormones, or neurotransmitters stimulated by the effects of the sermons or songs. This is akin to that thrill that permeates your body when you hear a powerful speech, only a hundred times more powerful.

Thousands of conflicts and millions of deaths have occurred because of religion, yet it is inevitable and necessary that human beings pay reverence and allegiance to a principle, a moral law that prevents the breakdown of society into lawlessness. This moral law does not have to be seen as an edict that God imposed on human beings but as a conscious self-imposed objective we take upon ourselves to make a more humane global society. When we perceive this moral law as an obligation that humans have to maintain, instead of an edict that God imposes on us, for which we will be punished by God if we disobey, then we will become more responsible for our actions.

Does God Abrogate the Laws of Physics?

If you have a die that is symmetrical in every respect, and you throw it on a perfectly-level surface a thousand times, the odds are that each of its sides will be facing up close to the same number of times as any other. A 6 will be thrown approximately the same number of times as a 5, 4, 3, 2, or 1. That is, each digit, from 1 to 6, would be facing up, close to 166 times out of a thousand throws, since 166 is the number of times each of the six sides (each digit) has a statical chance of showing face up in a thousand throws. Each digit will have an equal chance of showing its face. If one person or a thousand people pray and concentrate their prayers or "mental energy" for any particular digit to be thrown significantly more than the others, would their prayers be answered? If this experiment is done a thousand times with the same results, would these prayer groups be convinced that their prayers did not make any difference? My guess is that the prayer groups would just brush this off as the will of God that their prayers were not answered as anticipated. Whatever happens would be God's will. If this simple test is done and each digit shows face up approximately the same number of times, it would indicate that praying will not influence change in the results. We can make the inference that prayers did not produce the desired results. Would it make a difference if the test was done a thousand times? It most likely would not.

A logical evaluation of facts as presented by empirical evidence is more valuable to people living in a real and material world than stories born of imagination and fantasy.

Let us examine another hypothetical case. This could not be done as a test or experiment, but unfortunately, variations of this scenario happen in the real world every day. If a car with no airbags or seat belts were full of passengers and was traveling 5 miles per hour crashes into a solid immovable wall, the probability that there would be any fatality as a result of the crash would be very low. If no prayer were offered by or on behalf of the occupants, would this increase the probability of fatalities or serious injuries? If all the conditions remain the same except that now the car is traveling at 200 miles per hour and crashes into the same wall, would praying for the safety of the occupants prevent fatalities or serious injuries? Let us look at another scenario. Let us say that half of the number of passengers of the car had just prayed for God to deliver them from all harm. These passengers were evenly mixed among the other half who were atheists. Would the praying half escape injury or death and the atheists killed? If a sample of a thousand people who prayed for the safety of the car's occupants were asked why all or most of the occupants of the car traveling at 200 miles per hour were killed, regardless of their praying status, what would their reaction be? The consensus of opinions is that a significant majority of them would find rationale to justify why their prayers were not answered, even though there was no significant difference in the amount of the praying group who died and the atheists. They would most likely say that it was the "destiny" of these people, or it was God's plan to "take them to heaven to be with him."

Why would rational people who have the ability to make logical analysis of a situation so blatantly ignore logic and instead embrace positions that make no sense in the real world? Bias and passion seem to be the answer to this question. There seems to be a strange interplay among logic, passion, and bias. Some kind of bias may be an inherited trait, but the bulk of the bias that people display is more likely acquired bias. Observed human behavior over time and across different cultures indicates that religious, racial, and political biases are acquired; it is unheard of for a person born in a country with a monolithic religious culture to show preference for another religion without any exposure to the second religion. The ability to apply logic to evaluate these biases most likely depends on the intellectual capacity for logical reasoning, not necessarily education, of the individual.

A friend of mine once told me that she accepts unconditionally and literally everything in the Bible because it is the "word of God". "Even Exodus 31:15, which declared that 'whosoever doeth any work on the Sabbath day shall surely be put to death'?" I inquired.

Her response was, "I don't question what is in the Bible. I simply accept it because it is the word of God."

She accepts what the Bible says about killing people who work on the Sabbath, yet she herself does work on the Sabbath, and she does not kill people who work on the Sabbath; how illogical and ambivalent! This person is a college graduate, so you see, education does not necessarily equate to an ability to make a logical evaluation of facts. Bias sometimes overrides the decision-making ability of even well-educated people. If my friend knew the real history of the Bible, that God did not dictate it to "inspired men," that wars were literally fought and thousands of people died so that one sect of Christians could determine what would be the content of the Bible, would she be more open-minded to look at the historical facts in a more objective way?

There are others who make the case that the Old Testament is Mosaic law, and these laws were annulled by the coming of Jesus Christ. This notion destroys the whole premise that the Bible is the authentic words of God. It is either the authentic word of God as a whole or a collection of writings from various authors.

It is evident that when we pray, we may or may not have a positive response to our prayers. Our bodies respond to the laws of physics. Everything that is a construct of matter obeys the laws of physics. The entity we identify as God has never, in any controlled test or experiment, interfered with the laws of physics. You may believe that Jesus Christ walked on water; after all, it is in the Bible, so it must be true. This would be an abrogation of the laws of physics; it is contrary to scientific principles. According to the gospel, Jesus walked on the sea of Galilee to get to his disciples on the other side of the sea. Even more importantly, Peter started walking to Jesus but eventually started to sink because, according to Jesus, he had "little faith." The deduction here is that according to Christian theology, a mortal person (Peter) can walk on water if he or she has enough faith. So is there no one on earth who has ever had enough faith since no one else has ever walked on water? You can believe that Jesus or God or whatever other supernatural powers abrogated the laws of physics and science in general to make this happen, and you do accept that everything in the Bible is literally true, or you can believe that this story is just another myth.

There is a strong argument in favor of praying, whether your prayers are to God or to a divine providence, whatever that is, or the remarkable ability of your body to heal itself. It is common knowledge that our bodies respond to our emotions by producing powerful hormones and neurotransmitters that cause reactions ranging from the well-known adrenaline rush to deaths by heart attack caused by emotional shock. Someone can drop dead just from hearing very bad news or can be healed from a deadly disease because of the hormones and neurotransmitters their bodies produce as a result of sincere prayers.

Prayer can cause our bodies to produce healing effects that few medicines can. In fact, as powerful as antibiotics are, they do not cause healing of our body's tissues. All they do is to kill the bacteria that are invading our bodies, especially the injured tissues, so that the body can heal itself. If you break your arm, the marvelous and mysterious power that your body possesses starts manufacturing protein that fuses this broken bone together, even stronger than it was before. A doctor has to properly position the parts of this bone and put it in a cast to keep the broken parts together so that this miraculous "glue" can join the parts together, but ultimately, it is the body that heals that broken bone, not the doctor or his cast. Our bodies have limitations; however, it can only use the tools and the chemistry that is available to it. These tools also include our emotions, which can be enhanced by prayer or other positive affirmations.

Cancer is one of the worst scourges that humans have to deal with. Our immune system is very aggressive in catching and killing foreign bodies that enter our bodies. Unfortunately, our bodies do not recognize cancer cells as a foreign entity because they are not. Cancer cells are produced by our own bodies and were originally intended to perform legitimate function of the body, but somewhere along the road, the instructions coded in the DNA got mutated, and the original function is compromised. These cells have now become like a blind bull in a china shop, just growing and growing without the ability to perform any useful function.

This ability of our immune system to seek out and destroy foreign bodies is a function of the chemistry of our bodies. There is no evidence or any credible body of facts to indicate that any healing is a function of God or any holy spirit miraculously causing it, except the fact that prayer can change the chemistry of our bodies and invoke a healing process. It has been established that a positive mental attitude and prayer sometimes aid and stimulate our immune system to promote healing, but no controlled study has ever been done that shows that any controlling energy, whether to heal a person's body or to determine which side of a die shows face up, has ever been presented for public scrutiny or peer review.

Neither has it ever been credibly demonstrated that our bodies or any part of us has any form of energy that can be transmitted telepathically to another person, another thing or to God. If we pray for someone and that person knows that we are praying for them, that may cause that person's body to be stimulated to produce resources to cause healing, physically or emotionally. However, if the person being prayed for does not know that he or she is being prayed for, these prayers may be in vain since it has never been credibly demonstrated that prayer in this context is effective. This also applies to nonhuman things that cannot comprehend your prayer. I have seen someone praying for the healing of sick cats and dogs. If the animals get better, its healing would be attributed to the prayers; if it did not, then it would be God's will that the animal should die.

Some time ago, there was a severe frost that hit our community and killed a woman's avocado plant. Before the plant was completely dead, the woman was praying for God to heal it and bring it back to life. If you believe that God has human attributes that enable him to respond to your prayers, and that he has omnipotent power, why should it not be reasonable to expect him to heal your avocado plant? The fact, though, is that it has never been demonstrated in a controlled environment that the ability of a tree to live or die can be changed by prayer.

There is a Bible story (Mark 11:12–25) where Jesus cursed a fig tree, causing it to wither and die because he was hungry and there was no fruit on it for him to eat. The probability that this story is just a folklore is very strong. It has never been credibly or scientifically demonstrated that God the Father or Jesus the Son has ever caused the laws of physics to be abrogated; in this case, cursing a tree to make it wither and die. You may be one of those people who believe that everything in the Bible is literally true. On the contrary, if you can get rid of this proclivity, then it should not be difficult to have doubts about this story and cast it in the dustbin of folklore.

Does this propensity to depend on God or to pray for everything have to do with the god gene that we are believed to have in our genome?

I come from a rural community where chickens used to be reared in the yard adjacent to the house. Back then, we called them fowls. The name "chicken" was reserved for the young ones that were still taken care of by their mothers. "Chick" was singular, and "chicken" was plural, much like "child" and "children." "Chickens" (with an "*s*") was not in our vocabulary.

You could say that these fowls were semiautonomous. They mostly depended on us for food. To supplement this, or, more appropriately, as an instinctive attribute, they would forage around the yard, scratching to find additional food such as worms and insects. They roosted at night in a nearby tree. The hens built nests where they laid their eggs. Even though they did their best to hide these nests, we found them and took most of the eggs, leaving just enough for them to produce new chickens. They tried to hide their nest where we should not find them, but they were not always successful. After sitting on these eggs for the appropriate number of days, the hens would march out with a brood of fluffy white chickens, beautiful to behold. The mother hens constantly put out a homing call, "cluck-cluck-cluck," while the chickens responded with "pee-pee-pee." This interplay of calls kept mother and chickens together. This behavior of hen and chickens gave rise to a common expression in the community, "pee-pee-cluck-cluck." If you are a person who blindly follows and idolizes a person, ideology, or religion without any questions, you are deemed to have the "pee-pee-cluck-cluck" mentality. If you accept what someone says without trying to ascertain if it is factual, you are a "pee-pee-cluck-cluck" person; you are following your leader, "pee-pee-cluck-cluck." In other words, you are following your leader or ideology unquestioningly.

Before human beings became less civilized, that is, less dependent on a social order, did we have a more powerful "pee-pee-cluck-cluck" instinct to enable us to stay together for survival as a family? Do we still exhibit this primordial instinct why we tend to have this groupthink mentality? Since we no longer have a monolithic society with universal ordinance, could there be a lot of subconscious "pee-pee" going on but not enough benign "cluck-cluck" to provide the mother hen's guidance? This would leave the population quite vulnerable to people with dominant personalities to assume the roles of the mother hens, consciously or subconsciously. There are cults and cult leaders who people gravitate to for no logical or sensible reason. In most cases, the reasons they give for their actions have no grounding in logic or rationality. What is even more profound is the feedback effects of the utterances of these leaders that amplify the passion that the followers bring to the group. We have seen cases where sports fans trash cities in their euphoric bliss to celebrate the victory of their favorite team. Political parties and dictators use this innate passion of the people to amplify their particular causes and inculcate other people with their dogmas. These dogmas usually spread without proper scrutiny.

Another manifestation of the "pee-pee-cluck-cluck" syndrome is the influence religious and other organizations have on people in general. Do you ever wonder why it is that so many people want so much to proselytize to others? Apart from the money-grubbing aspects of these ventures, they are also satisfying their "cluck-cluck" syndrome. Religious leaders and their members are always trying to recruit new members and are quite elated when they succeed. Same thing with political parties, gangs, sports fans, and other groups. In these cases, we can see the interplay among passion, bias, and logic.

Humans and other animals appear to be born with this passionate devotion to pursue some sort of activity. Some of us have more of this passion; some have less. This passion is combined with our bias and will also combine in varying degrees with our ability to apply logic to moderate this compounded passion.

Our mental faculties interact with our physiological faculties and vice versa. This is an awesome characteristic of the human personality that sets human beings apart from other animals. We can see this situation play out in phenomena such as hypnosis, acupuncture, and the use of placebo. Prayer is also one of these phenomena. With these phenomena, you convince yourself that the particular course of action that you indulge in will make the requested event or healing happen. If you believe enough in a particular course of action, let us say that you pray to be healed of a disease, and if the physiological parameters that will effect your healing are within the physical limits of your body, then you will be healed. Your cancer may be healed by any of these procedures if you sincerely believe in it. Your pain may go away, or your fear of the voodoo spell may disappear; but if the result of your course of action is the desire to grow two more eyes in the back of your head to achieve a 360-degree vision, your body, (or God for that matter) will not oblige because that is outside the functionality of your body. That is not one of the things your body was programmed to do. Neither has it ever been reasonably and logically demonstrated that God has ever granted any favor of this nature to anyone.

Neither can you, (or a multitude of you) pray to make a hurricane or tornado wither and die. That is because this phenomenon obeys the laws of physics only. Even though the laws of physics are what cause your body to heal itself by responding to your emotions and producing the appropriate hormones and neurotransmitters to stimulate the proteins that do the healing, the emotions that you invoke cannot cause changes outside your own body, except for instances where you have influenced someone else to invoke their own emotional response. Praying with someone or participating in a riot with someone are examples of invoking the emotional responses of others.

In spite of millions of supplications from human beings, it has never been scientifically and logically demonstrated that God has ever granted any favor of this nature to anyone. Of course, people claim that their prayers stop natural disasters, but these claims are just delusions. In terms of proof, these claims have never gotten past the realm of their imagination. Individual delusions or mass delusions will happen as long as human beings imagine and conceptualize things that have no grounding in the real world.

People ask God to override the laws of physics that they proclaim he created, putting him in an untenable predicament. There are people who pray for God to divert hurricanes. If the hurricane is diverted, as the laws of physics dictate and as predicted in advance by meteorologists, they claim that God hears their prayers, even though the hurricane devastates another community. If the hurricane is not diverted, then they claim that it is God's will or even that it is punishment for the sins of the people impacted. There are people who pray to God asking him to punish their enemies on their behalf. Most of these people take their cue from the Bible. King David's prayer for God to punish his enemies, from Psalm 109, is quoted below. It emphasizes how human beings can cast God in their own human image, even in their most despicable image. Here, King David is asking God to place the most egregious curse on his so-called enemies and even the enemies' children. Should we accept without question that this is the same merciful God to which we pray?

Psalm 109 (KJV)

{Hold not thy peace, O God of my praise;
For the mouth of the wicked and the mouth of the
deceitful are opened against me: they have spoken
against me with a lying tongue.
They compassed me about also with words of
hatred; and fought against me without a cause.
For my love they are my adversaries: but I give
myself unto prayer.
And they have rewarded me evil for good, and
hatred for my love.
Set thou a wicked man over him: and let Satan
stand at his right hand.
When he shall be judged, let him be condemned:
and let his prayer become sin.
Let his days be few; and let another take his office.
Let his children be fatherless, and his wife a widow.
Let his children be continually vagabonds, and
beg: let them seek their bread also out of their
desolate places.
Let the extortioner catch all that he hath; and let
the strangers spoil his labour.

Let there be none to extend mercy unto him: neither let there be any to favour his fatherless children.

Let his posterity be cut off; and in the generation following let their name be blotted out.

Let the iniquity of his fathers be remembered with the Lord; and let not the sin of his mother be blotted out.

Let them be before the Lord continually, that he may cut off the memory of them from the earth.

Because that he remembered not to shew mercy, but persecuted the poor and needy man, that he might even slay the broken in heart.

As he loved cursing, so let it come unto him: as he delighted not in blessing, so let it be far from him.

As he clothed himself with cursing like as with his garment, so let it come into his bowels like water, and like oil into his bones.

Let it be unto him as the garment which covereth him, and for a girdle wherewith he is girded continually.

Let this be the reward of mine adversaries from the Lord, and of them that speak evil against my soul.

But do thou for me, O God the Lord, for thy name's sake: because thy mercy is good, deliver thou me.

For I am poor and needy, and my heart is wounded within me.

I am gone like the shadow when it declineth: I am tossed up and down as the locust.

My knees are weak through fasting; and my flesh faileth of fatness.

I became also a reproach unto them: when they looked upon me they shaked their heads.
Help me, O Lord my God: O save me according to thy mercy:
That they may know that this is thy hand; that thou, Lord, hast done it.
Let them curse, but bless thou: when they arise, let them be ashamed; but let thy servant rejoice.
Let mine adversaries be clothed with shame, and let them cover themselves with their own confusion, as with a mantle.
I will greatly praise the Lord with my mouth; yea, I will praise him among the multitude.
For he shall stand at the right hand of the poor, to save him from those that condemn his soul.}

This was King David's prayer to God to destroy his enemy. It should also be noted that according to the Bible, David was chosen to be king of Israel because David was a man "after his (God's) own heart" (1 Samuel 13:14). Humans usually ascribe to God a character that is like their own.

Recently, I had the opportunity to tour South Africa. Among the sites we visited were the Table Mountain and the Blyde River Canyon. At both sites, one of my traveling companions stretched out his arms with his palms facing the sky. He solemnly proclaimed, "How could anyone not believe that this is God's handiwork?" If there were a geologist on this tour, I am sure he or she would be saying, "Just reflect on the awesome forces of nature, the powerful seismic activities that threw up these magnificent mountains, and the river that carved out this awesome gorge." It is so easy to say that God created everything simply because we do not know how it came about or how it was created.

Saying that God created it is meaningless. Can we say that God just wishes everything into existence? This is so simplistic. The fact is that we do not know how these things initially came into being, and we are too arrogant to admit it. We know that over the eons, earthquakes and volcanoes threw up these mountains and gorged out these canyons, then the rivers eroded them, but our intellect is too limited even to have a concept of how it all began. Scientists gave us the big bang theory, and the theologians gave us the creation theory, but even if any of these theories are correct, there would be so many dark shadows behind it that by venturing into it, we would be even further lost than where we are now. We should keep exploring but never be arrogant enough to say that we know how it all began.

The beautiful flowers that we so often describe as gifts from God to inspire us, is nothing more than the reproductive (sexual) organs of the plant. They really outdo human beings in their functionality as reproductive organs. Their sweet nectar, advertised in grand style by beautiful petals and aromatic fragrance, attracts bees, butterflies, and other insects. These insects unwittingly transfer the pollen (analogous to the human sperm) from the anther, the male part of the flower, to the stigma. From the stigma, it grows through the style and enters the ovary, which is analogous to the human ovary and uterus, since the eggs are produced, fertilized, and developed in the ovary. So the beautiful rose that we admire so much is just the sex organ of a flowering plant. The fruits that we love so much are just mechanisms to disperse the seeds of the plant.

The flower has both male and female organs. It can be pollinated with its own pollen, or it can be cross-pollinated. Cross-pollination provides a larger gene pool to ensure that its offspring have a better chance of surviving in a changing ecosystem, but just in case cross-pollination does not take place, it can fall back to self-pollination. You have to admit that the functionality of the roses far outweighs the romantic allure that we ascribe to it and that its functionality is intended for the propagation of the flower rather than to provide a feel-good sense of adoration that we believe God wants us to have when we see the flower.

If a goat sees a branch of flowers, it will evaluate the flowers to find out if it is edible. It will either eat it or walk away, but even if that goat has the physical ability, it would not cut the flowers and put them in a vase like humans do and admire them until they fade and wither. Nor would that goat lay out a canvas and start painting a picture of the flowers. This attribute seems to pervade only human beings. The goat was able to evaluate the flower to ascertain if it was edible. That is all. It did not have the mental capacity to ponder if the flower was beautiful or not. The phrase "casting pearls before swine" comes to mind. Neither the swine nor the goat has the level of abstract concept to place any meaning on beauty. Beauty is really just an arbitrary abstract concept. Neither the goat nor the pig has the ability to ask why they exist, who made them, who made the universe, or ponder the existence of God.

To see beauty in a bunch of roses, wonder in awe about the gorges and crevasses of a canyon, is a peculiarity of the human personality. This ability to admire a rose means that our pursuit of abstract concepts is stronger than that of the goat or the pig. The pursuit of abstract concepts gives us the ability to ask questions and seek answers; it also gives us the ability to pursue mathematical concepts.

"Mathematics is the language with which God has written the universe," Galileo Galilei famously said. He said this long before great minds such as Albert Einstein proposed the universal equation for energy, $E = MC^2$, and James Maxwell's equation for electromagnetic waves. Mathematics has to be one of the first abstract concepts that early humans dealt with. Simple truisms such as "the shortest distance between two points is a straight line" is the cornerstone of modern mathematics. These mathematical concepts are logical, intuitive, basic, and form the core of our ability to reason. We are able to build on these core concepts to formulate more complex mathematical theorems. After we learned to count objects, then we learned to multiply. If we have eight families, each family having five people, we can multiply eight by five and concluded that there is a total of forty people, instead of adding each person head by head.

This ability to pursue abstract concepts is an additional dimension in the human psyche that recognizes and appreciates what we perceive as beauty and art and to indulge in spiritual and abstract pursuits. We do not need an appreciation of beauty and art to survive, but it is essential for the development and self-actualization of our inquiring mind. Admiring flowers may have more to do with our culture than our gene.

According to people who believe in natural evolution (Darwinian), humans were just like that unsentimental goat. We evaluated things only for food, safety, or sex, which were necessary for our survival. The contours of a canyon or the colors and arrangement of the petals on a flower meant nothing to us back then. As we evolved, we started to paint pictures on cave walls and started to see beauty in things that do not necessarily satisfy the needs that are essential for our survival.

"Not so fast," proclaimed the theists. "God made human beings in our present form, physically and intellectually. God made us one or more dimensions above other animals so that we can recognize him and worship him." The only obvious truth here is that both sides of this argument cannot be correct.

We also appreciate and admire all these spiritual things which we really do not need to survive. All these human attributes fall into what psychologist Abraham Maslow described as the fifth level of his hierarchical pyramid—self-actualization, the realization or fulfillment of one's talents and potentialities. According to Maslow, this pyramid of hierarchical needs is physiological, safety, love, self-esteem, and self-actualization.

Our brain, more appropriately, our neurological system, has taken this giant leap to endow us with the need for self-actualization. This also comes with the questions of "Who am I?" "Where am I from?" and "Why am I here?" We have now become self-aware. There is now a dimension to our existence that stops seeing other things only as food to eat or foe to flee from, a sanctuary or a snare, a mate or a rival, a member of the clan or an outsider. We can now smell the rose for its fragrance rather than its edibility. We have now evolved into a thinking, self-conscious entity. We now have an abstract dimension that can now envision a flower for what we conceive as beauty, which is an abstract concept. The goat or the pig could not sense this attribute of the flower. A bee or butterfly sees the same thing, but they sense food instead of beauty. We can now paint on the walls of caves the human figure or any other figure that we now have the mental ability to conjure. This is when we start to ask the questions "Who am I?" "Do I have a soul that occupies my body?" "When my body dies, what happens to my soul if I have one?" "Where does this vast expanse of energy and matter around us come from?" and "Is it a construct of an omnipotent, omniscient god that created this incomprehensible universe?"

Microphysics and Metaphysics

Scientists have demonstrated that our brain has evolved from a simple biological entity to this awesome supercomputer, millions of times more potent than the most potent supercomputer built by humans. As reference, these scientists cite no-brain organisms such as the paramecium, which literally has no brain, up through the evolutionary chain, to the human brain. In addition to controlling our basic motor functions, such as walking, talking, swallowing, digestion, and respiration, our brain, along with the neurotransmitters that it produces, along with the hormones in the body that it manipulates, and also along with conscious feedback and conscious actions from our bodies, has made us into a self-aware, aspirational, and spiritual being. It has also created in us a new dimension which is referred to as a metaphysical dimension.

There are many ways in which a computer system may be compared to the human neurological system. A computer has hardware "drivers," which are parts of the computer program that has detailed information about every piece of hardware that it controls. You cannot successfully instruct a computer to print a document unless the computer has all the operating parameters of the printer ready to use for that process. Similarly, you could not literally lift a pin if your brain does not have all the parameters for your fingers, arms, eyes, and every other part of your body and every muscle that is involved in the lifting of that pin. Having a stroke (Cardiovascular accident) is obviously a situation where this chain of command is broken between the desire to do something and the expected result. Is it not interesting how an apparently nonphysical entity as a thought can generate a physical action such as lifting a pin or a log? It has been demonstrated that thoughts generate electrical impulses in this supercomputer, (the brain.) These electrical impulses go through a lot of processing, then the brain spits out another set of electrical impulses to our muscles to do the required task. Is it not interesting how little we humans know about what goes on between that thought and the lifting of the pin? Is it not also interesting that we as human beings have so little knowledge of what goes on in the brain, yet we are so convinced and so self-confident that we know so much about who or what we are?

Our brains have all the critical information for every part of our bodies. This information has continuously been acquired ever since we were born. Everything we see, hear, feel, or do has been stored in our memories. No one is really sure if this information stays permanently in our memories. Neither do we know how much control we have over recalling it. We do believe, however, that all that information that gets into our memory bank is part of what makes us who we are. A young baby cannot understand when we speak because he or she has not yet gathered enough information in his or her memory bank to process our words into meaningful information. For the same reason, his or her babbling conveys no meaningful information.

Our brain has the functionality of the arithmetic logic unit (ALU) found in a computer—it has a memory, and it has its peripherals, such as our eyes, ears, hands, feet, heart, and lungs. These elements of functionality are not as discrete as in a computer and are as undefined as the metaphysical dimension that we are purported to have.

Our brains have developed the intelligence to interpret rapid changes in air pressure, otherwise called vibration, particularly changes in frequency and intensity. It converts these variations into electrical impulses that are replications of the changing air pressure. These electrical impulses, which we sense as sound, are sent by the ear to the brain. Our entire world of verbal communication is built on this simple wave of compression and decompression of the air around us.

Our brains have also developed the intelligence to interpret changes in the frequency and intensity of a particular spectrum of electromagnetic waves, the spectrum that we know as light, into usable electrical impulses. The retina in our eyes is able to sense thousands of pixels of light simultaneously. This gives us the ability to see different wavelengths (frequency) in the spectrum as different colors and the variations in the intensity of the light as the brightness. The changes of the wavelength (color) and the brightness are sent to the brain as electrical impulses. Our brain interprets this data from the eye as our vision, which enables us to see material objects. (There is no evidence that this physiological mechanism enables us to see ghosts, angels, or other nonmaterial things.) The images that we see are simple variations in the frequency and intensity of the part of the electromagnetic spectrum that our brain has utilized to create vision. Our sense of vision, our sense of hearing, and our other physical senses have created a vast network of sensory awareness and a vast treasure trove of information that have become part of our consciousness, our psyche, our culture, our behavior, and our language.

These impulses are stored as new data in our brains and are modulated and given meaning by the enormous volume of stored information and directives that we have acquired since we were born. These data are interpreted as words and intonations, also images, that make sense to us. This results in our recognizing an image as a bird or a car or your son or daughter. If you have ever heard an audio recording played in reverse, this is what someone who is hearing sound for the first time would hear when someone speaks to that person—totally unintelligible as if it is an unknown language. Similarly, if you ever watched an analog color TV (TV before the digital standard was introduced a few decades ago) with no input signal, all you would see are small random rapidly moving colored dots. This is how a person who is seeing for the first time experiences his newfound sense of sight.

This accumulation of data results in thoughts and words that have the ability to invoke strong emotional and physiological reactions in our bodies and our minds. As a result of these inputs, the brain also generates electrical output which it sends to the relevant muscles and organs to take action. It may send out commands for you to start running or fighting. Your brain has to send out thousands of impulses to different muscles and organs. At the same time, it has to monitor thousands of inputs that it uses to control the ongoing operation. To do this, the brain has to know where to find each input and each output element and what kind of signal it is sending and receiving from each. This is not unlike a computer needing "driver" software to instruct it how to communicate with its peripherals.

Here, we start to get into a conversation of metaphysics, since our words and their intonation, our gestures, and our movements can have the effect of causing other people and animals to alter their behavior without any apparent physical interaction. If you make some horrible and aggravating comments about someone who was not aware of what you said, it will have no effect on him. However, if he hears you, it can have a profound effect on him, even though there was no physical contact. On hearing these remarks, his blood pressure may shoot up to alarming levels, his heart rate may spike, his adrenaline level may spike, he may now be prepared to fight, and he may even drop dead from a heart attack.

Since there was no physical contact between you and the abused man, you could say that there was a metaphysical contact, just like when you pray for someone who hears you praying for them or knows that you are praying for them. So prayer can bring healing, but it is not necessarily a divine deity that is miraculously causing the healing; it is the chemistry of your own body. Conversely, mental abuse can have debilitating effects or even cause death.

Now if you look keenly enough, you will find the missing physical link between your words and the man's reactions. When you speak, your vocal cord and your mouth make a pattern of vibration which is replicated in the air flowing through your mouth. This pattern of vibrations spreads through the surrounding air as a wave of compression and decompression of the air. We associate specific words with this vibration pattern. When this wave hits the eardrum of the abused man, it sets up a pattern of vibrations that is a replica of the vibration in the mouth of the abuser. Therefore, there is a "microphysical" chain of events that cannot be found in so-called metaphysical events such as telepathy or the allegation of God talking to someone. How do we distinguish between someone's imagination or hallucinations and God talking to them? If the voice cannot be recorded on an audio recorder it is not a sound coming from an external source, but an electrical impulse generated in the brain of the person hearing the sound. Theoretically, God may have generated this electrical impulse in that person's head, but this has never been established to be the case. We may never know if this can happen. On the other hand, it has been established conclusively that hallucinogenic drugs or neurological disorders do cause anomalies in the brain that cause people to hear or see phantoms.

When we see an image, the movement of the image, and other things near the image, the reservoir of our stored experiences conjures up a new experience in our psyche where we do not necessarily see any obvious physical link between one event and the other. We are not conscious of an array of light pixels changing into electrical impulses, the brain comparing these impulses with stored information, then concludes what these light pixels mean to the person. Instead, this scenario is perceived as one "metaphysical" event, having no physical process. You may see a person running toward you. Depending on the information you have stored in your brain, and how you are able to process it, you may perceive your son coming toward you for a hug, or you may perceive a murderer coming toward you to kill you.

A person just does not exist as a physiological entity, but as a construct of their physiological body, their behavior, their memories, the memories that other people and animals have of them, the relationship that they have with other people, other animals, and other things. The apparently nonphysical attributes of the human psyche, we will consider as metaphysical. The general characterization of a person would be that he or she has physical and metaphysical attributes.

The word "metaphysical" has acquired mysterious as well as mystical meanings over time. To a lot of people, metaphysics has come to mean mysterious events that they believe do happen, but they cannot explain it in physical terminology; events such as one's thoughts acquiring the ability to cause a material object to move from one place to another (psychokinesis), the ability to communicate with an entity from the "spirit world," or telepathic communication between human beings. Another popular belief of this metaphysical power is that people can get together to do things such as praying for rain to fall to break a devastating drought or for a hurricane or tornado to be diverted by prayer. One spiritual organization defines metaphysics as "The science of Being; that which transcends the physical." This ambiguity gives them the latitude to define their unique interpretation of many biblical or other spiritual narratives as the "metaphysical interpretation" of such narrative.

None of these definition of metaphysics is what we are discussing at this time. In our discussion, what appears to be metaphysics as defined by conventional grammar may be more aptly defined as microphysics, or a series of small unobserved physical events as was demonstrated when the horrible comments were directed to the man. We are not talking about actions that are perceived to happen outside the realm of known physical science. The apparent metaphysical process that appeared to have happened has physical process and does not abrogate the laws of physics.

A so-called metaphysical phenomenon will not cause a hurricane to change course because a group of people pray for that to happen or for guardian angels to be watching over someone so that no harm comes to him or her for two reasons; first of all, it has never been demonstrated in any scientifically-controlled way that this process is anything other than a figment of the imagination. Second, there is no known active energy source that transmits this information or any medium that carries it. Imagining that these things may be possible cannot be construed that it is reality. The metaphysics that we are talking about is one that has physical processes, albeit nuanced enough so that we tend to see the bigger picture rather than the microphysical ones. Because the small physical steps are usually not observed, we tend to extrapolate these processes into actions by God. We believe God makes them happen and we can talk to God to influence his actions.

Going back to that little girl wondering what happened to the puddle of water, you can believe one of two things: (1) You can believe the miracle-based version of metaphysics that God, who is omnipotent, just miraculously made the water disappear. Or (2) you can believe the science-based version of metaphysics that all physical actions obey the laws of physics even though we are mostly unaware of the microphysics behind the scenes. The microphysics here is that all forms of liquids can turn into vapor, given the right conditions of temperature, pressure, and the level of saturation of the vapor in which the liquid is being absorbed. The laws of physics are very well understood at the molecular and even the atomic level.

At the subatomic level, however, we humans do not have sufficient knowledge or probably even the intellectual ability to comprehend it all. We have an inkling of knowledge about weak forces and strong forces, the Higgs boson, gauge bosons, leptons, gluons, mesons, quarks, dark matter, dark energy, and antimatter; but what we humans know only humiliatingly exposes our lack of knowledge. Scientists still do not know how life was created in the beginning. Scientists have become experts at splicing DNA and literally making biological cells perform the functions of other organisms, but they cannot create a living cell from nonliving chemicals, even though they know which chemicals and the chemical formula for these cells. This is where scientists have run into their limitations; they cannot create life, and they are completely baffled by subatomic particles and mysterious things, such as dark matter and dark energy.

Theists do not have these limitations. They just declare that God made these things happen; the wishes of the gods simply materialize. In the case of Judeo-Christians, God just simply commanded the heavens and the earth into existence, then he commanded all living things into existence, then he made man from the dust of the earth, then he plucked out one of the man's ribs and made the woman. Proof or reasonable deduction is not required. The stories theists believe to be true are handed down from generation to generation, sometimes recorded on clay tablets. We, who are members of the more recent generations, have the responsibility to fact-check, as much as possible, beliefs that are so central to our very existence.

Undoubtedly, there are infinite and powerful forces in the universe, forces that become more mysterious and unknowable the more we study them. But are these powerful forces (or maybe it is just one force or power) synonymous with the entity theists know as God? Does this entity have humanlike attributes with which we can communicate, or is it just the source of the laws of physics? Can humans receive favors or benefits that override the laws of physics from this entity? An example of this favor is praying for a hurricane to change course.

Friends of mine who I discuss this subject with just brushed this aside with the comment "But it's God who made the powers of physics. He made everything!" To this, my answer is, "Which God? Brahma, the Hindu high god? The African god and goddess Oluron and Olokum, who allegedly made the earth habitable out of a watery mess? Or the Hebrew God who just willed the universe, including the earth, into existence?" We tend to be dismissive of other people and other religions, but if all we have to offer is the same kind of myths with only faith to back up our religion, what makes ours the true religion and the others, myths? My friends also say, "We have the Bible to prove it." But other religions also have their holy book as proof of their narrative. Majority of people on this planet worship the Abrahamic God because of the influence of the Roman Empire and Europeans in general. This does not mean that other people worshipping other gods are less credible. Our proof of authenticity is our holy book and our faith. Their proof of authenticity is also their holy book and their faith. Why is one more authentic than the other?

How Is Intelligence Defined?

Theists believe that we can intelligently communicate with God as we do with other human beings. To get a better understanding of how we use the word "intelligence," we have to understand the difference between "artificial intelligence," "natural intelligence," and "human intelligence." Natural intelligence is the basic laws executed by natural processes, such as photosynthesis or the evaporation of water. This is not a formal classification and is only mentioned here to complete the discussion of intelligence. These processes are not hard to understand if you have any knowledge of chemistry, but they can also be classified as intelligence since they follow the same laws of physics as the other classification of intelligence.

Fundamentally, there is not much difference between human and artificial intelligence. Both are the logical manipulation of bits of information. One is done by the human or animal nervous system; the other is done by man-made computers. Both have humble and simple beginnings. As powerful and as awesome as supercomputers are, they evolved from curious people experimenting with logic circuits consisting of a few resistors and diodes. They developed a "truth table," whereby a particular set of inputs will deliver a particular output. For instance, an "and gate" must have all inputs "high" before you can have "high" output. Do not get confused by the words "high" and "low" or "zeros" and "ones"; these words refer to the state (example: absence or presence of voltage) at the inputs and output of these circuits. Throw several of these circuits together and add a few memory cells and the resulting combination can work wonders.

A computer executes instructions. When you power up your computer (which includes your phone and almost every appliance in your house, since almost every appliance has a microcomputer embedded inside), it first sees an instruction that tells it where to find the next instruction to execute. The phrase "telling it where to find the next instruction" does sound so unreal, but fundamentally, these instructions are just a series of "ones and zeros," represented internally in the computer by the absence or presence of a given voltage level at various points in the system.

What is generally referred to as "ones and zeros" are material or energy that are in one of two states, hence binary. It may be magnetic material either magnetized or de-magnetized. It may be a voltage source, usually transistors, with a voltage level representing logic zero and another voltage level representing logic one. It may be a light source, turned on or off. Each individual element may be in one of two states and is called a bit, (short for binary digit.) Each bit may be on or off, otherwise expressed as "high" or "low" or as a "1" or "0." To be more efficient in conveying information, these bits are grouped together to form "bytes" or "word."

The materials that are used to make the logic gates that execute these bits and bytes are usually silicon. Parts of these devices are doped with a small amount of aluminum to change the way they function. These earthly materials have taken onto themselves, (or rather, humans have conferred on them,) nonmaterial characteristics of magic and mystery. The megabytes and terabytes, by which we rate the memory of our computer; the megahertz and teraflops, by which we measure our computer performance; are well on their way to become as mysterious to the layman as the metaphysical phenomena, such as magic, telepathy, and psychokinesis, that we so often believe in. The only reason why computers have not yet reached this revered status is that we are generally familiar with the engineering process and the engineers who make it happen.

Modern computers can navigate robots on the surface of Mars. They can teach a robot to walk, which, when you think the whole thing through or try to write an algorithm for, is really a phenomenal task. Computers have dethroned the grandmaster of chess and have become the champion of champions of *Jeopardy!* They can give you highway directions and even drive your car for you. They even fly the airplane when you are up 30,000 feet in the sky. Without computers, the way we practice medicine would still be in the Dark Ages.

Just as computers are the mysterious expression of simple material things, couldn't all the metaphysical properties we ascribe to ourselves be the physical functions of our brains and other parts of our nervous system?

Inside all the science of physics and chemistry are energy sources, (or maybe one source that expresses itself in different ways) that are awesome and mysterious and is the ultimate source of all energy. No one knows where it comes from; no one knows how or when it comes into being. It may even be beyond our intellectual capacity to comprehend. All we know is that it obeys the laws of physics as we have come to understand physics. The laws of physics are an expression of this source of energy. It has never been demonstrated to have any human attributes, such as love, hate, empathy, sympathy, envy, jealousy, or the capability to react directly to human sensibilities. We also know that there is no instance where this awesome source of energy has been shown in any properly controlled test or study to abrogate the laws of physics in order to facilitate the prayers, hopes, and wishes of human beings. It is responsible for the existence of the universe and everything that the universe consists of. It is responsible for our thoughts, actions, aspirations, dreams, hopes, passion, love, and hate; not in the supernatural, metaphysical sense, but in the natural, physical, and biological sense. This is so because our physical abilities, culture, language, memories, and passion are driven by our core memory, our hormones, and neurotransmitters. All these elements are functions of the microphysics of our bodies.

Galileo stated that the language of the universe is written in the laws of mathematics. The way I understand this is that these are simple basic natural laws that are fundamental and universal. This fundamental source of all energy and the forces that manipulate this energy are usually referred to as Mother Nature by naturalists when the way they affect the planet Earth is considered. Beyond the Earth, they are simply referred to as the forces of nature. This mysterious phenomenon, the interaction of mysterious forces and mysterious energy, is the ultimate question on the minds of scientists: How did this energy and the forces that manipulate them come into being?

This particular phenomenon would fit squarely into the phenomenon that theists know as God, except for one great obstacle: this force and energy combination follows very strict, unyielding, and inanimate principles. It is called the laws of physics. Praying to it will not get you anywhere. Billions of dollars are spent each year on the Superconducting Super Colliders that seek to explore the nature of subatomic particles. This research seeks to understand the fundamental principles of these natural forces.

The theist's approach is to recognize this ultimate source of all energy as God. It is generally referred to as a male person and is ascribed human attributes; that is, he can love, hate, be angry, and be jealous. He makes anything materialize by just commanding it to be so. He willed the universe into existence. He made man from the dust of the earth, then because man displeased him, he destroyed everything by flood, except the occupants of the ark. You have to worship him otherwise he will cause great harm to you. If he gets angry, he will cause earthquakes, fires or tsunami to happen.

It may be quite true, as the theists claim, that this entity is God and has awesome powers, that it is responsible for the creation of everything in the universe by just willing it to happen. The lightning and thunder, which are natural phenomena caused by discharge of electrical energy, has now become the wrath of an angry God. A hurricane, caused by a rising current of warm air, has now become a punishment from God for the sins of the people. The rainbow, which is caused by the separation of colors by the water droplets because each wavelength is refracted at a different angle, has now become a promise from God not to destroy the world by flood a second time. This phenomenon must necessarily have been happening ever since the sun has been shining when there is rain falling from another part of the sky.

I have discussed this topic with many scholars of religion, and their answer to me is that God has endowed the human species with unique attributes to enable humans to serve him. Is this a logical, rational answer or just platitudes from people who think that they have answers for everything, simply because they do not know how very little knowledge the human species has when the totality of the human experience is considered?

I know of a beautiful little church on the top of a hill in Hartford, Connecticut, USA. Its tall, pointed, picturesque spire against the sky paints a picture that postcards are made of. Unfortunately, it happened that lightning struck the spire and started a fire in the church. The story that was going around was that there were hypocrites in the church and God was punishing them. The church was repaired, including the spire. A few years later, it was again hit by lightning. Now the story that was going around was that the second lightning strike was positive proof that the church members were wicked and hypocritical; that was why God was punishing them.

Do you believe that God was punishing the members for their wickedness? If you believe that God has humanlike attributes and was punishing the people as he did with Sodom and Gomorrah, then you may have no problem believing that God was punishing the members because they were sinful. Fortunately, someone had a more scientific idea and installed a lightning arrestor on the church spire. It has been several decades now, and there has not been any damage from a lightning strike since.

Lightning and thunder are natural phenomena that obey the laws of physics and are not a mystery anymore. They are not caused by God being angry with anyone, or God batting his eyes. As children, we were taught a poem in elementary school part of which goes like this: "He (God) batted his eyes, and the lightning flashed. He clapped his hands, and the thunder rolled."

Lightning is a giant electrical spark. Friction between particles in storm clouds strips electrons off atoms and causes a difference in electrical potential between one part of the cloud and another, or between the cloud and the earth. When this potential (voltage) builds up to where it overcomes the electrical resistance of the air, this giant spark occurs, this is the lightning. This lightning causes the air to expand and contract rapidly, setting up a to-and-fro movement of the air molecules, referred to as vibration of the air. This is sensed by our ears as sound and is called thunder.

The electrical potential of these lightning bolts are usually tens to hundreds of millions of volts and the current flow measuring thousands of amperes (amps). Of course, nobody can physically measure these values, but they can be inferred. For instance, it has been determined scientifically that it takes 30,000 volts to "jump" a space measuring one centimeter in air at normal humidity. We have seen lightning bolts that are tens of meters long. Calculate this and see how many million volts it takes to jump fifty meters. When this jump is made, the path between the negative and positive points becomes ionized, allowing a gigantic amount of current to flow. The electrical voltage between the cloud and the earth will find the path of least resistance to discharge through; therefore, the tallest object in the area that will conduct electricity is likely to be the object to get hit. The aerial rod of a lightning arrestor is made to be the tallest object in the area that will conduct electricity. If the conductor that connects the aerial rod to the ground rod is bulky enough, the electrical charge in the cloud that has the potential to cause a lightning strike will be safely conducted to earth. All this contraption has its limitations, however; some lightning charges are just too powerful to be discharged by a lightning arrestor without causing damage.

From this explanation of what causes lightning, you can deduce that some of what we hear about lightning are myths. For example, it is a myth that you are more likely to get struck by lightning if you are standing near a glass window inside your house in a thunderstorm than if you are away from the window. It is a myth that lightning is caused by God batting his eyes. It is a myth that God uses lightning to punish people.

People who live in regions where the winter temperature gets very cold sometimes, often unwittingly, create their own miniature lightning and thunder. When the heat is on in your house, meaning that the indoor humidity is very low, a walk across the carpet, reaching for the doorknob, usually produces a nasty static shock. The act of walking across the carpet produces the same kind of friction that produces the voltage in the clouds. This static discharge between your finger and the doorknob can be as much as 100,000 volts. Luckily, the number of electrons available to sustain a current flow is relatively small, and as soon as any current starts flowing, the voltage drops to near zero. The "static cling" when you are wearing nylon clothes or even when you are combing your hair are also instances of friction producing electricity.

My friend who believed that God caused the water to evaporate will also believe that God caused the voltage to drop from 100,000 volts to near zero volts so that nobody gets killed from a static discharge when you walk across the carpet in your house. There is no proof whether she is right or wrong, but I will repeat that it has never been demonstrated in any controlled study that any deity has ever caused the laws of physics to be overridden. Besides, static discharges do kill people; lightning is a good example.

When I was growing up, gasoline tankers had steel chains connected to its body, the other end left to drag on the road. This was to discharge static electricity that the friction of the tires caused while rolling on the road. With a volatile cargo as gasoline, static that may cause a spark that could ignite the gasoline could not be tolerated. With better technology in tire manufacturing, this hazard no longer exists.

If you have an old-fashioned AM radio receiver, which you can manually change the frequency that it is tuned to, you can hear static discharges in the clouds represented as audible crackle in the loudspeaker of the radio receiver. This used to be referred to as static or atmospherics.

An electrical charge that looks more like lightning can be made by a Van de Graaff generator. Here is an excerpt from Wikipedia describing it:

> *{A Van de Graaff generator is an electrostatic generator which uses a moving belt to accumulate electric charge on a hollow metal globe on the top of an insulated column, creating very high electric potentials. It produces very high voltage direct current (DC) electricity at low current levels. It was invented by American physicist Robert J. Van de Graaff in 1929. The potential difference achieved by modern Van de Graaff generators can be as much as 5 megavolts (5 million volts).}*

I cannot dispute that God endowed humans with inducement to serve him or deterrence not to serve him. Conversely, why should anyone accept this proposition simply by faith with no acceptable evidence or proof, or even the preponderance of realistic evidence? Because we do not know how or why something exists or happens does not mean that we have to invent an answer. We should strive to promote facts. "Fact" means an event that takes place in real time and real space and of which real record exists.

Since our brains are the total repository of all our knowledge, including the internal knowledge of all our body parts that only our brains are privy to, all our thoughts, everything that can be described as I or me, is it unreasonable to conclude that the functions of our brains are what we construe as our spirits, our souls, our psyche, or the spirit of God in us? Could it be the answer to "Who am I?"

There are some schools of thoughts that believe that a person's spirit or soul or whatever you want to call it, is a separate entity from the body, not a function of our physical body, and is incorporated in the body at birth by the process of reincarnation or some other unnatural process. Even more importantly, that this spirit survives the death of the physical body. If this were the case, wouldn't a newborn baby be able to understand spoken language and be able to speak intelligently instead of babbling, since this incarnated "life" had previously acquired knowledge and intelligence to use that knowledge?

Theists believe that this additional dimension that we as humans appear to have is the spirit of God in us, that God made humans special and his spirit dwells in us. This additional dimension envisions a world where gods and ghosts exist, where heaven or hell is the final destination of our immortal souls, where obeah and voodoo can cast spells on people for better or worse, where people can communicate telepathically or material things can even be transported from one place to another by psychokinesis; a whole new world where our thoughts and prayers can cause material things to come into existence and override the laws of physics to make unnatural things happen. Ultimately, with the invocation of the power of God, this added dimension could make any and all things we desire happen, where whatever we imagine can be made possible, where humans could even call upon the power of God to afflict his enemy. This is the word where people who are not scientifically inclined refer to as the metaphysical world.

The need to have God as a consideration in our lives should not be downplayed. Let us take another look at the pee-pee-cluck-cluck syndrome. Recall those fragile and helpless chickens, pee-peeing to make sure that their mother is nearby to protect and feed them. This is what the presence of God is like to a lot of people. I have also seen chickens that have lost their mother. In many cases, their mother was caught by a mongoose. Every other fowl, both mother hen and other chickens, kept pecking and harassing those motherless chickens to keep them away, to make it clear to them that they did not belong in that clan. They went around foraging for themselves in a state of nervous anxiety. If they were not given special attention by us humans, they usually would not survive to adulthood.

Humans who feel deprived of this "mother hen" protection may also feel this psychological deficit like the chickens who lost their mother. It appears that we as humans go to great extent to avoid being in this predicament. We tend to find a church, a clan, a gang, or a cult to embrace. Some of us do fall into that state of nervous anxiety, foraging by ourselves in the "Slough of Despond", as John Bunyan aptly puts it.

Religion is not the only inspiring course of action that a person can take to experience a positive and satisfying lifestyle. Secular humanism also provides an outlet for self-actualization and a lifestyle that is fulfilling but does not have to embrace religious dogmas.

Psychologists, with Sigmund Freud pioneering the hypothesis, strive to compartmentalize the human psyche into three parts: the id, the ego, and the superego. The id, they claim, is the animal instinct in us that is always seeking instant gratification. The id wants us to have sexual intercourse anytime the desire is aroused, while the ego says, "This is not the time or place." The ego is the part that strives to implement social boundaries. The id says, "There's food, I have to eat." The ego says, "It's not our food, I will eat when I get home." The superego, by definition, is the conscience of our psyche. This is what makes us feel guilty when we do something wrong.

Unfortunately, our brains do not have a social filter to separate right from wrong or good from evil. Like a giant vacuum cleaner, it sucks up all the data that come in via our five physical senses. It does not matter if these things are bad things or evil things. All these things go together to construct our psyche. Right and wrong are quite arbitrary. What one culture believes to be good may be repulsive and atrocious to another culture or even to the same culture in a different era. What our brains construe as right or wrong largely depends on the culture we live in. Even the idea of the spirit of God that we believe we have within us does not stop us from doing atrocious things. The prevailing argument is that God gives humans free will to do whatever we want to do, even ungodly things. This I find to be diametrically opposed to the idea of an omnipotent, compassionate, and loving God who we can depend on to protect us from all harms. Some people do believe both things at the same time; logic usually takes a flight through the window when religion walks through the door. This hands-off posture would surely make God redundant. There is no evidence that I am aware of where God told anyone that he gives humans free will to do whatever they want to do.

There is a danger in imagining and concluding about something without going through a process of logical and analytical evaluation. Logical evaluation, in scientific terms, usually means double-blind controlled tests, and peer review. The same can be applied to our everyday decision-making, albeit in a less formal way. Inside of this alternate dimension that we have created, there is no physical process by which we as human beings can measure the presence or absence of the spirit of God in us or when we believe God is talking to us; therefore, we have to be careful about any assertion that God has spoken to us.

I have a friend who was stalked and harassed by a woman who claimed that God revealed to her that my friend was her future husband. She was born in the United Kingdom and lived there for several decades, then she came to visit her sister in Connecticut, USA. This English lady was introduced to my friend who was living at an apartment that her sister owned. The woman became insanely enamored with this man. She swore that the man was her future husband because God revealed it to her. She claimed that on several occasions, God appeared to her and said that this man shall be her husband. This man had to leave his apartment and go to live where the woman could not find him. Apparently, he chose not to get a legal restraining order to avoid embarrassment to the woman's relatives. If he had gotten a restraining order, it is almost certain that the woman would not have complied.

Did God appear to her as she claimed? Was she hallucinating? Was she taking some psychedelic drugs, such as LSD? Was she mentally ill? Are other people who claim that God talks to them or that they talk to God any different? Unfortunately, there are no parameters by which these cases can be judged objectively; we just have to rely on objective and professional evaluation of the situation to make the best call.

To cultivate a healthy and rational psyche, one has to have a clear sense of direction about his or her personal philosophy as it relates to the rest of the world. A person can be like a rudderless ship. Even worse than a rudderless ship, this person (or ideology) can be like a rudderless ship with its engine running, ploughing headlong into other objects like a wrecking ball. We need to have a positive, analytical, and aspirational purpose in our lives. Most of us, perhaps all of us, at some time in our lives "lost faith" in our own ability to pursue a self-actualized life. We also need to develop an analytical thinking process that can be a healthy repository for empirical facts buoyed by a rational inquiring mind, not irrational dogmas and myths.

The following story and all stories in this book are factual, though the names of people are changed for obvious reasons.

Sister B is a good example of how the functions of our brains, (otherwise called our mind or our psyche,) can influence our health, physically and mentally.

Sister B was a kind and gentle person, very spiritual and religious. She would make sure that there was enough food in the house to give any acquaintances who happened to stop by on their way from the village square or the city. She was a devout member of her church. She was always reading her Bible and singing spiritual songs.

In her middle age, Sister B became susceptible to a lot of emotional and physical problems. She suffered from frequent seizures, which were usually preceded by severe headaches. She had been treated by several doctors, but the sickness persisted. She was also paranoid by the belief (rightly, wrongly, or partially) that her husband was having an affair with another woman. I happened to have firsthand knowledge that, in at least some of the instances that he was accused of visiting another woman, he was actually tending his animals on his small farm. There was not much peace in the house; the atmosphere was usually acrimonious and bitter.

Her church colleagues did not make the situation any better. The diagnosis of the problem by her church colleagues was that her mother-in-law's ghost was haunting her. The worst part of this conundrum was that these church colleagues did not express this as a belief or opinion; they claimed that it was revealed to them by the Holy Spirit in the prayer meetings. They would have prayer meetings at Sister B's house. While singing and praying, they would get "into the spirit" and "speak in tongues," which were uncontrolled hysterical expressions of vocal and physical commotions.

When the ruckus subsided, the "interpreter" in the group would announce in a very nuanced way what the Holy Spirit supposedly revealed. In this case, it was the ghost of Sister B's dead mother-in-law hurting her. The next round of the commotion was to "rebuke and discharge" the ghost. Generally, there was no change in the situation except for a general exhaustion of everyone that lasted a few hours. From time to time, other causes other than the ghost of Sister B's mother-in-law were identified. These other causes ranged from other ghosts to obeah spells cast by her enemies; yet there was no significant change.

It is so easy to assume something that is difficult or impossible to prove is false, like those stories that one has to accept by faith. How do you prove a story that a ghost is tormenting someone and making them sick? How do you disprove it? This is a great danger to those who believe without proper evaluation. The greatest danger is when these unverified stories are repeated, amplified, and take on lives of their own.

Eventually, the "prayer meetings" became less frequent. Most evenings Sister B got together with her grandchildren to sing. They mostly sang hymns, choruses, and songs from the Sankey songbook. This was not something planned but just happened spontaneously. From this point onward, Sister B started a gradual process of physical and emotional healing. The acrimony in the household was getting less. The idea that Sister B was being haunted by ghosts faded into the background; it was hardly mentioned eventually. The paranoia about her husband having extramarital affairs had also faded into the background. The seizures, headaches, and general poor health improved considerably over time.

Looking back on this situation, I have concluded that most of Sister B's problems were emotional problems that were expressed physiologically. She did not acquire the proper balance between verifiable facts, or at least circumstantial evidence, and falsehood that she accepted as the truth. This caused a situation similar to what is called "reset wind-up" in control systems parlance, which is explained below.

The background of this story is in a rural environment over sixty years ago. A lot of us may be smirking and saying, "How primitive was that!" Let me warn you that too many of us are suffering from a similar psychosis in our urban modern environment. You can substitute the ghost, prayer meetings, and "speaking in tongues" in Sister B's case for drugs (prescribed and unprescribed), conspiracy theories, reliance on erroneous doctors' advice or prescriptions, addiction to mentally-debilitating social media, and a debilitating approach to life in general. People's mental state have not changed over the years; only the tools they use to manipulate their emotions have changed.

"Reset wind-up" is a term used in electronic, pneumatic, or hydraulic control systems, where the control system is set to be controlled at a particular point. If the system cannot accurately sense the process it is controlling, it will keep increasing the control signal until this signal gets to its maximum possible level. Because of erroneous feedback, the controlling device (let us say a water supply valve) would have been driven wide open and stuff would start getting out of control.

To illustrate this situation, let us imagine that we have a holding tank that supplies water to a village. Water from a lake below is pumped into the holding tank. There is a controller (pneumatic, hydraulic, or electronic) that keeps the tank at 80 percent full. There has to be some sort of signal that tells the controller what the level in the tank is, the controller puts out a signal to a device (a control valve) that modulates the flow of water into the tank. What will happen if the tank level signal to the controller does not reflect the true level of the tank or even if this signal is disrupted? It is not hard to imagine that this tank will eventually run dry or will overflow, depending on which direction the error goes. Accurate feedback is necessary for all control systems, whether they control a water tank, a rocket on its way to the moon, or the thought process that controls the human mind. Accurate information is necessary for any system that has a control function. This is even more important for the control of the human mind. Distorting this feedback signal is what brainwashing is all about, especially in this era of the Internet-driven social media. As I am writing now, there are bizarre conspiracy theories circulating on the Internet that make you wonder if people who believe and act on these stories are really sane. The problem is that they are deprived of accurate information, and more importantly, their ability to evaluate this information is not functional for one reason or another.

There are many awesome and little-understood control systems in our bodies; most of them we know very little about, a few we have some knowledge of their operation. Among these few are our body temperature and our blood pressure.

Our normal body temperature is 98.6 degrees on the Fahrenheit scale. This may vary by about two degrees either higher or lower. When we consider the vast array of variables that would cause our body temperature to change considerably outside of this range, it becomes easy to visualize how intricate and precise this control system is. Our discussion is not about abnormal conditions, such as when we are having a fever, other internal physiological anomalies, or when we are exposed to extreme temperature conditions. Under normal conditions, we are subjected to changes in the amount of clothes we are wearing, the temperature of the air around our bodies, changes in humidity, changes in wind speed, whether we are walking, running, or sitting, or if we are directly in the sun or in the shade. All the above variables would cause drastic changes in our body temperature if it were not for this tight control system that holds our temperature at approximately 98.6 degrees. Our bodies go to great lengths to conserve, generate, or radiate heat to maintain this temperature. The blood flow to our skin is regulated to modulate our temperature. When we overheat our bodies sweat to cool us down, when we get too cold, our bodies shiver to generate heat.

Another system in our bodies that is heavily regulated is our blood pressure. Unlike our body temperature, our blood pressure is not controlled at a fixed value because its primary function is to provide a precise flow of oxygen, mainly to our brain and secondarily to the rest of our body.

CHAPTER 2

RELIGION VERSUS SCIENCE

The Galileo Story

Religion and science have been in conflict ever since the dawn of civilization. An infamous iteration of this conflict was the inquisition of Galileo Galilei. Other than the Eastern Orthodox Church, the Roman Catholic Church was the dominant Christian authority throughout Christendom. It wielded its power, religious and political, for hundreds of years and was the de facto governing authority in the flailing Roman Empire. It preached to its faithful followers that God made the Earth as the center of the universe, and the sun, moon, and all the stars revolve around the Earth.

Galileo was an Italian mathematician, astronomer, physicist, and engineer (sounds like a very smart guy). He made significant improvements to the telescope which was, at that time, a recent invention. He used his improved telescope to discover the moons of the planet Jupiter. He discovered that the Earth's moon was not the luminescent, romantic orb placed by God in the heavens to give us romantic moonlight, but a rather rugged unromantic chunk of rock, which only reflects light from the sun and did not generate light. He postulated that the sun was the center of the solar system and not Earth. This did not sit well with the leaders of the Roman Catholic Church; neither was his discovery that Jupiter's moons orbit that planet. Everything, according to the church, was supposed to revolve around the Earth. The church's doctrine was that the Earth was the center of the universe, and the sun, moon, and everything else in the universe revolved around it. The church's position was "Our way was the way God made it, the Bible said so."

Galileo published his discovery that the sun, not Earth, is the center of the solar system. He tried to soften the impact on the church by also publishing a counternarrative to the sun-centered hypothesis.

This gross violation of the divine doctrine must not be tolerated by the church. In 1633, Galileo was summoned to the Roman Inquisition; he was charged and convicted of "vehement suspicion of heresy." He was forced to publicly recant the "heresy" that earth orbits the sun, and that earth was not the center of the universe. Even then, he was placed under house arrest for the rest of his life.

Thanks to Galileo's research, astronomy has advanced to the point where mankind put a human being on the surface of the moon. The church imprisoned him for life but could not imprison the curiosity to acquire knowledge as a result of the study of factual evidence, rather than believing myth as a result of blind faith. Just like the moon, thousands of man-made satellites are now in orbit around the earth. They provide innumerable amounts of information that enable us to communicate seamlessly by phone, to watch live TV halfway across the world, see the vast and mind-blowing pictures captured by the Hubble Space Telescope, and capture information to improve weather forecasting. Now you can be in Tokyo, Japan, and watch who is approaching your front door in New York City in real time. Because of the Global Positioning System, which depends on satellites, we now have cars and trucks that drive themselves and airplanes that fly themselves. We put vehicles that drive around and perform prearranged tasks on the planet Mars. Without satellite communication, most of these things would not be possible. A limited amount of this transfer of information may be possible via cables laid across the floor of the oceans and radio relay stations across the planet, but just imagine how difficult and impractical that would be.

Let us pause for a moment and imagine what would be the result if the church had succeeded in squelching scientific research that is contrary to their philosophy. What if the church had prevailed in deluding the rest of the world that everything in the universe revolves around earth?

How did the church become the authority that could sentence someone to death (in the case of Galileo, to house arrest for life) for saying something that the church considered heresy?

Onward Christian Soldiers

The following information about the Roman Empire, its influence on the Christian religion, and the demise of the Empire were gleaned from sources such as, but not limited to, *Encyclopedia Britannica*, Wikipedia, *World History Encyclopedia*, History.com, and WesternCivilization.com.

During the halcyon days of the Roman empire, there was little tolerance for religion such as Christianity and Judaism. At the time when Judaism was an established religion, Christianity was a fledgling upstart. Christians were persecuted by both Jews and Romans. (Talk about being caught between a rock and a hard place.) Several of the early Christian were killed by the Romans. Then a period of serendipity happened to Christendom and the rest of mankind. Emperor Flavius Constantine I of Rome was facing a major battle. It is said that he had a dream that if he painted the emblem of the Christian religion on the shields of his soldiers, he would win the battle. He painted the shields, and he won the battle. He went on to win other battles under the emblem of Christianity. Constantine became a convert to Christianity. (He was not baptized and did not officially become a Christian until he was dying.) He soon used his power to address the status of Christians, issuing in the year AD 313 the Edict of Milan, which allowed the freedom of worship for Christians throughout the Roman Empire.

In AD 324, Emperor Constantine of the Western Roman Empire defeated Licinius, the Emperor of the Eastern part of the Roman Empire (the Byzantine Empire), and took control of a reunited empire. After this triumph, Constantine founded the city of Constantinople (now Istanbul, Turkey) on the site of the Byzantium. As Constantine's power grew, so did the power of the Roman Catholic Church, which, by then, was the universal authority that governed all of Christendom.

The Christian faith at this time was not a unified body. Just picture a relatively small group, the followers of Jesus Christ, being persecuted and killed by the greatest authority in the world, the Roman Empire, suddenly becoming the comrade in arms and the pawn of this powerful authority. During this period there was heated and continuing controversy over conflicting beliefs and written materials pertaining to different aspects of Christianity.

A major schism that plagued the early Christian church was Arianism, a sect of Christians who asserted that if Jesus Christ were the Son of God, he would be distinct from God the Father and would be subordinate to the Father and could not be one and the same as the Father (God). This is a logical deduction to be made by anyone who can step out of the indoctrination and cultural bias that pervades society, then, and now.

The Arian controversy (not to be confused with the Indo-Europeans known as Aryans or the race of people Adolf Hitler called the master race) was a discourse that occurred in the Christian church of the fourth century CE that threatened to upend the meaning of the church itself.

The Christian church, like the Judaic religion before it, was committed to monotheism. All the Abrahamic religions say there is only one God. The Christian church, which, by now, had become the religion of the Roman Empire, adopted the doctrine that God is one entity that comprises three "Godheads," the Father, the Son, and the Holy Spirit.

Arius who was a presbyter and preacher from Alexandra in Egypt, argued for the supremacy of God the Father; thus, he insisted that only God the Father had no beginning and that the Father alone was infinite and eternal. Arius attracted a significant following in the early Christian church, much to the chagrin of the leadership of the church in Rome. The Christian church was deeply divided over disagreements on Christology, (the nature of the relationship between Jesus and God).

The official doctrine of church was that the three entities of the "Godhead" are distinct yet are one and the same. (When religion enters a discussion, logic flies out the window!) This is somewhat hard to comprehend, but the Christian warriors went to war to assert this doctrine. The question of an anthropomorphic God, the attribution of human characteristics or behavior to a nonhuman God, and other characterization of God was a philosophical conversation that was widely discussed in that era, as opposed to the current era where a significant percentage of the people on the planet have coalesced into the acceptance of the Abrahamic God of the Jews, Christians, and Muslims. [New World Encyclopedia: https://www.worldhistory.org/religion/]

To settle these various contradictions, the Roman Emperor Constantine convened The First Council of Nicaea, which was the first ecumenical council of the Christian church. This council produced the Nicene Creed which became the official religious doctrine of the Roman Empire. Most significantly, it resulted in the first uniform creed of the Christian church. With the creation of this creed, a precedent was established for subsequent local and regional councils of bishops to create statements of belief that properly define the doctrine for the whole of Christendom. Christian sects, such as the Arians and the Gnostics, which did not conform to this creed, were disbanded from the church.

At the dawn of Christianity, there was one Christian church whose main message was the teaching of the gospel (the good news), even though there were many controversial sects to this doctrine. During the reign of Emperor Constantine, the Roman Empire adopted Christianity as their de facto religion. Over time, an ever-growing rift took place between the Christian doctrine in the eastern half of the Roman Empire (the Byzantium) and

the Western Roman Empire. Remember that the Byzantium and
the Western Roman Empire had always been in conflict, either
military or verbal conflict, except for occasions of cooperation
that benefit their mutual interest. The Christian church of
the Byzantium is now more generally known as the Eastern
Orthodox Church. The church of the Western Roman Empire
was the Roman Catholic Church, which is now split into the
Roman Catholic Church and various Protestant churches.

It is unfathomable that one of the lasting rifts between the
eastern church and western church was whether leavened or
unleavened bread should be used in the Eucharist, a Christian
ceremony commemorating the Last Supper, in which bread and
wine are consecrated and consumed. Another one of those trivial
rifts was that the Eastern Orthodox Church began dipping
the bread in the wine, which was condemned by the Roman
Catholic Church. Another more substantial bane of contention
was that one sect viewed Jesus as having two natures (human
and divine), while others thought Jesus was only divine. This
conflict had to do with the Arian doctrine that Jesus Christ
could not be God and the Son of God at the same time, if one
believed in a monotheistic God. The Eastern Christians favored
Arianism, while the western church rejected it.

There were other rifts that led to the Great Schism that became
official in the year 1054. The Western Roman Catholic Church
unilaterally inserted extra words into the Nicene Creed to
promote the divinity of Jesus Christ; the eastern church strongly
objected to this. The western church believed that the pope, the
religious leader of the western church, should have authority
over the patriarch, the religious authority of the eastern
church. The eastern church disagreed. Each church recognized
their own leaders, and when the western church eventually

excommunicated Michael Cerularius and the entire eastern church, the eastern church retaliated by excommunicating the Roman pope Leo III and the Roman church with him. While the two churches have never reunited, over a thousand years after their split, the western and eastern branches of Christianity came to more peaceful terms. In 1965, Pope Paul VI and Patriarch Athenagoras I lifted the longstanding mutual excommunication decrees made by their respective churches.

There was no single canonized (collection of writings sanctioned by the church) collection of texts that Christians used, even after Christianity became the official religion of the Roman Empire and after the Nicene Creed. Since early Christians were dissidents of the Jewish faith, and their fledgling religion was a deviation of Judaism, they had grounding in the Jewish Torah and other Jewish literature. There were also numerous contemporary literatures by the early Christians and other scholars. Several attempts were made by the early church to canonize some of these manuscripts so that Christians could have one common set of writings, but these attempts were often unsuccessful. The Turkish church leader Marcion was expelled from the church by the Roman Catholic authority for attempting such a canon. The Syrian writer Titain also attempted to canonize some of these writings, but he also failed. The Muratorian Canon, which is believed to be dated AD 200, is the earliest compilation of canonical texts resembling the New Testament.

The Torah, which is the first five books of the Bible as we know it, existed originally as stories told orally by the ancient Palestinian Semites, particularly the Hebrews who practiced the Jewish religion called Judaism. Among these stories were the stories of the creation (Genesis), the freedom of the Hebrew (the

Israelites) from slavery in Egypt (Exodus), the teachings that the Hebrew people said God gave them to govern themselves (Leviticus), the genealogy of the Hebrew people (Numbers), and God's covenant with Moses (Deuteronomy). As writing became a part of the culture, those stories were written down and have been changed and edited over the years. Along with the Torah, other writings of prophets, judges, kings, and scribes were added into a collection called the Jewish Bible, which is now a part of the Christian Bible called the Old Testament. In the early years of Christianity, several and diverse conflicts erupted concerning the fledgling Christian religion. Many texts were written about the life of Jesus, the apostles of Jesus also wrote letters to the new converts to Christianity.

After several attempts to produce a unified written scripture, Pope Damasus 1 at the Council of Rome in the year AD 382 canonized several early Christian writings (the New Testament), along with the Jewish Bible (the Old Testament), into what would be the earliest canon that roughly has a similar collection of manuscripts that could be identified as what we now know as the Bible. Books did not exist at that time; writing was done on scrolls of papyrus or parchment. The ancient Bible has gone through numerous changes to become the Bible as we know it. In medieval times, the Roman Catholic Church, which had supreme authority over all of Christendom, except the Eastern Orthodox Church, fought many battles and killed thousands of people to ensure that only their version of Christianity and no other religious dogma was taught anywhere in any part of the world that they could exert their influence.

There were many other Christian books that were excluded from this canon, including the Gnostic Gospels. This brought forth another controversy; what qualified some manuscripts and disqualified others from being included in the Bible?

This was the Bible in its earliest form; the Bible became the official holy book of the Christian religion. It has gone through various changes to get to where it is today.

Given the history of the Bible, should we, in blind faith, accept stories in the Bible with nothing to authenticate them? Just because they are in the Bible, we accept them without question. Does it not look like we are still being brainwashed by a pope and his gang that died nearly two thousand years ago?

When I was growing up, I asked my mother who wrote the Bible. Her answer was quick and unambiguous as if she had practiced this answer over and over. "The Bible was written by inspired men of God," she said. She obviously was brainwashed by a lot of people into believing that a group of sages were sent in a room, and God directly dictated the Bible to them, much like the story of the Ten Commandments. She, like most other people, is not aware of the history of the Bible, or the history of Christianity for that matter, except as it appears in the Bible, which we erroneously believe was narrated by "inspired men of God."

In spite of all the creeds and canons decreed by the early Christian church, it has never been able to become a united entity. The schism between the Eastern Orthodox Church and the Western Roman Catholic Church that started from the beginning of the Christian era still exists today.

The western church, also called the Roman Catholic Church, which incorporated the Holy Roman Empire and the Papal States, was shattered by the Protestant revolution in Europe.

This is how *[history.com] introduced* an article on the Reformation:

> {*The Protestant Reformation was the 16th-century religious, political, intellectual and cultural upheaval that splintered Catholic Europe, setting in place the structures and beliefs that would define the continent in the modern era. In northern and central Europe, reformers like Martin Luther, John Calvin and Henry VIII challenged papal authority and questioned the Catholic Church's ability to define Christian practice. They argued for a religious and political redistribution of power into the hands of Bible- and pamphlet-reading pastors and princes.*}

The Reformation in Europe was mainly sparked by Martin Luther, a German monk and professor of theology at the University of Wittenberg. In 1517, according to tradition, he posted his *95 Theses* on the door of the Castle Church in Wittenberg, Germany. This was a list of statements that expressed Luther's concerns about certain church practices, largely the sale of "indulgences."

The sale of indulgences was a practice where the church acknowledged a donation or other charitable work with a piece of paper (the indulgence) that certified that your soul would enter heaven more quickly by reducing your time in purgatory. If you committed no serious sins that guaranteed your place in hell, and you died before repenting and atoning for all your sins, then your soul went to purgatory, a kind of halfway station where you finished atoning for your sins before being allowed to enter heaven. The "indulgence" you purchased would guarantee you a shorter stay in purgatory. In other words, people were paying priests to pray their persona out of purgatory.

Pope Leo X had granted indulgences to raise money for the rebuilding of St. Peter's Basilica in Rome. These indulgences were being sold by Johann Tetzel not far from Wittenberg, where Luther was professor of theology. Luther was gravely concerned about the way in which getting into heaven was connected with a financial transaction. But the sale of indulgences was not Luther's only disagreement with the institution of the church.

About this time in Europe, the church was seen as an institution plagued by internal power struggles. At one point, the church was ruled by three popes simultaneously, all claiming to be the true pope. Popes and cardinals often lived more like kings than spiritual leaders.

Other leaders of the revolution who made contributions with the aim of reforming the church in Europe were John Calvin and Huldrych Zwingli.

King Henry VIII of England also made significant contributions to reform the church, even though his persuasion was a personal one. He broke from the Roman Catholic Church because the pope would not agree with him to divorce his wife, Catherine of Aragon. Henry VIII consolidated his break with the Catholic Church by establishing the Church of England.

In response to the Reformation movement, the Roman Catholic Church, including churches in the Holy Roman Empire, launched a counter-revolutionary war that lasted for centuries and killed millions of people. At least one third of the German-speaking population of Europe was killed, a mortality rate twice that of World War 1. Inquisitions were set up by the church for the eradication of all "heretics," and numerous wars were declared on states that did not comply with the edicts from Rome.

What role did God play when all these atrocities were being committed in his name? Can we continue to bury our sense of logic and honesty by saying that he allowed humans to have their free will to slaughter millions of people because they did not agree with a particular version of Christianity? When "indulgences" were being sold ostensibly to shorten the time your soul stayed in purgatory, would God not do something about that ungodly extortion?

With the Edict of Thessalonica in AD 380, Emperor Theodosius I made Christianity the official religion of the Roman Empire. The authority of the Roman Catholic (universal) Church did not decline with the decline of the Roman Empire; instead, it grew. Christian zealots took the message of the Roman Catholic doctrine into the "barbarian" territories, whose inhabitants were now occupying the flailing Roman Empire. Irish monks played a major role in preserving the structure of Christianity and the records of the Roman antiquity.

The church, using their newfound power, amassed armies of "Christian soldiers" to wage war on non-Christians who they called barbarians, and also Christians who did not conform to the official doctrine of the church. These armies of Christian soldiers were incentivized by church policies that they could keep whatever loot they took from the people they slaughtered and the assurance of the pope that if they take part in the Crusades against the "infidels," all their sins would be forgiven when they die, and they will all go to heaven. This brings back to my memory the Sunday school song we were taught as children and sang with great enthusiasm:

> *Onward Christian soldiers, marching as to war*
> *With the cross of Jesus, marching on before. Christ*
> *the royal master, leads against the foe. Forward*
> *into battle, see His banners go.*

I always thought that this song was an allegorical expression of the Christian faith, but given the fact that it was written in 1871, not too far removed from the Christian carnage in Europe, it may well have been a literal battle hymn.

As the power and the glory of the Christians increased, so did their militancy and the atrocities they committed. One of their early objectives was to capture Jerusalem from the Muslims who had been occupying that area for 450 years in harmony with the Jews, Christians, and other ethnic brethren. In that period of European history, Jerusalem was believed by Christians to be the center of the cosmos where Jesus Christ was crucified, buried, and resurrected. They believed that Jerusalem was where God resided, and Jerusalem would have to be purged and sanitized for God to send down the "New Jerusalem" on earth.

Here is a quote from the Bible, Revelation 21

{Then I, John, saw the holy city, New Jerusalem, coming down out of heaven from God, prepared as a bride adorned for her

husband. And I heard a loud voice from heaven saying, "Behold, the tabernacle of God is with men, and He will dwell with them, and they shall be His people. God Himself will be with them and be their God. And God will wipe away every tear from their eyes; there shall be no more death, nor sorrow, nor crying. There shall be no more pain, for the former things have passed away."}

This is the Christian doctrine that was canonized in the Bible. Unfortunately, this doctrine is still preached and accepted as reality in these modern era. After the call of Pope Urban II in 1095 that initiated the First Christian Crusade, the main objective of the Christians was to gain control of the "Holy Land," There are numerous accounts in the annals of history of the savage brutality with which the Christians massacred the inhabitants of Jerusalem.

The following are two excerpts about the capture of Jerusalem by the Christian Crusaders and the carnage that ensued. The first is from the *[World History Encyclopedia]*, and to give some balance to the story, the other is from Bar-Allan University in Israel, captioned, "Jerusalem in the Crusade."

> From the [World *History Encyclopedia:* https://www.worldhistory.org/article/1254/ the-capture-of-jerusalem-1099-ce/]
>
> *{The capture of Jerusalem from Muslim control was the primary goal of the First Crusade (1095–1102 CE), a combined military campaign organised by western rulers, the Pope, and the Byzantine Empire. After a brief siege, the city was captured on July 15, 1099 CE and the population massacred. A Muslim relief army was defeated three weeks later,*

and the First Crusade was hailed as a remarkable success in the west. The huge problems of logistics, famine, disease, a formidable enemy, and internal rivalries had all, somehow, been overcome, but the future defense of the Holy Land would require many more crusades over the next two centuries, and none would be as successful as the first.}

From [Bar-Allen University: https://www2.biu. ac.il/js/rennert/history_9.html]

{The Crusaders savagely murdered the Jewish and Moslem inhabitants of Jerusalem. The dimensions of the massacre were so horrific that "rivers of blood" flowed through the streets and even covered the horses' hooves. William of Tyre described the victorious Crusaders "dripping with blood from head to foot, an ominous sight which bought terror to all who met them.}

The brutality with which the carnage was implemented had few parallel. Almost all the 40,000 inhabitants were slaughtered. The few that were not killed were sold at the gate of the city as slaves. The Jews were locked in the central synagogue and burnt to death. When they were finished murdering thousands of innocent people the Crusaders gathered at the Church of the Holy Sepulcher to give thanks to God for the victory he had afforded them. It is hard to imagine that people, especially Christians believed that God supported them in executing this carnage.

This bloody conquest of Jerusalem, where almost all 40,000 of its inhabitants were slaughtered, was how the European

Christians practiced their religion. Muslims, Christians and Jews had coexisted in Jerusalem for hundreds of years until the European Christian church, under the leadership of Pope Urban II, on November 27, 1095, called all Christians in Europe to war against Muslims and Jews in Jerusalem to reclaim the Holy Land, with a cry of "Deus vult!" or "God wills it!"

After the conquest of the city was secured, the Crusaders selected Godfrey de Bouillon as the city's ruler. He was given the title "Advocate of the Holy Sepulcher" and established Jerusalem as the capital of the country which he called, "The Crusader Kingdom of Jerusalem."

The Crusade to capture Jerusalem was only one of many church-sanctioned Crusades fought by armies of Christian soldiers. The first Crusade began in 1095, when the Christian church undertook to capture Jerusalem, which was, at that time, occupied by the Muslims. After this victory, the Christian church expanded the idea of waging war against territories controlled by the Muslims. They also waged war against their own Christian brethren who dared to disagree with the official doctrine of the Roman Catholic Church. These wars were fought to combat what the church saw as paganism and heresy and to resolve conflict among rival Roman Catholic groups or to gain political and territorial advantage. The difference between these campaigns and other Christian religious conflicts was that they were considered a penitential exercise by the church—that is, those who fought in these Crusades would have their sins forgiven.

Our contemporary Western civilization is very silent or very ignorant about these atrocities. We uphold the model of Western civilization as God's model, the way God intends it to be, or as Pope Urban declared, "God wills it!" Wherever it looks messy, we avoid looking at it, covertly suppress it from our history books, or sanitize it. During the slavery era, Europeans purposefully conclude that slavery was justified because they were doing Africans a favor in "civilizing" them and that black people inherited a curse from Noah, which made them slaves perpetually.

Religion has always been used to justify atrocities. What part does God play in all this manipulation of religion for evil deeds? Is it really God's will that causes or allows these things to happen? Is it okay to massacre millions of people and justify the evil deed by making the excuse that it is the will of God? Would humans continue committing these atrocities if, instead of making the excuse that they are doing it in the name of God, they were honest enough to admit that they are doing it to satisfy their own greed for power, and they will be subjected to the logical consequences?

Religious wars and atrocious killings are not unique to the Christian religion, but the scope of this book does not allow me to include all religious wars in all religions. In fact, that would be almost impossible. Therefore, I am restricted to critique religious practices in the culture that I am familiar with.

In following and researching the history of the Bible, a few things become very evident: The Bible, in its beginning, did not exist as a holy canonized "word of God," revealed to "inspired men" by God, as I was taught as a child, and what most Christians believe; rather, it was put together from various and sundry manuscripts that had been in existence for some time. The Christian church, which was mainly the Roman Catholic Church at that time, amidst much heated and conflicting opinions, chose the contents of the original Bible. There have been many changes from the original Bible to what we know now as the Bible.

There is a natural schism between most religions and scientists since science is based on the established proof of a theory on which empirical studies have been done, procedures for repeatability done, and peer review by other scientists done. Religion, on the other hand, is a belief in something that is not proven or of which there is no factual evidence. These beliefs may be rooted in a dream by someone a very long time ago, as in the case of Abraham and Judaism, or not so long ago, as in the case of Joseph Smith and Mormonism.

As with the conflict between Galileo and the church, another conflict between the Christian community and the scientific community is the question of evolution versus creation. Most Christians believe in the Bible version that God created the heavens and the earth in six days.

"In the beginning," the Bible declares in the book of Genesis, "God created the heavens and the earth." On the first day, he created the earth. The earth was dark, so he created light. He separated the light from the darkness and named the light "day" and named the darkness "night."

On the second day, God made a "firmament." (The King James Version of the Bible calls this structure a firmament, the New American Bible calls it a dome, the New International Version calls this structure a "vault," which God named "sky"; how confusing? Should not there be just one meaning?) In the King James Version, God named this firmament "heaven."

This structure divides the waters above the firmament from the waters below.

On the third day, God commanded the waters under heaven to be collected in one place so that land appeared. He populated the land with grass and fruit trees of every kind.

On the fourth day, God created two great lights; the greater one to govern the day and the lesser to govern the night.

On the fifth day, God populated the oceans, seas, and lakes with all the aquatic creatures.

On the sixth day, God created all land animals. Then he said, "Let us make man in our own image and after our own likeness." So God made man in his own image on the sixth day of his creation of the universe. Then God gave the man he created dominion over all living things that he created.

On the seventh day, God rested.

What appears to be another account of the creation of man appears in the second chapter of Genesis; God molded a man from the dust of the earth in his own image, blew the breath of life in his nostrils, and man became a living soul. Sometime later, as if by an after-thought, God reckoned that this man needed a partner, so he put the man (Adam) in a deep sleep, removed one of the man's ribs, and created a female partner (Eve) from the rib of the man.

This is the sum and substance of the creation theory. It is easy to see how much of a challenge Galileo's discoveries were to the church; his discoveries completely unraveled a fundamental tenet of the Judeo-Christian faith. The church was super powerful at that time, so it threw in all its powers to squelch Galileo's scientific discovery. The Christian church's persecution of Galileo, who history has proven to be monumentally correct, should be in such a state of embarrassing contrition that no unsubstantiated claim should again be embraced and defended; yet in this age of scientific revolution, the majority of Judeo-Christians accept this version of the creation and tries to invalidate geological and radiometric proof of evolution in favor of the biblical story of creation.

To whom did God say, "Let us make man." He is purported to be a monotheistic God, just one entity; not a family of gods with sons and daughters. I am often told that God was addressing his son Jesus, who, I am told, was in heaven at that time; but we cannot have it both ways. He is either a monotheistic God or a divine family of Gods akin to the Greek family of gods and goddesses. Christians claim that Jesus Christ is God's son; simultaneously, they also claim that God is a monotheistic deity. This is one of the confusing dissonances that is characteristic of the Christian religion. This was the cause of the schism between ancient Arianism and the Roman Catholic version of Christianity.

In the same creation story in Genesis, where God created man from the dust of the earth, is the story of God creating the firmament or "dome." It may be an elusive task to prove how man was created, so why don't the creationists prove the existence of this firmament? They should not just sit by and wait to criticize research done by scientists. If they believe in the biblical story that God created a firmament to separate the waters above the earth from the ones below, go prove it! The firmament should still be there waiting to be discovered.

In the summer of 1977, NASA launched two satellites: *Voyager 1* and *Voyager 2*. They made fly-by of the planets in the solar system, sending back spectacular pictures and other useful data of the planets. Both satellites have now exited the solar system and are heading into interstellar space. As of February 2018, *Voyager 1* was 13.2 billion miles from earth. It is a humbling experience to see a picture of earth as a small blue dot that the satellite sent back. Since creationists are still clutching to the biblical version of creation, shouldn't they come up with some proof that there is a physical firmament or dome above Earth or accept the fact that there is none?

During the great space race between the USA and the Soviet Union, the Soviets were the first to put a man in orbit around the earth. The Soviets claimed that their cosmonaut, Uri Gagarin, said that he looked around when he was up there but did not see any God. Not to be outdone, when the Americans put their man, John Glen, in orbit, he declared that when he looked on the earth and looked at the stars, he saw the handiwork of God. Here is a quotation from him: *"To look out at this kind of creation and not believe in God is, to me, impossible."* This is paraphrasing the very popular quotation from Psalm 19 in the Bible, *"The heavens declare the glory of God, and the firmament showeth his handiwork."*

Some proponents of this biblical version of the creation have made the claim, without any credible evidence, that this creation happened about 10,000 years ago. Another popular variant of biblical creation theory are the believers in "intelligent" design. These believers, in their avid desire to support the biblical creation theory, claim that life is too complex to have come into existence by chance. (Evolution is not a game of chance; it is the survival of the most adaptable mutant in a changing environment.)

The "evidence" presented to support intelligent design theory is mainly pseudoscience since no systematic study comparable with standard scientific procedures has ever been presented, to my best knowledge, to show any research that substantiates any hypothesis of the biblical creation story. Usually, only baseless critiques of scientific findings are presented.

On the opposite side of the biblical version of creationism are scientists and anti-creationists who support the Darwinian theory of evolution and other studies involving fossil, ancient artifacts, geological dating, DNA analysis, radioactive element dating (radiometric), and other scientific techniques. Let us take a look at some of these techniques.

Material Dating versus Intelligent Design

The following information on material dating may be found in the public domain and represents information from various sources.

In the nineteenth century, some geologists realized that the vast thicknesses of sedimentary rocks meant that the earth must be at least hundreds of millions of years old. Charles Darwin reinforced this idea by pointing to the time that must have been required for the evolution of advanced life from primitive forms.

Radioactive materials have played a pivotal role in material dating. Some elements, such as uranium, are unstable and spontaneously mutate into other elements, radiating energy in the process. The instability in these elements is associated with atoms that have more neutrons than protons in their nuclei. They have the same chemical characteristics as the normal atoms, but they have a greater mass. These elements are called isotopes and are characterized as being radioactive because of the energy they radiate when this mutation takes place. Because of this phenomenon, the original radioactive element changes its physical characteristics, becoming a different, stable daughter element at the end of the process. This change takes place at a known fixed rate, determined by the half-life of the isotope. The half-life is the time required for one half of the original amount of radioactive isotopes to be converted to the stable daughter element. In each of this period, one half of the remaining parent isotope will again be converted.

Some radioactive elements used in radiometric dating have relatively long half-lives. A good example is rubidium-87, which changes to strontium-87 at a rate of one half every 50 billion years. Therefore, a rock can be dated by measuring how much of its original rubidium-87 content has changed into strontium-87. Another key element in the dating process involves uranium-235 transforming to lead-207 at a rate of one half every 713 million years. Scientists have used these methods to place the age of the earth to be 4.5 billion years old.

The carbon-14 method of material dating involves the conversion of radioactive carbon-14 to stable nitrogen at a rate of one half every 5,700 years. The carbon-14 method of dating is only used to date organic materials and is accurate only for material that have died for less than 50,000 years. Scientists are able to tell fairly accurately how long ago an animal or plant died by using radioactive carbon-14 dating.

Radioactive carbon-14 is constantly being created in the atmosphere by the interaction of cosmic rays with atmospheric nitrogen. The radioactive carbon-14 is evenly distributed all over

the planet. It is an unstable version of the carbon element and
starts decaying at a very precise exponential rate as soon as they
are formed. These carbon-14 atoms, along with other isotopes of
carbon, combine with oxygen in the atmosphere to form carbon
dioxide. Plants use this atmospheric carbon dioxide to create
carbohydrates that plants and animals consume. As long as the
plants and animals are alive, they recirculate fresh carbon-14 in
their structures. Once they die, their uptake of carbon-14 stops,
but the decay of carbon-14 in the dead structures continues at
a precise rate. Therefore, the level of carbon-14 in the structure
of the dead plant or animal is a function of how long it has
been dead.

Beyond 50,000 years the sample of carbon-14 becomes small;
therefore, the accuracy of the test gets unreliable.

The DNA in living cells mutates; it was found that they mutate
at a constant rate. Scientists use this mutation to determine that
humans (*Homo sapiens*, not *Homo erectus* or other humanoid
species) evolved in East Africa about 200,000 years ago.

The mitochondrial DNA in women of different races of people
around the world were analyzed, then extrapolation was done
back to a common ancestor and a specific time. This common
ancestor was dubbed "Mitochondrial Eve."

The manuscript of the original draft of the mitochondrial
research was submitted to *Nature Magazine* in late 1985 or early
1986 and published in January 1987. The published conclusion
was that all humans of the *Homo sapiens* species (everyone
currently living on earth) originated from a single population
from East Africa, at the time dated to between 140,000 and
200,000 years ago. Radiometric dating of early human fossil

placed the earliest human in East Africa roughly about the same time, 200,000 years ago.

As would be expected, there was widespread disbelief and anger among some white people when it was revealed by the scientific community that the original ancestors of everyone on planet earth were black nomads from East Africa. Many scientists jumped on the bandwagon just to disprove this finding, but being scientists with integrity, they ended up confirming it. Since the initial study, many other studies have been done, which further confirmed the authenticity of this body of work. This DNA study is collaborated by geological and radiometric studies done on fossilized remains of humanoids found around the world. It is now undisturbed by anyone with any scientific training and any integrity that every person currently living on earth has a nomadic tribe of black people from East Africa as their original ancestor.

There is a credible hypothesis that the skin of people whose intermediate ancestors lived further away from the equator, where the sun's rays are less intense, mutated to a whiter color to strike a balance between the vitamin D manufactured from sunlight and the skin cancer that sunlight causes. The melanin that causes the dark pigmentation in a person's skin is the active ingredient that inhibits skin cancer, but it also inhibits the ability of our skin to utilize the rays of the sun to manufacture vitamin D. Therefore, in regions where the sun is less intense, a lighter skin will make more vitamin D without causing as much skin cancer—a great genetic compromise.

If it is a biological advantage that the air we breathe reaches our lungs near our normal body temperature, then our nose would have evolved into the proper shape to meet that objective;

therefore, if our intermediate ancestors (about a hundred generations up to the current one) lived in a non-tropical climate, a long, narrow nose with more inner surface area with warm tissues to warm the air would go a long way to meet that objective. A logical deduction would be that a long narrow nose and whiter skin is a genetic adaptation for people whose immediate ancestors have not been living continuously in the tropical regions of the world.

Those who seriously believe the Bible's version of creation must by logical deduction, also believe that the Garden of Eden (if it ever existed) was in East Africa, and Adam and his first lady were black people, since East Africa is indisputably identified as the origin of the human species by DNA analysis, radiometric analysis, and geological analysis. More importantly, in the Bible, God said that Adam was made in his (God's) image. Therefore, by extension of the creationists' story, God's image is that of a black man and vice versa. I am not advocating the creationists' story of Adam and Eve, or the Garden of Eden, or that Adam and Eve were made in the image of God. I am advocating that if someone believes the Bible's version of the creation, then the only logical deduction that person can make, after accepting the various scientific findings that the progenitors of the human race were black, is

    a) If the first humans were black and were created/evolved in East Africa, then the biblical story of the creation of humans and the findings of the scientific research refers to one and the same story. There can be only one beginning and only one creation of Adam. And

    b) If that person believes that man was made in God's image, then the only logical deduction that person can make is that the image of God is that of a black man and the Garden of Eden was in East Africa.

If you do not believe the Bible's version of the creation, then you are not bound by the logic of association to a Garden of Eden in East Africa, where a black God molded black Adam from a lump of clay.

Creationists have mounted various challenges to material dating in general, but there has always been valid rebuttal to these challenges. As far as I am aware, creationists have never presented a case study backed up by empirical or verifiable data to prove their hypothesis of creation; their modus operandi is to try to disprove facts or credible hypotheses presented by scientists.

If the fossil of a humanoid were found in a layer of sedimentary rock, how do we know how old it is? Scientists can test a sample of the rock to find out if it is radioactive. If it is, the next objective would be to find out what material is giving off the radiation. Further tests will be done to determine the ratio of parent and daughter elements. For example, if uranium-235 is found, it will be compared with the amount of its daughter element, lead-207. This ratio is a direct indication of how old the fossil is. More than one type of radioactive isotopes may be present; therefore, more than one radiometric test can be done to collaborate the accuracy of each other. Relative and geological dating may also be done to further collaborate the dates.

Let us make the following assumption. A date for this fossilized humanoid is established at approximately 4 million years ago. Sometime later, probably not in the same location, another fossilized humanoid was found. The second humanoid has the same basic anatomical features as the first one, but there are significant differences in terms of particular features, such as a more upright posture, shorter arms and fingers, skull that is shaped slightly different. Let us also assume that they were found in different strata of sedimentary rock, and geological and radiometric dating put them at a specific dates 20,000 years apart. Let us take this assumption even further. A third and fourth humanoid were found; they were separated in time by approximately the same 20,000 years; changes in features also happened. Wouldn't it be safe and logical to come to an educated conclusion that there is a process of evolution going on here?

To accept the foregoing scenarios, one has to accept that material consists of atoms, that the isotopes of some atoms spontaneously emit radiation and mutate into another form of matter, that there is a precise time scale in which this material conversion is done, and that the ratio between the mother and daughter material is an accurate measurement of time. If we concede to all these, why should we not concede that the radiometric dating process is a valid way of establishing the age of a fossil?

When rocks which have had an undisturbed history are analyzed, all methods reveal the same age. This uniformity demonstrates that these principles of measurements are reliable. Even more verification may be done if both dated artifacts and fossilized records of an important ancient exhibit exists; the artifacts can be tested to see if it complies with the dated records. This is often done.

By the way, materials giving off radiation is not such an unusual phenomenon. When we eat a banana, we swallow down a quantity of radioactive potassium. The carbon dioxide in the air we breathe contains radioactive carbon atoms. The carbohydrates and other food that we eat contain radioactive material. Even the water that is so much a part of us contains some amount of radioactive hydrogen atoms. Uranium ore, from which the radioactive material used to make the atomic bomb is made, is distributed generously around the world.

It is inevitable that the radioactive emissions from these radioactive atoms that are a part of our very existence cause mutations in the genes of living organisms. In which case, as a result of our close relationship with radioactive materials, innumerable mutations will occur in each organism over time. Some of these changes may happen in our epigenome rather than changing the coding of our DNA. Some will cause mutations that will enable us to have a better chance of survival in our environment. It may cause the mutant to see better, hear better, or run faster. It may cause the amount of melanin in our skin to decrease, thereby making us more susceptible to skin cancer but at the same time, make our skin lighter in color, with more ability to make vitamin D. Some of these mutations will have no apparent effect. Some will cause harmless tumors and harmless mutations; some will cause cancer. Those that affect our reproductive organs will cause mutations that cause divergence in the offspring of the individual. The mutations in reproductive genes will enable the mutants that are more suitable for that environment to survive better, while those which are less able to survive in their environment to die out. As the environment changes, those mutants that are more suitable to the new environment will have the best chance of survival and propagation. This process takes a long time.

Scientists who believe in natural evolution have built their cases on the fundamental principles of physics. The creationists' case rests on what is in the Bible, and that the Bible is the word of God, and that the Bible has to be accepted by faith—no proof or test is required.

If someone has faith that something happened, that faith-based thing only exists in that person's mind and the minds of like-minded people if it cannot be verified that it exists in the space and time where real material things exist. In the prehistoric world, where no science existed, where nobody knew that clouds were droplets of water that will fall to the earth when the right atmospheric conditions exist, when the highest anyone got off the ground was when he or she climbed a tree, it was easy for most people to believe that "God made the firmament (dome) and divided the waters which were under the firmament from the waters which were above the firmament" *[Genesis 1]*.

This great blue dome that we see above our heads that we call the sky really looks like a solid structure, a firmament; it really is nothingness, and we are seeing stars that are millions or even billions of miles away. Seeing dangerous lightning and earsplitting thunder coming from this endless blue dome had to lead ancient humans to believe that there was a powerful God up there executing all these powerful miracles.

It is now quite evident to everyone that there is no physical barrier above our heads separating the waters above the firmament from the waters below, so some creationists say that this part of the story of creation is a metaphor. If one part of the creation story is a metaphor, then the whole thing is. Without any scientific knowledge, it is quite understandable that this is how ancient people understood the world around them; and there was no divine entity that revealed it to them. What would be quite damaging is that people would hold on to unsubstantiated belief, even in the face of information that contradicts this belief, and worse, to force or incite others, especially their children, to conform to this belief. This was what happened in the Galileo saga.

Faith is accepting a concept without testing or questioning it. Some people take faith even further; they refuse to evaluate any other concept that is contrary to the one they believe. The Roman Catholic Church (meaning almost the entire Christendom at that time) believed the biblical version of the creation; therefore, they rejected proof presented by Galileo that the earth was not the center of the universe, even though this proof was overwhelming. He was summoned to the Roman Inquisition, charged, and convicted of "vehement suspicion of heresy." He was forced to publicly recant the "heresy" that the earth orbits the sun and that the earth was not the center of the universe. Even then, he was placed under house arrest for the rest of his life. What travesty and arrogance!

There are defenders of creationism who try to rationalize the six-day creation by saying that six days mentioned in the Bible is equivalent to tens of thousands of years. They make reference to Psalm 90:4, which states, "For a thousand years in your sight are like a day that has just gone by," and 2 Peter 3:8, which states, "With the Lord a day is like a thousand years, and a thousand years are like a day."

What we do not hear when this point of view is articulated is the passage from the Bible, Psalm 90:10, that reads, "The days of our years are threescore years and ten; and if by reason of strength they be four score years." This is a clear indication from the same Bible that one year in this biblical text correlates with one year as we know it, and the life expectancy of humans is seventy to eighty years, as we know it.

More unfortunate, though, is the use of circular semantics, using texts from the Bible to justify texts from the same Bible, using those that help the case and ignoring those that do not.

Following the story of the creation in the Bible is the story of the flood. This is the story of how God destroyed every living thing on earth by this great flood that inundated the entire earth. Could he not just command the death of everyone, except Noah, his family, and the selected animals? Better still, could he not just change the people's wicked ways? God regretted that he made man because man became so wicked. God did things, then regretted it? So he is not omniscient? Only Noah and his sons and their families were righteous in the sight of God. God commanded Noah to build an "ark," wherein they could stay safe when the earth was flooded. One version of this story in Genesis said that God told Noah to take in one pair of every animal; the other version says that seven pairs of every "clean" animal and one pair of every "unclean" animal came into the ark. Which version is true? Both cannot be correct.

This is an unlikely story. Whereas local floods are common, you cannot have a flood that inundates the entire earth because the total amount of water on the planet does not change; it is only displaced from one area to another when it rains or when there is a flood. When there is a flood in one place, the water has to come from another place on earth. This water evaporates in one area, usually from the ocean, and falls in the area where the flood is. Where the rain falls, from a shower to a flood, and where the wind blows, from a gentle breeze to a hurricane, is determined by well-known meteorological conditions. In the case of the wind, warm areas on the land or water heat the nearby air, its weight per volume decreases, a given volume weighs less than before. Therefore, it rises in the atmosphere because a given volume is now lighter; cooler air flows in to take its place. This is the basic principle of a gentle breeze to a tornado to a category 5 hurricane.

There are instances such as in a derecho or downburst, where cooler air actually falls out of the sky and causes strong wind. In these cases, atmospheric conditions cause air in the upper atmosphere to cool and fall to the ground.

Creationists will immediately counter this narrative by saying that God has the ability to create the extra thousands of trillions of gallons of water to cover the 29,000 feet Mount Everest. Compare the above Hebrew folklore of the flood to the following Greek folklore.

In Greek mythology, Icarus is the son of the master craftsman Daedalus. Icarus and his father planned an escape from Crete by means of flying with wings that his father constructed from feathers and wax. Icarus's father warns his son not to fly too low or too high so that the sea's dampness would not clog his wings nor the sun's heat would not melt them. Icarus ignored his father's instructions and flew close to the sun; this caused the wax to melt. When the wax in his wings melted, he tumbled out of the sky and fell into the sea where he drowned.

Why would someone believe that the folklore of the biblical flood has credibility and the folklore of Icarus's flight does not? One is a Hebrew folklore that happened to get mentioned in the Bible but has no credible evidence to authenticate it; the other is a Greek folklore that is told in many books but was not included by Pope Damasus I in his canonization of what has now evolved to be the Bible. Scientists have come up with a solution; it cannot be credible if it only exists as a "miracle" in writing or folklore without any factual evidence of its occurrence, and there is no instance of it being repeated if all the same physical conditions exist. Miracles exist only in the domain of the imagination, in folklore, or instances where normal physical processes are misunderstood. The laws of physics have never been shown to change to facilitate any folklore, prayer, or the desire of any living being.

Many ancient civilizations from Africa to North America have folklore of the creation of life on earth or the creation of the universe. This creation story is usually accompanied by some great flood. The Roman Catholic popes and bishops, who decided which manuscripts should be canonized in the Bible, chose to include the Hebrew folklore of the creation and the flood.

Praying will not stop hurricanes from developing because the laws of physics have never been proven to be abrogated. The only way prayer will help is to galvanize the majority of people on the planet to practice lifestyles that will not cause an increase in the average temperature of the planet. The path of a hurricane is determined by where the air is warmer or cooler relative to another area, where a low pressure or high pressure area forms. The laws of physics have never been proven to be overridden. Claims to this violation of physical laws by miracles invoked by God is common, but proof is usually a scarce commodity. I have never seen, read, or studied any event where the laws of physics were annulled to facilitate a particular request by any human or groups of humans.

Several years ago, there was a severe drought in an area of Texas in the USA. Some religious groups led by the then governor of Texas got together in a prayer crusade for rain to fall. This prayer crusade became a national event among Christians. They prayed and prayed, but the rain did not fall for a considerably long time. The crops dried up and cattle died. To the prayer groups, though, it was not that God did not answer their prayers, but it was that God has mysterious ways of answering prayers, which was not apparent to them. He answers them in ways mere mortals cannot understand. To the naturalist, prayer does not change the laws of physics. Rain could have fallen shortly after they prayed as an instance of coincidence. No one would be able to tell if it were coincidence or God answering their prayers. They would claim that God answered their prayers and took credit, even though nothing was proven.

Another part of the flood story is the appearance of the rainbow in the sky. It states that God puts a rainbow in the sky as a promise to Noah that he will never again destroy the world by a flood.

Here is the relevant quotation from the Bible, from the book of Genesis:

> *{I have set my rainbow in the clouds, and it will be the sign of the covenant between me and the earth. Whenever I bring clouds over the earth and the rainbow appears in the clouds, I will remember my covenant between me and you and all living creatures of every kind. Never again will the waters become a flood to destroy all life. Whenever the rainbow appears in the clouds, I will see it and*

remember the everlasting covenant between God
and all living creatures of every kind on the earth.}

Does God need an icon to remind him of something?

Once again, the laws of physics have never been shown to be invalidated. One of the basic laws of physics is that when light travels from one medium to another (in this case, from air to the water droplets), the angle of refraction is different for each wavelength. Each color in the light spectrum is a different wavelength; therefore, a separation of the colors occurs. Mostly everyone is familiar with a prism. When sunlight, or any artificial source of "white" light, which is an aggregation of all the colors in the light spectrum, is shone on one face of the prism, a rainbow of colors emerges from another face. We do not even need a prism to create a rainbow; all we need is a garden sprinkler when the sun is shining. If you, the sprinkler, and the sun are placed at the correct angles relative to one another, there will always be a beautiful rainbow to be seen.

People of ancient time did not have any proper prism. They may have seen different colors coming out of natural material and attribute it to some magic; they could not have even imagined a garden sprinkler. It is obvious that they saw these spectacular rainbows in the sky and conjured up this story that it is a promise from God. Do any of us still believe that a rainbow in the sky is a promise from God not to destroy the world by flood again? What about the rainbow from your garden sprinkler? Is that also God's promise?

Myths have been with us as humans ever since we acquired the ability to imagine. Whenever we see or hear or feel something, we acquire the notion that we know everything about it.

In prehistoric times, when there was no science, people just conjured up their own explanation. These explanations were not confined just to things that they could feel, hear, and touch; they spanned the whole range of the human imagination. Each culture has their own collection of myths, including some that they borrow from other cultures. One of these myths is usually a creation story.

In Greek mythology, the Gorgons were horrifyingly ugly monsters who lived at the edge of the world. Their hair was made of serpents, and one look from a Gorgon's eyes would turn a person into stone. Perseus killed the Gorgon Medusa by beheading her while looking only at her reflection.

The following is an excerpt from an article by Joshua J. Mark in the [*World History Encyclopedia:* https://www.worldhistory.org/article/225/enuma-elish---the-babylonian-epic-of-creation---fu/#:~:text=The%20Enuma%20Elish%20(also%20known,the%20creation%20of%20the%20world.] This article is a description of the Mesopotamian creation myth; its similarity to the Hebrew creation myth and the fact that since it predated the Hebrew creation myth, it is likely to be the inspiration for the Hebrew creation myth.

> {*The Enuma Elish (also known as The Seven Tablets of Creation) is the Mesopotamian creation myth whose title is derived from the opening lines of the piece, "When on High". All of the tablets containing the myth, found at Ashur, Kish, Ashurbanipal's library at Nineveh, Sultantepe, and other excavated sites, date to c. 1200 BCE but their colophons indicate that these are all copies of*

*a much older version of the myth dating from long
before the fall of Sumer in c. 1750 BCE.*

*As Marduk, the champion of the young gods in
their war against Tiamat, is of Babylonian origin,
the Sumerian Ea/Enki or Enlil is thought to have
played the major role in the original version of the
story. The copy found at Ashur has the god Ashur
in the main role as was the custom of the cities of
Mesopotamia. The god of each city was always
considered the best and most powerful. Marduk,
the god of Babylon, only figures as prominently as
he does in the story because most of the copies found
are from Babylonian scribes. Even so, Ea does still
play an important part in the Babylonian version
of the Enuma Elish by creating human beings.*

Summary of the Story

*The story, one of the oldest, if not the oldest in
the world, concerns the birth of the gods and the
creation of the universe and human beings. In the
beginning, there was only undifferentiated water
swirling in chaos. Out of this swirl, the waters
divided into sweet, fresh water, known as the god
Apsu, and salty bitter water, the goddess Tiamat.
Once differentiated, the union of these two entities
gave birth to the younger gods.*

*These young gods, however, were extremely loud,
troubling the sleep of Apsu at night and distracting
him from his work by day. Upon the advice of his
Vizier, Mummu, Apsu decides to kill the younger*

gods. Tiamat, hearing of their plan, warns her eldest son, Enki (sometimes Ea) and he puts Apsu to sleep and kills him. From Apsu's remains, Enki creates his home.

Tiamat, once the supporter of the younger gods, now is enraged that they have killed her mate. She consults with the god, Quingu, who advises her to make war on the younger gods. Tiamat rewards Quingu with the Tablets of Destiny, which legitimize the rule of a god and control the fates, and he wears them proudly as a breastplate. With Quingu as her champion, Tiamat summons the forces of chaos and creates eleven horrible monsters to destroy her children.

Ea, Enki, and the younger gods fight against Tiamat futilely until, from among them, emerges the champion Marduk who swears he will defeat Tiamat. Marduk defeats Quingu and kills Tiamat by shooting her with an arrow which splits her in two; from her eyes flow the waters of the Tigris and Euphrates Rivers. Out of Tiamat's corpse, Marduk creates the heavens and the earth, he appoints gods to various duties and binds Tiamat's eleven creatures to his feet as trophies (to much adulation from the other gods) before setting their images in his new home. He also takes the Tablets of Destiny from Quingu, thus legitimizing his reign.

After the gods have finished praising him for his great victory and the art of his creation, Marduk consults with the god Ea (the god of wisdom) and

decides to create human beings from the remains
of whichever of the gods instigated Tiamat to
war. Quingu is charged as guilty and killed and,
from his blood, Ea creates Lullu, the first man,
to be a helper to the gods in their eternal task of
maintaining order and keeping chaos at bay.

As the poem phrases it, "Ea created mankind/
On whom he imposed the service of the gods, and
set the gods free" (Tablet VI.33-34). Following
this, Marduk "arranged the organization of the
netherworld" and distributed the gods to their
appointed stations (Tablet VI.43-46). The poem
ends in Tablet VII with long praise of Marduk for
his accomplishments.

Commentary

The Enuma Elish would later be the inspiration
for the Hebrew scribes who created the text now
known as the biblical Book of Genesis. Prior to
the 19th century CE, the Bible was considered the
oldest book in the world and its narratives were
thought to be completely original. In the mid-19th
century CE, however, European museums, as well
as academic and religious institutions, sponsored
excavations in Mesopotamia to find physical
evidence for historical corroboration of the stories
in the Bible. These excavations found quite the
opposite, however, in that, once cuneiform was
translated, it was understood that a number of
biblical narratives were Mesopotamian in origin.

Famous stories such as the Fall of Man and the Great Flood were originally conceived and written down in Sumer, translated and modified later in Babylon, and reworked by the Assyrians before they were used by the Hebrew scribes for the versions which appear in the Bible. Although the basic paradigm of the biblical narratives and the Mesopotamian stories align closely, there are still significant differences as noted by scholar Stephen Bertman:

Both Genesis and Enuma Elish are religious texts which detail and celebrate cultural origins: Genesis describes the origin and founding of the Jewish people under the guidance of the Lord; Enuma Elish recounts the origin and founding of Babylon under the leadership of the god Marduk. Contained in each work is a story of how the cosmos and man were created. Each work begins by describing the watery chaos and primeval darkness that once filled the universe. Then light is created to replace the darkness. Afterward, the heavens are made and in them heavenly bodies are placed. Finally, man is created. These similarities notwithstanding, the two accounts are more different than alike.

In revising the Mesopotamian creation story for their own ends, the Hebrew scribes tightened the narrative and the focus but retained the concept of the all-powerful deity who brings order from chaos. Marduk, in the Enuma Elish, establishes the recognizable order of the world - just as God does in the Genesis tale - and human beings are expected to recognize this great gift and honor the deity through service. In Mesopotamia, in fact, it was thought that humans were co-workers with the gods to maintain the gift of creation and keep the forces of chaos at bay.}

Let us take a look at the "'human-ness" of God. It is still a popular belief that God created this "Goldilocks" planet called earth for the benefit of the human species.

He created a climate ideal for our existence. He provided enough water, oxygen, and sunshine for our sustenance. In fact, everything on the planet ostensibly was created to benefit human beings. There are billions of stars in the universe, and each of these stars are likely to have one or more planets with the same characteristics as earth. Whether or not there is any life form on them, we do not know, and we are not likely to find out. These planets are so far away that we cannot even imagine the distance. That being the case, we will not waste time discussing if *Homo sapiens* on earth are the only living beings God created to serve him.

Now that we are back on Earth, is there really such a special relationship between the *Homo sapiens* species and God? Various material-dating techniques, along with paleontological and archeological data, have established that millions of other species have existed on planet earth millions of years before human beings. The lowly stinking cockroach has been roaming planet earth for 300 million years and is still going strong.

Fossilized cockroach has been found in rocks that are dated to be about 300 million years old.

Humans in our present form (*Homo sapiens*) have been living on earth for only about 200,000 years. Even if we include earlier forms of the human species, such as *Homo erectus* (upright human), the first of the humanoid species to walk upright, they lived on earth between 100,000 and 2 million years ago. Compare that with the length of time that the cockroach has been around.

It is quite popular for creationists to challenge these findings, but fossils of these ancient humans have been discovered and material-dating tests have been done. The fossils still exist in various museums around the world. Creationists are free to do their own studies and come up with their own hypothesis with regard to the age of the fossils and what they are. They chose not to do so. Instead, they find every reason to dispute the scientific studies.

The dinosaurs inhabited the earth for 170 million years. Compare this length of time to the tenure of the *Homo sapiens* species on earth; as we saw previously, a mere 200,000 years.

Except for those that could fly, the dinosaurs died off 66 million years ago, when a massive asteroid plunged onto the earth off the Yucatan Peninsula in Mexico, creating a crater 150 kilometers wide. Scientists have conducted extensive core-boring in the area to bring up samples from miles into the earth. These samples were dated with the different methods of material dating. The layers of the core were studied. Data from these and other bores showed that after the asteroid hit the earth, most land animals and vegetation died off around the earth. This was because of a cloud of dust that blanketed the earth and prevented the sun from shining through for a long period. All this information was deduced from the core-drilling and other rock analysis around the world.

The dying off of the dinosaurs gave the smaller mammals a chance to propagate and thrive. The mammals eventually took over the dominant spot that the dinosaurs held. This is the lineage from which the human species evolved. How do we know all this? Fossil records tell us. Various fossil records dated over the millions of years, along with the approximate dates that these animals died, give us a kaleidoscopic vision of the transformation from one stage of development to another over hundreds of millions of years.

A Goldilocks environment was not made for humans; humans evolved to fit the environment they found themselves in. As the script from *Jurassic Park* puts it, "Life will find a way." Scientists have found microbes in nuclear reactors, microbes that love acid, microbes that swim in boiling-hot water, bacteria that feed on penicillin that was developed to kill them and has been killing them for decades. Thanks to overuse and misuse of that drug, they are now immune. There are bacteria that do not need oxygen to survive. There are whole ecosystems that have been discovered around deep sea vents where sunlight never reaches, and the emerging vent water is hot enough to melt lead.

A culture of bacteria was placed on the International Space Station in an environment where it was exposed to all the hazards of outer space. It was exposed to microgravity, harsh ultraviolet radiation, loss of atmospheric pressure, and temperatures near absolute zero. After one year in this out-of-this-world environment, it was reevaluated and was found to be doing quite well. It underwent some physical changes, but it survived. Life will always find a way! [This story was adapted from *BusinessInsider.com*.]

We are living in an atmosphere that exerts a force of 14.7 pounds on every square inch of our bodies. To counter this, the internal pressure in our bodies is pushing back with the same force. This is separate from the force of gravity trying to pull us down to the center of the earth. If an astronaut were to step out of his space suit in outer space, he would instantly explode like a bomb since the normal internal pressure of his body would be 14.7 pounds per square inch pushing outward, and the pressure of the atmospheric that he would have stepped into would be almost zero. Instinctively, you would believe that no one could survive with 14.7 pounds of matter (air), pressing inward on every square inch of their body, but here we are, quite comfortable under the load. We have evolved in this environment; this is our normal.

If there were no oxygen on earth, life could still have evolved. There are many anaerobic organisms that we have to deal with in our daily lives. These organisms live happily in an environment where there is no oxygen. They are the main cause of food poison in canned food that is not properly processed. We have made this environment on earth our normal environment. If we had evolved in an environment where there is no oxygen, no gravitational force, temperature close to absolute zero, that would be our Goldilocks (normal) environment. The environment on earth would be hostile and forbidding for us.

Whenever there are complex systems that humans encounter, we tend to dismiss the micro-operations that take place between the input stage and the output stage. If we do not understand what goes in between these stages, we simply pass it off as one of those things that God routinely makes happen. We are too arrogant to admit that we do not know and that it can be caused by many other processes other than God's will. This microphysics is also at play within the physiological and psychological systems of our bodies. Our thoughts interact with our physiological processes through hormones and neurotransmitters to produce apparently mystical and metaphysical effects. Instead of concluding that we do not know how it happens and we should pursue further knowledge, we simply concede that God made it happen. It is believed that the Muslims, who were the forerunners in chemistry, medicine, mathematics, and other branches of higher learning, became complacent, and their interest in these fields declined because of their gravitation toward more interest in religion.

We have placed delineation between chemical and physical processes, but a chemical process is just the more obvious molecular part of the overall physical process. What we define as chemistry is a process where electrons in the atom of one element bond with the atom of another element to form a new compound. Conversely, they can also be separated if they are induced with the required amount of energy to do so.

Two atoms of hydrogen gas bond with one atom of oxygen gas to produce water, always with an explosive force of energy. It is quite intriguing that two gasses bond together to form a liquid. This gives us an insight into how little we know as a species in relation to all the knowledge that we still do not have.

Very often there are accidents where spectacular explosions happen when hydrogen or other explosive gases are mixed with the oxygen in the air. If you feel inclined, you can say that God made the bond between hydrogen and oxygen happen, so if you pray, he can prevent the explosion, but once again, it has never been shown where God has ever abrogated the laws of physics. You can pray for this explosion not to happen when these two gasses are mixed, but your prayers will not be answered if the explosive gas in the mixture with oxygen exceeds the lower explosive limit (LEL) and a spark or any temperature higher than the ignition temperature of the gas is produced in that mixture. The chemical bonding of the two gasses will happen in spite of your prayers, the bonding will release a large amount of energy to cause a spectacular explosion, and water will be produced as a result.

Many of us use natural or propane gas to cook. If this gas leaks into your house, there will be a horrible explosion if two conditions are met. First, if enough gas is leaked into the house to meet or exceed what is called the lower explosive limit, this is a point where enough gas is mixed with the oxygen in the air to sustain an explosion. Second, a source of ignition occurs, such as a spark. At this point, there is no if or but about an explosion happening; there is going to be an explosion. You can pray all you want, but the laws of physics will not be changed to satisfy your prayers. If we could pray to stop this explosion from happening, we would never need any safety measures to prevent accidents. All we would have to do is pray incessantly that there would be no accidents.

This bonding of atoms which releases the energy that causes explosions, or the un-bonding that requires energy, is what scientists call chemistry. We also know that this happens to satisfy the valency of each atom, which is an urge that each atom has to fill the outer shell of its structure—its valence shell. Here, we get from chemistry into microphysics. Scientists know that this urge to fill the valence shell is caused by an interplay of forces inside the atom. This force also makes its presence felt down to the subatomic level, where elements actually mutate and radiate energy. Billions of dollars were spent to construct particle accelerators at the Fermilab facilities in the USA and the CERN particles accelerator operated by the European Union to learn more about these strange forces. One of the things that they have established so far is that these forces behave in strict compliance with physical laws. No amount of prayer will make them deviate from established physical laws.

Human and Artificial Intelligence

A simplified comparison can be made between the ways humans perceive the microphysics of life as being the creation of an all-powerful God having human characteristics, with the microphysics of a computer system. Most of us humans see life in general as a product of an intelligent designer with human attributes such as emotions, but there are other intelligences, such as artificial intelligence and natural intelligence. Artificial intelligence is pure logic that exists in the arithmetic logic unit (ALU) of a computer. The ALU is a product of human engineering; its output is always a truly logical result, devoid of human (or godly) bias or emotion. To implement a functional computer system, the ALU is amalgamated with other computer systems to give the computer the ability to execute instructions. Because of the instructions that the computer can now execute, human biases can now be programmed into it. Those who advocate intelligent design advocate that changes over time are extremely limited. Natural intelligence, as scholars of Darwinian evolution advocate, is a slow process of natural changes happening over millions of years. Artificial intelligence, as seen in the computer, has a humble beginning with people experimenting with logic gates. Fundamentally, all intelligent processes are simple functions which manipulate the inputs that they are given to derive a logical output.

If you are standing a mile from your friend on a dark night, you can communicate with him with a flashlight. Just by shining the light, you can inform your friend to execute a plan. If he does not see the light, he will know that he should not execute the plan. Of course, the plan of action has to be prearranged. In computer parlance, this prearranged plan is called a protocol.

Switching the light on or off only manipulates one bit of information. Only two specific instructions or set of instructions can be implemented. If the light is on, the instruction will be implemented; if the light is off, the instruction will not be implemented.

Let us imagine that you and your friend decide to extend the usefulness of this method of communication. Your protocol is that you will send pulses of light, each group of pulses consists of long pulses and short pulses, and the arrangement of long and short pulses represents each alphanumeric character. For instance, transmitting the following signal, "short-pulses, short-pulse, short-pulses" would represent the letter S, and "long-pulse, long-pulse, long-pulse" would represent the letter O. Therefore, you can send out an "SOS" message on your flashlight, assuming that you and your friend have previously agreed on this protocol. This is actually the internationally recognized code for a distress signal.

Unfortunately, for you and your friend, this would bring you no fame or fortune since this was used more than three hundred years ago by a gentleman called Samuel Morse. His invention facilitated the advent of the telegraph. He did not use light waves but radio waves. Radio waves and light waves are in the same electromagnetic spectrum but different wavelengths. Light waves can be sensed by the eyes of human and other animals; radio waves cannot. The advantage of radio waves, though, is that they can travel great distances, even around the world and back almost instantaneously. Radio waves travel in a straight line unless they are reflected or refracted. The ionosphere around the earth serves as a medium to reflecting radio waves around the earth. Various methods are used to transduce the radio waves into signals detectable by humans.

With the advent of computers, Morse code and telegraph are not as popular as they used to be. The ASCI code and its extended version, EBCDIC code, are the codes utilized by computer engineers to represent alphanumeric characters. As an example, the eight-bit (one byte) arrangement of ones and zeros for the character A is 01000001.

Each character on your computer keyboard is represented in the computer's memory by an array of these ones and zeros corresponding to the EBCDIC code. What you type goes into the computer memory as ones and zeros, which can now be manipulated by the computer since it has the same language as the instructions stored in the computer. You may be writing an essay, so that text editor you are using stores what you write as a text file. You may be doing a calculation with the calculator application on your computer, so the calculator software does operations (multiply, divide, etc.) as you instruct it to, then the software writes the result on the computer display.

This process seems similar to the way our bodies process information. The input devices— our eyes, ears, and other physical senses—are analogous to the computer keyboard and other input devices.

The brain looks out for inputs from the various input devices (eyes, ears, etc.). These inputs then go to a processing center in the brain, which can be compared to the applications (programs) in the computer, the processing takes place, and the final output is sent to an output device, such as muscles in your arms and legs. It is also stored in your memory so that you can remember what you just did. It also becomes a part of your database.

We tend to be oblivious of what goes on between the input and the output of the computer. We simply leave that to the experts and the engineers. Aside from the computer, we treat other equipment in our lives the same way. This is inevitable since we cannot have more than a cursory knowledge of all the equipment in our lives. The experts and the engineers do know what is between these inputs and outputs. They may not know why the silicon chip in a transistor behaves the way it does when a voltage is applied to it, but they know that they can design with these silicon chips because their behavior never changes if the input conditions do not change. It does not matter if you pray to God to change the behavior of these microchips; the laws of physics will never be changed to comply with anyone's desire or prayer. The whims of a deity have never been seen to cause a change in the laws of physics.

When it comes to living organisms, including human beings, the attitude seems to be even more pronounced in terms of ignoring the small steps between input and output and just assume it to be "metaphysical"; then we take metaphysical solutions to an

infinite degree by imagining that the omnipotent, omnipresent
invisible hand of God is at work, manipulating everything.

No Evidence of Intelligent Design

Recently, I read a book written by Dr. Francis Collins, *The
Language of God*; the subtitle is *A Scientist Presents Evidence
for Belief*. The book excited my curiosity because Dr. Francis
Collins is not just another scientist, but he is also the preeminent
microbiologist, physicist, and physician. He discovered the
genes associated with a number of diseases and led the Human
Genome Project, which mapped the complete human genome
for the first time in the history of mankind. He is the director
of the National Institutes of Health. He has been elected to the
Institute of Medicine and the National Academy of Sciences
and has received the Presidential Medal of Freedom, and the
National Medal of Science. Needless to say, he is no run-of-the-
mill scientist. He is also a practicing Christian and a believer in
an anthropomorphic God who is benevolent and loving, who
listens to and answers the prayers of his creatures, and who
encodes a system of Moral Law in the conscience of mankind,
at the same time gives mankind the choice of free will to do
as they please. Dr. Collins's philosophy is that God initiated
and controlled a Darwinian evolution. This paradox is very
interesting, so I became interested in finding out more about
his philosophy by reading this book.

Dr. Collins is certainly not a believer in Young Earth Creationism
(YEC). This is a subset of the creationist believers who advocate
the literal translation of the book of Genesis in the Bible.
They object to the scientific theory that the earth is billions
of years old and that human beings evolved from other species

approximately 200,000 years ago. Instead, their worldview is that Adam, who is purported to be the progenitor of the human race, was created in the present form of humans by God from the dust of the earth between 6,000 and 10,000 years ago. The scientific theory of evolution is supported by Darwin's study of the evolution of the species, radiometric dating, mitochondrial DNA studies, geological dating, and other technologies.

There are no verifiable studies or experiments that are used by Young Earth Creationists in particular or creationists in general to validate their hypothesis. Generally, all they do is attempt to invalidate the works of evolution scientists. Their only "proof" of young-earth creation is the Bible, which is mostly a collection of folklores, allegories, and writings that are contemporaneous with first-century era and earlier.

Dr. Collins wrote in his book,

> {*After all, there are clearly parts of the Bible that are written as eyewitness accounts of historical events, including much of the New Testament. For a believer, the events recorded in these sections ought to be taken as the writer intended -- as descriptions of observed facts. But other parts of the Bible, such as the first few chapters of Genesis, the book of Job, the Songs of Solomon and the Psalms have a more lyrical and allegorical flavor, and do not seem to carry the mark of pure historical narrative.}*

Dr. Collins dedicated several pages of his book to demonstrate from a scientific point of view why the idea of "irreducible complexity" is not a valid argument. Intelligent design advocates claim that complex biological systems, such as the human eye, could not have evolved by a Darwinian process because if you remove any part of the eye, the remaining parts, without the missing part, would be useless for seeing. This conclusion, however, does not properly address the situation. It is more likely that a light-sensitive area that stimulated the nervous or other systems of the body first developed on the organism. This could be helpful in many different ways, but more importantly, it would not be a disadvantage that causes the organism to be less likely to survive than it was previously. When a mutation occurs that causes the tissue in front of the light-sensitive spot to grow into the shape of a convex lens, it performs the function of the lens of the eye, so the organism can start seeing objects. This would be a gradual process over millions of mutations, but each mutation that caused the clear spot to shape more like a lens, the more functional the formative eye became. As Dr. Collins and other scientists pointed out, from an engineering point of view, the functionality of the eye in its present state of evolution could be improved if the light-sensitive cells were more strategically placed. This could happen in the next hundred generations if the driving factors are right. The primary driving factors would be that the mutants who have the improved eye would have a distinct advantage of surviving over those who do not.

This is the nature of evolution; the mutations that cause the mutant to be more viable in a particular environment would give the mutant a better chance of survival, and the mutations that do not, would inhibit the survival of the unimproved mutants. If this process continues over millions of years, these gradual changes can make an organism take on completely different appearance from what it looked like in the beginning. I have had creationists telling me that God made all creatures in its present form and evolution is responsible for only small changes. The example they give is that a bird's beak may become modified to facilitate what they eat. My response is that a million small changes make for one great change if you cannot see the small changes in between.

There are organisms existing today that only have light-sensitive spots instead of eyes. Some species of worms and shellfish fall in this category. In the one-celled organism called Euglena, the eyespot is located in the gullet, at the base of the flagellum (a whiplike locomotory structure). The light-sensitive region apparently influences flagellar motion in such a manner that the organism moves toward light.

Another factor that affects evolution is the environment. I arbitrarily picked a hundred generations to see any significant improvement in the functionality of the eye, but this is entirely dependent on the environment in which the organism lives. In our modern scientific era, natural selection is inhibited by modern technology. If someone was born with a 20/20 vision, and the ability of an owl to see in relative darkness, and you have only average vision, that person is no more likely to survive than you can in this technological age. You can always get glasses to correct your vision, and you get your food from the supermarket rather than having to compete with the owl for your food. Therefore, you and your offspring will get along fine in our technological environment. There are fish that live at the bottom of the ocean, where it is dark, that have no eyes. The evolution of eyes would not be an advantage for their survival.

It probably took more than one hundred generations for the eye to evolve; that would be thousands of years. Our life span is so short compared to evolutionary events that we tend only to be able to envision a very short span of this spectrum of time. We seem not to realize that human existence is just a "tick in time and a speck in space."

Our scientific environment inhibiting evolution is not necessarily a good thing. While we are inhibiting our ability to evolve, other organisms are evolving full speed ahead. I can remember one morning about fifty years ago, I took up the newspaper and was ecstatic to see an article on the front page with the bold prediction that within the decade, bacterial infections would be a thing of the past. The article stated that so many powerful antibiotics were being developed that all bacteria would be eliminated in a few years' time. Lo and behold, sometime ago, many decades after reading the article proclaiming the imminent demise of bacteria, I read another article describing how some bacteria were found to be feeding on penicillin, the very medicine that was produced to kill them and has been killing them for a long time. They have not only evolved to be resistant to the thing that was supposed to kill them, but they have also now begun to use it as their food.

Do creationists who believe that God ordered everything to happen believe that he ordered the bacteria to become resistant to penicillin and to start feeding on it? This line of reasoning has no other rationale but to justify their opinion that God conceptualizes everything and makes those concepts reality by the power of his thoughts. It is more likely that the ongoing process of mutation caused mutants to emerge that are more survivable in the environment in which they find themselves, which is an environment with penicillin.

A brand new virus that causes severe respiratory and other diseases suddenly showed up in China in December 2019. This is the deadly SARS-CoV-2 virus which causes the COVID-19 disease. It is an airborne virus that hangs in the air for some time after an infected person breathes, talks, sings, sneezes, or coughs, just waiting for hapless people to breathe it in. It also hangs out on surfaces like doorknobs, countertops, and other places, just waiting to be picked up by people who touch these surfaces. The one thing scientists know for sure is that this virus is very infectious; in the twenty or so months that it has been around, it has spread to every corner of the globe and has been categorized as a global pandemic. It has, so far, infected more than 200 million people worldwide and killed over 4.5 million. These are official estimates, but the actual number may be two or three times greater.

Scientists were very proactive in developing vaccines to combat this pandemic. By the end of January 2021, they had developed four different vaccines, most of them were about 95 percent effective in combating the virus, but the virus was not about to surrender and die. Several mutants, otherwise called variants started to pop up around the world. There was the Italian variant, the Brazilian variant, the UK variant, the Vietnamese variant, the USA variant, and the South African variant; all proved to be easier to spread than the original virus. Scientists were keeping their fingers crossed. It was too early to tell if these new variants were more deadly or more resistant to the vaccine, even though, initially, that appears to be the case.

Then came bad news out of South Africa. They had to stop dispensing one of the more popular types of vaccines because it was becoming evident that their variant has developed a significant level of immunity to it. Some of the variants are more infectious and more deadly than the original virus. The news media was reporting that "the virus found a way to evade the vaccine." However, the scientists would have been more appreciative if the reports were more accurate, stating that "the new variant was a more viable mutant that was able to survive and propagate in spite of the vaccine." It was simply the survival of the fittest. In other words, the survival of the variant that is most compatible with the environment that it finds itself in.

Like a race to the finish line, the Delta variant of the virus came out of India like a category-5 tornado. In only a few months it has overtaken all other variants and has caused eighty percent of all the new cases worldwide. It is considered to be multiple times as virulent as the other variants, and is more likely to cause severe sickness and death.

Did God direct and control these mutations, or was it a result of natural, Darwinian, Mother Nature survival of the most compatible mutants? Was it that God decided to play a game of Whac-A-Mole with scientists, and when the scientists were in sight of success, he threw in a more challenging variant? It is either that, or Darwinian evolution is the driving factor behind these increasingly potent mutants.

It is the belief of some creationists that God sent this plague on the nations of the world so that they will realize who is in charge. The fact that both believers and unbelievers are dying makes a lot of sense to them. "The good will have to suffer for the bad," they declared.

Here, we can envision a scenario similar to the conflict between Galileo and the church, only mitigated by the fact that at this point in time, the church does not have the authority to hold inquisition for scientists. Thanks to the powers that be for the separation of church and state. Theists may be inclined to suppress information about mutations of organisms and genetic engineering because it does not comport with their idea of an omnipotent and anthropomorphic God. They will have the tendency to believe and rely on the biblical account of frightening goats with speckled sticks to achieve genetic changes, instead of natural mutations leading to the survival of the most adaptable mutants.

In the biblical account of Genesis 30:25–43, Jacob made an agreement with his boss Laban that as payment for his labor, all spotted or colored goats or sheep would be inherited by Jacob and the rest would remain in Laban's possession. Jacob then came up with the very "high-tech" scam of placing a speckled piece of stick in the animals' watering troughs. Presumably, when the animals saw this speckled stick, they would produce speckled offspring. He even went further by exposing the speckled sticks only to the best animals.

According to the Bible, Jacob became very wealthy because of this genetic manipulation of Laban's livestock. He should not have been rewarded by God for scamming his boss, but lo and behold, according to the Bible, he was. How many of us believe that this scam actually worked?

Most bacteria are now immune to most antibiotics. Soon they all may become immune to all antibiotics. This is a serious situation. It is important to pause at this point and ask what role does God play in this scenario of bacteria becoming immune to antibiotics? Is he not paying attention? Are we not praying enough for God to intervene? Is this a test that he is giving scientists? Maybe God just allows the laws of physics, including biophysics, to take its course. Maybe this is not the nature of the God we pray to; he may just be a "metaphysical" creation that is neither anthropomorphic nor gracious and is not expressed in a "physical dimension." Maybe all this has to do with the forces and energy of Mother Nature interacting with atoms, molecules, valence bonds, genes, and DNA.

Should we pray and pray some more for God to work a miracle to stop the bacteria from becoming resistant, or should the scientists go to work to find a solution? This is a serious situation that cannot be left unattended.

While Dr. Collins is a strong advocate of Darwinian evolution, he is a believer in an anthropomorphic God, who created the universe, then used the elegant mechanism of Darwinian evolution to propagate life and establish the world as we know it. This doctrine is based on theistic evolution, otherwise called BioLogos. After presenting six principles of theistic evolution in his book, Dr. Collins wrote,

> *{If one accepts these principles, then an entirely plausible, intellectually satisfying and logically consistent synthesis emerges. God, who is not limited in time or space, created the universe, and established natural laws that govern it. Seeking to populate this otherwise sterile universe with living creatures, God chose the elegant mechanism of evolution to create microbes, plants, and animals of all sorts. Most remarkable, God chose the same mechanism to give rise to special creatures who would have intelligence, a knowledge of right and wrong, free will, and a desire to seek fellowship with him. He also knew these creatures would ultimately choose to disobey the Moral Law.}*

A few paragraphs later, Dr. Collins commented,

> {*After twenty-eight years as a believer, the Moral Law still stands out for me as the strongest signpost to God. More than that, it points to a God who cares about human beings, and a God who is infinitely good and holy.*}

First, in Dr. Collins's words, "God chose the same mechanism to give rise to special creatures who would have intelligence, a knowledge of right and wrong, free will, and a desire to seek fellowship with him." This is not Darwinian evolution, which Dr. Collins said he endorses. Darwinian evolution is the natural inclination of the most survivable mutant of a species to survive better in a particular environment than the other mutants, without any interference from any supernatural entity.

Second, Dr. Collins pointed out that the Moral Law, (a mandate by God to observe moral code of ethic,) is his strongest signpost to God, yet he said that God knows that these creatures (humans) would ultimately choose to disobey the Moral Law. A statement that God knows that his creatures (humans) would choose to disobey the Moral Law implies that the Moral Law is not being observed or obeyed by most people. If it is generally not observed by mankind as a moral force pulling everyone toward God, then how could this moral law be a signpost pointing toward God? Is it not as impotent as an insignificant rock on the side of the road instead of a signpost? Many people (I wish I could say most) do feel the urge to observe a moral law as defined by their culture, but given the level of immoral deeds that pervade most cultures, it is hard to envision that the moral law was one of God's objectives in creating mankind.

Third, what moral law? The very survival of any species depends on how good their ability is to kill other species or even members of their own species. Human beings are no exception. In fact, we are the worst perpetrators, or the best, depending on your point of view of this behavior.

Even in prehistoric times, war, conflict, and brutality have been the hallmark of the human race. Just in the past two hundred years, hundreds of millions of human beings have been killed by international conflicts. About the same amount may have been killed by domestic warfare. During this time slavery and colonialism devastated nations which did not arm themselves to meet the aggressions of unscrupulous and ungodly people who conquered their land and enslaved their people. Rapacious capitalism is the cause of most of the human suffering that happened and is happening around the world. This is a phenomenon where humans strive to acquire and accumulate more material things than they can consume and to get it by whatever means necessary, fair or foul. This is not an analogy of the squirrels hiding nuts in the summer to sustain themselves in the winter; it is an insatiable greed to expropriate material things that other people have. The more vulnerable a country or group of people is, the more targeted they are. Rapacious capitalists are usually an arm of various governments or have extreme influence on the government. Their spheres of operation are usually national and international. "Greed is good" is the mantra of the rapacious capitalists. Greed begets envy, covetousness, and wars eventually. Most international wars are started by one country wanting to take what the other country has. Within a country, rapacious capitalists only need to have laws enacted to ensure that the most influential people get richer, and the poor get poorer.

According to the Federal Survey of Consumer Finances, the wealthiest 1 percent of American households own 40 percent of the country's wealth. This is the antithesis of any moral law. In the light of all this inhumane practice, it is inconceivable that a God, who is merciful and humane and who created humans to serve him by observing his moral laws, could stand by and not act. Moral laws have to be an objective of the human species without any religious bias; it has to be consciously recognized and implemented by human beings. To believe that God has written moral law in a DNA code is as much a facade as Christians using the Bible to justify slavery. What happens when people who believe that God laid down moral law for them to follow and see no consequence of their atrocities? They go to their vast arrays of imaginary rationale; example: God put a curse (hex) of perpetual slavery on black people at Noah's request because Noah's son saw his father's "nakedness", or that God favors one ethnic group of people over other ethnic groups, and therefore, whatever that favorite group does is the will of God.

It is difficult or maybe impossible to determine the attributes or characteristics of the entity who we refer to as God. In scientific terms, God only exists as an imaginary concept. Theists say that he can only be experienced by faith, which, in this context, is another word for one's imagination. In other words, no physical or material characteristic can establish the existence of God. There has never been any controlled double-blind study backed up by an independent review that demonstrates that God has ever caused an event to happen that would bypass the laws of physics to satisfy the hopes and prayers of an individual or a group of people. Nothing that conclusively demonstrates the existence of any entity or being that is anthropomorphic, omnipotent, and omniscient, let alone loving, merciful, and kind, has ever been established. People who are skeptical about these glorified attributes of God are not necessarily denying the existence of God; that would be arrogant. No one has so much knowledge that they can declare or prove that there is no God. It is impossible to prove a negative concept. The dilemma, though, is the theists who declare the existence of God by citing the Bible or other holy books, with nothing else to substantiate their claims. It is apparent that humans go through these phase-shifting rituals to identify themselves with what they conjure up as a loving and benevolent God, who they can only reach by faith (imagination), then they come back to the world of reality where material things happen.

As stated in his book, Dr. Collins believes that God is not limited by time or space. The only thing that cannot be proven scientifically to be limited by time or space is the ability of the human mind to imagine things. For anything to exist means that it occupies time and space. Only if God is an imaginary concept will he not be limited by time or space. If he is not just an imaginary concept, then it must be possible for him to express himself in material ways. This material "dimension" is the only one in which humans exist in spite of unfounded claims by some people. If God is talking to someone, it should be possible to record his voice on an audio recording device; otherwise, what that person hears only to himself or herself may very well be caused by a neurological or mental disorder. The same is true for things people claim to see that have never been video-recorded or corroborated by independent sources. Sound is a function of rapid compression and decompression of air impacting our eardrum or the effects of this compression and decompression process traveling through the tissues of our bodies. The same is true for what we see, which is rapid changes in the frequency and intensity of light waves. These are physical phenomena obeying the laws of physics. Sight and sound are not happening if these elements are absent. What our brains tell us we are hearing or seeing is not necessarily from an external source but maybe a function of our thoughts driven by a mental or neurological anomaly. If it is some incident that someone experienced and claimed that it is a miracle executed by God, then that person has the obligation to prove its veracity and that it could not have happened naturally. Even this would not prove that God made it happen.

It is irrelevant to believe or imagine that God is not limited by time or space; what is relevant is to show even one instance, in a controlled scientific environment, where God has nullified the laws of physics to cause an event to happen or stop an event from happening that would not have happened naturally. One can speculate and imagine things in the absence of credible material evidence, but this speculation will remain a figment of the imagination until something tangible is presented. Imagination can be used constructively to create novels, plays, and other literary works. Scientific and engineering projects have to be imagined before they can be implemented, but if humans continue to create a false sense of reality by just the power of their imagination, just envision how chaotic and untethered society could become.

Juxtaposed to the philosophy of Dr. Collins's BioLogos, otherwise known as theistic evolution, is the philosophy of secular humanism. The secular humanist believes that human beings are capable of being ethical and moral without religion or belief in a deity.

The following paragraph is an excerpt from an article in Wikipedia on secular humanism:

> *{The humanist life stance emphasizes the unique responsibility facing humanity and the ethical consequences of human decisions. Fundamental to the concept of secular humanism is the strongly held viewpoint that ideology—be it religious or political—must be thoroughly examined by each individual and not simply accepted or rejected on faith. Along with this, an essential part of secular humanism is a continually adapting search for truth, primarily through science and philosophy.}*

The humanist is a spiritually liberated human being. He or she does not have to live in the virtual reality that God is providing his or her daily bread, then having to revert to the real world and dashes off to work to earn some money to buy his or her daily bread, because, if he or she does not, he or she will end up hungry and homeless, sleeping under a bridge somewhere. In spite of his or her beliefs, God will not give him or her food or shelter. If someone offers a handout to a hungry and homeless person sleeping under a bridge, what other process other than one's indulgence in a religious dogma would lead someone to believe that it was God that caused that gift to happen? If this were a situation where other human beings are not able to help, this hungry homeless person would die from hunger or exposure to the weather. How do we know? It has happened every time that help was not available from other humans.

If a relative of the humanist dies from a disease after every effort was made to save that relative, the humanist would accept that his relative's body succumbed to the onslaught of a pathogen.

The relative will be sadly missed, but the humanist would be assured that every effort that was humanly possible was taken to save his relative.

On the other hand, the theists would believe that it was the relative's time to be called to heaven by God and that he would now be in heaven dancing with the angels. They would believe that God had a good reason for not answering their prayers the way they anticipated it would be answered. They would believe that God has his reason why their prayers to heal their relative were not answered. The theists would not go through the thought process that if it were the relative's time to be called to heaven by God, their prayers and the medication would be totally useless and unnecessary.

According to the Council for Secular Humanism the following statements which is an excerpt from *Wikipedia*, describe the worldview of the organization:

> *{Need to test beliefs* – *A conviction that dogmas, ideologies and traditions, whether religious, political or social, must be weighed and tested by each individual and not simply accepted by faith.*
>
> *Reason, evidence, scientific method* – *A commitment to the use of critical reason, factual evidence and scientific method of inquiry in seeking solutions to human problems and answers to important human questions.*
>
> *Fulfillment, growth, creativity* – *A primary concern with fulfillment, growth and creativity for both the individual and humankind in general.*

Search for truth – *A constant search for objective truth, with the understanding that new knowledge and experience constantly alter our imperfect perception of it.*

This life – *A concern for this life (as opposed to an afterlife) and a commitment to making it meaningful through better understanding of ourselves, our history, our intellectual and artistic achievements, and the outlooks of those who differ from us.*

Ethics – *A search for viable individual, social and political principles of ethical conduct, judging them on their ability to enhance human well-being and individual responsibility.*

Justice and fairness – *an interest in securing justice and fairness in society and in eliminating discrimination and intolerance.*

Building a better world – *A conviction that with reason, an open exchange of ideas, good will, and tolerance, progress can be made in building a better world for ourselves and our children.}*

Underlying all the faith based belief in miracles and the belief that God will defy the laws of physics to answer the supplications of human beings, is the lack of empirical data to buttress these claims. There are simple studies that could be done to test the theory of telepathic (intercessory) prayers, whereby it could be reasonably determined if people could be healed by someone or a group of people praying for them, even though the recipients would be unaware of anyone praying for them. I have made Internet searches and have found no instance of any double-blind independent study of this being done previously, probably because the advocates of telepathic healing have already closed their minds to any empirical studies that may prove them wrong. I have found tests, but they do not meet scientific standards and show no positive results.

The following is a simple study that may be done to find out if telepathic prayers where the recipients are unaware of being prayed for, are effective.

This proposed study should involve a sizable sample for greater accuracy; let us propose about four hundred cancer patients. These patients should meet the following criteria: They are not aware of anyone who regularly prays for them; they have the same type of disease. Cancer would be a good disease to use for this test since each type is clearly defined and treatment normally takes some time. It should be the same type of cancer. The patients should have had cancer for the same length of time, they are approximately the same age, and they are undergoing the same type of treatment. Let us randomly select half of the patients; each half would have the same amount of male and female patients. One half will be prayed for on a regular basis; no prayer will be offered for the other half. The patients' names, photographs, and whatever other items the people praying need, but the patients should never be alerted that they are being prayed for.

After some time, probably a year, the result should be analyzed. If there is divine intervention, everyone receiving prayer should be cancer free while only average results take place in the other group; since God is supposed to be omnipotent and can make every cancer go away, he would have no problem healing everyone in this group. If there is some other kind of telepathic healing energy that goes from the prayer group to the patients, then a significant percentage of the group being prayed for, compared to those not prayed for, should be healed. If the percentage of patients cured in each group is close, then this experiment would demonstrate that prayer by telepathic media for unaware recipients has not been proven.

There are so many instances in the Bible where God invoked his power to demonstrate his supremacy, yet none of these shows of power or potency has ever been seen in modern times, except those uncorroborated episodes of fantasy that people often have. A lot of people also gloat that they are "spirit beings" (souls) in a physical body, meaning that their "soul" or consciousness is not a function of their physical body. Again there is no empirical data to even suggest that there is any truth in this claim. It is just the imagination of the individual that invokes this conviction or the collective imagination of a group of people.

Many people have had near-death experiences, especially when they were being operated on at a hospital. They claimed that their "spirit" left their bodies, and they were able to look down from above and have a visual aerial tour of their surroundings. Usually, they would claim to have experienced a bright and "loving" light at the end of a tunnel that symbolizes the presence of God. There have been instances where hospital staff put hard-to-miss unique icons in places where the patients would not be able see them from their operation table but would be quite visible looking down from above. Icons such as a large red painting of the number 8 on a piece of cardboard placed on the floor. In no instance when these out-of-body travelers were questioned about what they saw, did they ever mention seeing these easily visible icons. If there were no instance where the patients reported seeing objects that were placed after the operation started, then the logical conclusion has to be that their experience was akin to the stuff that dreams, and hallucinations are made of.

People will tell graphic stories of their personal interaction with God or some guardian angel. These stories are always illogical and hardly based in the world where reality exists. The following is a dialogue I had with someone some time ago. I shall call the person Tom.

> **Tom:** I am positive that God spoke to me and prevented me from having a car accident.

> **Author:** How come?

> **Tom:** I was pulling out of my driveway a couple days ago. I forgot to check before I entered the road. I heard this strong urgent voice saying, "Stop! Stop!" I slammed on the brakes, just in time to see a car barreling down the road. I avoided the accident only by a split second. If it wasn't God speaking to me, it was my guardian angel.

> **Author** (after some thought): Do you mean that God or his angel literally spoke to you?

> **Tom:** Literally! Literally! I never heard a voice like that before. It was loud and clear.

Author: You may have seen the car in your peripheral vision, or heard it coming, or you may have remembered just in time to look. The voice you heard may just be a vivid imagination caused by the fright.

Tom (agitated): I am sure it's God or an angel. Nobody can convince me otherwise.

Author: And there can be no other explanation?

Tom: No.

I always wondered why God would wait until a few milliseconds before the impact to alert Tom.

Since this conversation took place only about ten years ago, Tom had two separate collisions with pedestrians, one with a tractor-trailer and one with another car. I saw Tom some time ago; he was still talking about how God saved him from the accident. I ask him why God or the guardian angel did not stop him from having these other accidents. He did not have an answer but held on to his story that God protected him from the first account. Did God shout at him to stop the car in the first near-miss then abandon him in the accidents? Is his account of the incident the only possible explanation of what happened?

One day, about fifty years ago, I was driving, and a front tire of my car blew out. I was traveling at a fast speed down an inclined road. The car overturned and rolled over one or two times; I am not even sure how many times. I was lucky to come out of the car alive and without serious injury. I climbed out of the wrecked car, stood up, felt myself for broken bones or laceration, then with a deep sigh of relief, I spontaneously said, "Thank God!" Then I made an evaluation of what went wrong. Before the accident, I was aware of a noticeable bulge on the side wall of the tire that eventually blew out. I was driving too fast with that defective tire. I made a pledge to myself never again to drive any vehicle with a defect that I am aware of that can cause an accident. Instead of just depending on God to keep me safe, I try to do everything I can in the realm of this material world to keep this promise. Fifty years on, I think I can tap myself on the shoulder for a very good driving record.

Imagined "reality," without material facts to establish proof, has promoted conspiracy theories, belief in myths, magics, obeah and voodoo rituals, fairy tales, old wives' tales, folklores, and even gods. Ancient Greeks looked on the majestic cloud-covered peaks of Mount Olympus. They saw lightning flashing between the high mountain peaks and distant clouds. They heard earsplitting blasts of thunder from the mountains. They had good reason to *imagine* that this must be where the gods lived. So the Greeks imagined into existence an entire family of gods living on Mount Olympus. Like us, the Greeks' power of imagination was unlimited by time, space, or reality. A material link between the imaginary gods on Mount Olympus and facts based on reality was not provided and was deemed not to be necessary. According to ancient Greeks, Zeus was the chief god that ruled on Mount Olympus. He was the god of the sky, lightning, and thunder and was the ruler of all the other gods on Mount Olympus. The conversation can be made that like the ancient Greeks, a significant percentage of the people of our present culture makes important decisions on moral and religious issues without due diligence to factual considerations; therefore, we face the same risk of coming to erroneous conclusions. In our present society, we have seen how easily conspiracy theories, without any basis in actual facts, can be propagated. We see how easily normal people can gravitate to cult leaders. We also see how easily traditionally religious people can accept untested religious dogmas and conspiracy theories while rejecting proven scientific facts.

The ancient Greeks were intelligent people. In fact, a lot of the knowledge we currently have as a society is built on the works of Greek philosophers, mathematicians, and scientists. We have a vast scientific knowledge base to draw from, whereas they did not. We know (at least we can learn from our knowledge base) that lightning is caused by the discharge of electricity created by friction in the clouds and thunder from the vibrations that this discharge causes. The ancient Greeks did not have that knowledge base so they can be forgiven for relying on their imagination that gods live in the mountains.

God and the forces of nature are most likely one and the same entity with two important differences: First, God is perceived to possess human attributes, such as the ability to communicate with humans, has empathy, can feel love, hate, and anger; while the forces of nature are inanimate and uncompromising, they follow strict natural laws. Second, natural occurrences that seem mysterious or unexplainable to humans are attributed to the omnipotent power of God. However, the existence of God has never left the realm of human imagination. In spite of all the proclamations and pontifications, there has never been anything to demonstrate that our belief in God is any more credible or any more factual than the Greeks' belief of Zeus and his family of gods on Mount Olympus.

Whatever humans cannot explain, it is assumed that God made it happen. Even when there are simply scientific explanations, God is given the credit to have caused the scientific process. When humans could not explain a bolt of lightning, it was assumed that God made it happen. When humans could not explain how an organic molecule became a living cell, it was assumed that only God could make that happen. Our immune system gets little credit for curing diseases in our bodies; the credit always goes to medicine, prayer, or some herbs that we took. Prayers, medicine, and herbs play a role in the healing process, but without the mastery of our wonderful ability to self-heal, other factors would be useless in most cases.

God is believed to have human attributes, including human cognitive abilities and human emotions, but these attributes have never been proven or credibly demonstrated. On the other hand, the entity that we conceptualize as God may be the four inanimate uncompromising forces of nature that physicists defined as gravity, the weak force of nuclear interaction, the strong nuclear force, and electromagnetic force. According to scientists, these four forces of nature are the creators of everything in the universe, from the microphysics of the DNA that gives us life to the energy-giving light from the sun, to the planets and central star in the solar system, to the vast expanse of the universe. These forces define the parameters that bond the atoms of one element with the atoms of another element using the well defined valence bonding, which causes various forms of chemical compounds to be formed. They bind neutrons and protons together in the nucleus of atoms, which forms isotopes that transform themselves into other elements and produce radioactive discharge and other sources of energy.

In the process of photosynthesis, these forces manufacture carbohydrates, the source of food on which humans depend for our very existence. These carbohydrates are synthesized from the abundantly available carbon dioxide and water. This process releases oxygen, of which every breath of our lives depends. This process uses another form of natural energy, sunlight, to accomplish this seemingly miraculous task. Without carbohydrates and oxygen, we could not exist as human beings in our present form. This and other natural processes are well known from high school students to research scientists. The meat and other forms of protein that we eat are derived from vegetation that the animals eat. Some plants also provide protein. The process of valence bonding is well known. The process of the energy from the sun overcoming the valence bond and regrouping these elements into life-giving oxygen and carbohydrates in the plants are also well known. This process can be described as natural intelligence. It happens as a matter of logical, mathematically verifiable scientific process. It is not responsive to prayers or other human supplications. This natural process has some of the attributes that we ascribe to God; it provides us with food and oxygen for our sustenance. Another perspective is that humans have evolved to use these products that the plants produce. Because of this natural process, we have evolved into humans who have the ability to probe into our very existence and worship various gods.

In a nutshell, energy from the sun causes the production of the food that sustains us. Energy from the sun causes rain to fall to nourish the plant and animals and fruits that we depend on for our sustenance. Energy from the sun causes the production of oxygen, without which we cannot live for more than a few minutes. We give God thanks for these life-sustaining essentials each day, even though God's involvement is still unclear and is still unexplainable; whereas it is scientifically proven that energy from the sun causes these things to happen.

I can hear the theists shouting, "Don't leave out the divine intelligence that created the sun, oxygen, water, and the process of photosynthesis that synthesizes things for our sustenance." Sorry, people who believe in logical processes based on empirical evidence have to exclude the "divine intelligence" because, so far, the theists have not provided any tangible evidence to substantiate the work of the "divine intelligence."

Energy from the sun needs no adulation or gratitude to provide us with our daily sustenance; it is an inanimate entity. It happens because it is responding to the laws of physics. Theists dutifully adhere to the teachings of the apostle Paul: "I (Paul) have planted, Apollos watered, but God gave the increase" (1 Corinthians 3:6). They have based our Christian principles on this quotation, which has no factual foundation in the real world, yet we blatantly ignore the scientifically proven fact that the energy from the sun produces photosynthesis, which gives us the food we eat. It gives us the oxygen we breathe, it causes the rain, it causes the wind, it causes lightning and thunder, and it will not respond to our prayers.

In the real world, Paul may have planted, Apollos may have watered, but the increase came from the energy of the sun through the process of photosynthesis that synthesizes the food (carbohydrate) from carbon dioxide and water, in addition to some minerals in the soil. At the same time, this process produces oxygen, without which we could not exist as humans. If anyone really thinks that it is God who makes the plant produce food and not energy from the sun, for a couple of weeks, cover the plant with an opaque box so that the plant is in darkness. Not only will it stop producing, but it will also die. Can someone tell me that God could not get through the box to sustain the plant and make it continue producing food? Or am I going to hear the tired cliche that God does everything for a wise purpose? Must we continue to deny things that are blatantly obvious in favor of our faith in imaginary concepts that have never manifested itself in the real world?

When the laws of physics dictate that this natural source of energy is manifested in the form of a tornado, hurricane, or flood, so be it; prayers will not help.

Physicists working to find a grand unified theory of the four fundamental forces of nature—gravity, electromagnetism, the weak nuclear force, and the strong nuclear force—aim to demonstrate that these four forces are one and the same entity expressed in different ways. Models of this unified theory have been proposed by some scientists, but they are yet to present anything acceptable to the scientific community. If this theory is proven, scientists would have discovered the theory of everything, a theoretical framework that could explain the entire universe. This would be the equivalent of the entity we recognize as God, with the exception that this unified force responds to human emotions and prayers only to the extent that these emotions and prayers may cause physiological changes in the human body.

If God is this caring, loving deity that is so omnipotent, having the power to make any and everything happen by just willing it to happen, then it is mind-boggling to understand why he created the universe, particularly human beings, and then walked away, leaving us to fend for ourselves. The oppression and brutalization of one class of people by a more malevolent class has continued since humans inhabited this planet. The notion that God gives man freedom to perpetuate these atrocities for thousands of years can only be valid to appease the conscience of the people who commit these atrocities. The belief by the evildoers is that if it were not the will of God, he would not permit it. A believer in natural evolution could never make the claim that God allows humans to have free will to commit atrocities. The humanists believe that humans have to create for themselves a moral law to have a viable society, rather than believe that God has given them any moral law but accepts the fact that they may disobey it if they choose to.

Thousands of innocent people are murdered in the United States each year by gunmen who are not guided by any moral law, who manifest their perceived superiority and authority by the cache of high-power firearms in their position and the allure to settle their grievances or act out their psychotic delusions with a gun. Each time the murderous rampage happens, "thoughts and prayers" are what the people who are entrusted to provide security for the citizens have to offer. That phrase absolves them of all responsibilities, and nothing is usually done. If only we could see ourselves as the entity that bears responsibility for doing something about the carnage rather than passing the responsibility to God in our "thoughts and prayers."

Recall this excerpt from the song written by John Lennon:

> *Imagine there's no heaven It's easy if you try No hell below us Above us, only sky*

If we can just imagine that the buck stops with us.

The daily claims that most people make about the goodness and omnipotence of God have never been substantiated with any verifiable facts. To a great number of people, everything beneficial that happens to them is effected by God; everything that is bad is effected by the devil. Just as Tom claimed without any substantive evidence that God prevented him from t-boning another car, people make daily irrational claims that have no factual relevance.

The Malaria Malady

Malaria is a disease that has killed millions of people worldwide over the past thousands of years. It is caused by parasites that infect the red blood cells and cause the cells to swell and burst. These parasites are injected into the human bodies by a particular type of mosquitoes; therefore, malaria most frequently occurs in tropical or subtropical regions where these mosquitoes thrive best.

For some reason that I do not believe is clearly understood at this time, the malaria parasites do not infect red blood cells that have a sickle shape; therefore, this dreaded disease is mitigated by blood cells with sickle shape. This story would have a happy ending if it had ended at this point, but it did not. Sickle-shaped blood cells also have a debilitating, painful, and deadly effect called sickle cell anemia. This condition happens because these abnormally shaped cells tend to clump together and cause obstruction (roadblock) in the blood vessels.

Here, we have a clash of evolutionary processes that clearly demonstrate that living organisms are propagated by Darwinian evolution rather than an intelligent designer. The situation has boiled down to which disease kills more people or inhibits the propagation of the affected organism, malaria or sickle cell anemia. Sickle cell anemia has become prevalent in areas where malaria is also prevalent. The logical deduction is that even though it is a painful and debilitating disease, if you have sickle cell anemia, the chance of getting malaria is small. Therefore, even though sickle cell anemia is a serious disease, for people living in a malaria infested area, having sickle-shaped blood cells gives them a better chance of survival. For people who are not living in a malaria infested area, having sickle-shaped blood cells does not give them any advantage as survivors of the fittest. Bear in mind that over the thousands of years that this scenario was being played out, the people affected were not aware of what was going on.

Would this compromise be the objective of an *intelligent* designer? If God were this intelligent designer, who can make things happen by simply willing it to happen, would he have been satisfied with this botched job when he can just make a simple correction in the DNA code for the blood cells?

> {It was all because of one single letter in the DNA that is misplaced, a "T" that should have been an "A." And that was profound. You could have all of that happen because of one letter that was misspelled.}

That was the response given by Dr. Francis Collins on a CBS *60 Minutes* broadcast about his team of scientists repairing the DNA code of the blood cells of a woman with sickle cell anemia. The woman showed considerable relief from her symptoms, and her body started to make normal red blood cells instead of sickle-shaped cells. This team of scientists led by Dr. Collins was aware of the DNA code for the normal red blood cells, and they observed that there was one displaced letter in the code sequence for the sickle-shaped cells. The team undertook the difficult task of repairing the DNA code. This is complicated stuff; you do not just go in with a scalpel and start cutting. This technique called recombinant DNA technology is a very advanced bioengineering technology that is revolutionizing the medical profession. What the team did was get stem cells from the bone marrow of the woman, where stem cells for the blood cells are produced; extract the misspelled DNA, get the DNA from an HIV virus (HIV has a way of using other human cells to do its dirty work); extract the virus DNA; insert the healthy blood cell DNA into the virus; and reimplant it in the woman's bone marrow. Instead of doing their dirty work of using the cells of the host to make new HIV viruses, these viruses are now instructed to make healthy red blood cells. It is still too early to evaluate the long term problem that this procedure may cause, but at the moment, the woman is enjoying her newly derived healthy status.

Letters of the alphabet are used to conceptualize the structure of the DNA molecule, just like ones and zeros are used to conceptualize a computer program. The planetary system is also used to conceptualize an atom. If you have a very powerful microscope and look at the DNA, you would not find a string of Ts and As, or 1s and 0s in computers, or a planetary system for an atom.

Scientists have done a good job in prying into the functionality of living organisms. They can now tell the DNA code from which a heart or a kidney will be constructed. They have been using this knowledge to implant the DNA of one organism into others in a genetic engineering process called recombinant DNA technology. The DNA that produces insulin in the human body has been implanted in bacteria to produce insulin on an industrial scale. This is a big boom to people with diabetes.

The human genome and the genome for any other organism, the part that contains the instructions for causing any particular trait, can now be edited out or edited in with a bioengineering technology called CRISPR (clustered regularly interspaced short palindromic repeats). This gene-splicing technology can be employed for many genetic diseases. If it is done in an embryonic cell, this would mean that the offspring of this person, who develops from this modified embryo, will carry this modified trait as if it were a natural mutation.

There is a frightening side of this bioengineering technology that bioethics advocates are concerned about. The parents of a child can now custom order the traits that they want their child to have. If you want a child with blond hair, blue eyes, tall, handsome, and with high IQ, the technology is now available for that child to be custom made for you. This technique is not yet perfect, and mistakes can be enormous. Ethical considerations are also of great concern. A Chinese scientist has already modified an embryo that has now produced two girls who cannot get the AIDS disease.

Here, humans have an incredibly potent tool, and apart from controlling genetic diseases, our greatest motivation for using it may be personal biases that have no vision into the long-term, future consequences.

We have seen the emergence of eugenics in the 1880s in the USA, when sterilization and other wanton methods to control the quality of the population was employed. We have also seen cruel and genocidal use of eugenics by the Nazis in German, aiming to eradicate everyone who did not qualify as a member of the so-called master race.

There are people who try to make the case that it is God who gives scientists the knowledge to enable them to do these works. This makes no sense. Would God wait for millions of people to die then give scientists the knowledge to come up with a solution to solve these problems? Millions of people have died over the years from both malaria and sickle cell anemia. Over the millennia, Darwinian natural selection has caused sickle cell anemia to emerge as a cure for malaria, even though sickle cell anemia is itself a serious disease. God did nothing over these thousands of years to alleviate these suffering and deaths. This is not a case of God allowing humans to have free will, which is the first thing you will hear from theists. In this case it is a parasite having free will, and in the case of the sickle shaped blood cells, a DNA code in the embryonic stem cell of someone got miscoded by a natural event, probably a radioactive discharge from an atom or a chemical that disrupts a DNA code.

It is logical that in natural Darwinian processes, a DNA code can get miscoded and start a chain reaction that over thousands of years ended up as the scourge of the sickle cell disease. It is not logical that a loving God would create the sickle cell disease or would allow it to be created for millions of people to suffer and die from, simply because they were exposed to infected mosquitoes, no matter if they were good or bad, righteous or wicked, pious, or powerful. All it took to cause or to cure the disease was to replace one letter of the DNA sequence. After thousands of years, millions of deaths, and unbearable suffering, scientists are learning to replace this one letter in the

DNA code. God, being omniscient, must have known how to fix this all along. This is not like taking a pill, though; it is not a routine procedure. At the moment, it is a very high-tech series of operations that costs millions of dollars per person and takes a long time to complete. It is still in the experimental stage. God could just say the word and everyone whom he wants cured would be cured, but alas, this does not happen, not in the sickle cell anemia cases, not in the cases of cancer or any other disease.

Of course, there are stories of individual divine healing; the divine process is always unverifiable. What would be the reason for God to single out one or two people out of tens of millions who have similar sickness to make their ailments suddenly disappear? These individual cases of miraculous cures may have happened, but why jump to the conclusion that only God could make it happen? Is this not like the English lady who swore that God told her that a particular man was destined to be her husband, or Tom swearing that God told him to stop his car ten millisecond before an eminent crash?

After thousands of years and millions of deaths by these diseases, are we not just champions of denialism to continue advocating that God is answering our prayers? Are we to believe that if we pray hard enough, God will cause all the malaria parasites to die out miraculously? A practical solution to this problem would be eradicating the mosquitoes that carry the malaria parasites. It also appears that maybe in the near future, scientists may have a tool to mitigate the suffering of sickle cell anemia.

One instance for this kind of divine intervention is the biblical story of God killing every firstborn Egyptian child and every firstborn Egyptian animal as the tenth plague to free the Israelites from bondage. Can this horrible story from the Bible be accepted as factual? Why would God kill these innocent people, including babies, when he could simply make the pharaoh change his mind? It is appalling how many people believe these folklores to be literal facts even though, it is impossible to equate this action with a loving God.

Theists will swear how God is good to them even in the face of adversity. I know this man who is pious, humble, and religious. At an early age, he went to study to become a minister of religion. After graduating, he had an accident and has been having severe back pains, which made him almost immobile for over fifty years now. His condition is gradually getting worse in spite of daily sincere prayers. His faith in God is still unfaltering. He uses the biblical Job as his role model, and he believes that God is testing him. Since he is now eighty years old, my belief is that he will die with this problem. Is it reasonable to believe that a loving God is testing this man for fifty-odd years? Or that he is a victim of circumstances in which God has no input or interest? This is only one example of millions of people in similar predicaments.

I know a woman who started to develop multiple sclerosis at about age twenty-five, and now she is about fifty years old. Her condition gradually got worse since she developed the disease. For the past six years, she is permanently immobile in bed with all the typical suffering of an advanced stage of the disease. She also is a devout Christian who prays several times each day for healing and expresses praises to God for keeping her alive. In this and other cases, there are large groups of people who pray with them and pray for them, in person and remotely. Is it reasonable to continue believing that a loving God who has the power to heal just simply ignores the perils of these people? This is just another example of millions of people in the world who are in a similar predicament. Can we continue to believe this is caused by God giving humans free will even though these illnesses were not caused by the actions of humans?

It is understandable why these people have to believe in a God who will deliver them from their suffering. They also believe that when they die, they will go to heaven, where they will be free of all pain and all handicaps. Not to be disparaging, but it is a popular cliche that when ignorance is bliss, it is folly to be wise. It is better to have that hope of a cure, even though it only exists in the realm of the imagination, than to believe that constant pain then eventual death is all that is to be expected for the rest of one's life after suffering so much. There has to be some light at the end of such a dark tunnel. If they did not have this utopian belief, imagine the kind of mental doldrum they would be living in. They need to have something to keep their spirits alive, even to the extent of deluding themselves that God will perform a miraculous relief which will be coming soon.

A minister of religion in Brooklyn, New York, sent his young son off to school one morning. The child did not reach school; he was missing for several days, probably weeks. The police and the entire community were involved in trying to find him. It turned out that a criminal-minded man had somehow enticed the boy into his house, sexually abused him, then killed him, dismembered his body, and put his body parts in a freezer for gradual and convenient disposal. The father was devastated, he could not stop grieving. When he was interviewed by the news media, he cried that he cannot understand why God did this to him. He cried that he was a loyal servant of God, he prayed to God every day, yet God chose to do that to him.

Many people were angry with this minister. They claimed that he had blasphemed. Some people reassured him that God will not give him more grief than he can bear, as if that were not enough burden. Some say that like Job, he was being tested by God.

The minister had said nothing that was irrational. He had every right to question why God had done that to him. Most people would have the same question but would not dare to utter them in public for fear that they would be accused of blasphemy. Those who were criticizing him were either indulging in denialism or hypocrisy. Is it a human trait to deny reality consciously or unconsciously, to see facts staring them in the face and consciously or unconsciously do not acknowledge it.

On June 17, 2015, a young man who was identified to be a white supremacist casually walked into the Emanuel African Methodist Episcopal Church in Charleston, South Carolina, USA. He joined the meeting as if he wanted to be a participant. After a few minutes, he got up, took out his gun, and started to shoot. When it was all done, nine African American people were massacred.

God did not protect those who were praying to him from this depraved monster whose hatred and bigotry made him into a psychopath. An omnipotent, loving, and caring God could have easily changed the mind of this young murderer. It will be said by many that God gives humans free will to do whatever they want. Is this not just another episode of denialism? Some people cannot face the fact that for whatever reason, God, with all his awesome powers, did nothing to protect those who were praying to him, from a deranged evildoer who was possessed with the demon of bigotry. Like the amateur ball player, the believers changed the narrative to say that God works in mysterious ways, and there are hidden benefits that God had in his plan for this massacre. The believers believe that God could not, or chose not to, make his plans manifest itself without the massacre, and that humans cannot comprehend the intricacies of God.

This quote from the French philosopher Voltaire is as relevant today as it was in his time: "It is difficult to free people from the chains they revere." Here is another relevant quote from Voltaire: "Those who can make you believe absurdities can make you commit atrocities."

Since the actions of God have never been demonstrated in any scientific or logical way to be any mystery that is not a result a physical processes, why do people continue to believe in an anthropomorphic God who is powerful beyond imagination, who is loving and kind, who is the good shepherd who would give his life for his sheep, whose followers need to fear no evil, even though they walk through the valley of the shadow of death? Yet this loving and powerful God allowed an evildoer to walk into a church and massacred people who were praying to him.

The wife of a prominent member of the church was killed in this carnage. When asked to give his opinion, his response was that his wife was "in heaven now, dancing with the angels." If there was such a benevolent result of the carnage, why was it also called such a despicable act?

On Sunday, September 16, 1963, worshippers were having a choir practice just before their scheduled Sunday service at the 16th Street Baptist Church, Birmingham, Alabama, USA, a church with a predominantly black congregation that also served as a meeting place for civil rights leaders, when a bomb planted by members of the Ku Klux Klan exploded, killing four innocent young girls and injured twenty other people. This was just another instance of the reign of terror that was unleashed on African Americans by white supremacists during that era. The only motive for the bombing was hatred and bigotry. The people who were targeted were not at war with anyone. In this instance, they were in their church, singing praises to their God, asking God to protect them. God did not protect them. Why did God not stop the terrorist? Why do we continue to believe that God is protecting us when it is blatantly obvious that he is not? We should not have to delude ourselves that it is just another way that God is showing how much he loves us. Sometimes these cliches are the only consolation that are available to people who are marginalized by societal biases.

There are other aspects of this faith in God that can have pernicious results. Some religious leaders use this blind faith that people have in religion to commit grievous atrocities. According to a 2004 research study by the John Jay College of Criminal Justice for the United States Conference of Catholic Bishops, 4,392 Catholic priests and deacons in active ministry, between 1950 and 2002, have been plausibly (neither withdrawn nor disproven) accused of underage sexual abuse by 10,667 individuals.

These priests betrayed the faith that these victims have in God, and by extension, these messengers of God, by committing these crimes that have, or will have damaged the psyche of the victims for the rest of their lives. How could a loving God who has the power to prevent these atrocities allow this to happen? The popular answer is that God gives humans free will to do whatever they want. This in really an irrational response; the victims who are the ones suffering from these horrible crimes did not have any free will in those actions. I put this question to a friend of mine recently, and her response was, "They may have committed some crime in their past life." What ridiculous level of denialism can we allow our minds to indulge in!

I know of a case where a minister of religion had been seducing a sixteen year old high school girl and had been having sexual intercourse with her. This minister was married, with a wife and children. I know this story because the girl gleefully told it to a friend of mine who told me about it sometime later. This minister was notorious for this kind of behavior. The parents of the girl were suspicious that their teenage daughter was having an illicit relationship, but little did they know that it was with the minister. They asked the minister to counsel her. The minister agreed but advised that the counselling is best done in private, and to be effective, it should be done on a continuing basis. This was done, as the minister suggested. The minister and the girl locked themselves in the girl's room several times for their counselling sessions, which were actually sex sessions. The parents were naive enough, or to put it another way, had faith enough in the minister, to allow this to happen. This is a true story as are all the other stories in this book. It is also what can happen when one has blind faith in a person, a religion, or an ideology.

It is one thing to contend that God gives humans free will to commit atrocities, but to use his name and his authority to facilitate these crimes is stretching this rationale extremely thin.

Sometime ago, I read a story in the newspaper about a little girl whose mother had just died. I do not recall the state or town in the USA where this incident happened, but it is a typical story that could have happened anywhere in the world that the Abrahamic religion is practiced. After the death of her mother, the little girl was overwhelmed with grief and was inconsolable. The relatives reassured her that her mother was not really dead; she had just "transitioned," she had just left her earthly home and had gone to her heavenly home. She is in heaven now, "dancing with the angels."

This poor little girl had not yet learned the ambivalent nature of the human psyche -- where humans have learned to live in the real world and an imaginary world at the same time. She did not know that her relatives' consolation was not real and should be understood only in an imaginary context. She pondered that if her mother had transitioned to this beautiful place called heaven, and she will someday be transitioned to heaven herself, and there will be this glorious reunion between her and her mother, why should this transition not happen as soon as possible?

There was a train track not far from the little girl's house where the train passed frequently. She was always warned not to go near the train track because the train could kill her. If getting killed by the train was to be transitioned to heaven, why not do it now rather than wait for "someday"? When she heard the train coming, she peacefully went and laid across the track. She was crushed to death.

That is the consequence of hypocrisy and denialism. We have created a world of fantasy from our imagination, with nothing from the real world to substantiate it.

CHAPTER 3

THE GOD GENE IS NOT NECESSARILY A GOOD GENE

Religion and the Roman Empire

One would believe that the concept of a god gene would be associated with peace, love, and the best attributes of humanity. This turned out to be farthest from what actually happened. An analysis of historical data shows that the rise of Christianity to a status of privilege in the Roman Empire unleashed one of the most brutal eras in the history of mankind.

The following information about the Roman Empire as it affects Christianity was gleaned from, but not limited to, the following sources: *Encyclopedia Britannica*, *National Geographic* magazine, Wikipedia, Western-Civilization.com, and History.com.

To put this in context, even before the Roman administration was converted to Christianity, they practiced the most savage and brutal lifestyle imaginable. Their main sport, which they built grand arenas to watch, was having gladiators fight each other to their deaths with swords and other contrived weapons. These gladiators were not volunteers; they were forced to do it; else, they were horribly put to death. They fed live human beings to hungry wild animals and cheered when these animals tore into the flesh of those unfortunate humans. While they were basically tolerant of religions in general, if they felt politically threatened by any religion, or if that religion threatened to cause any disruption in the society, they were very ruthless in dealing with it. The Jews and the fledgling Christians fitted this description and were mercilessly dealt with by the Romans.

The Roman emperor, Flavius Constantine I, after winning battles under the emblem of the Christian church, became sympathetic to Christianity and the Christian religion. Christians were subsequently excluded from any more persecution. Later, Christianity was declared the official religion of the Roman Empire. We all know, however, what happens when religion and government merge into one entity: Other forms of religions get crushed, and religious dogmas become the law of the land.

Unfortunately, Christianity did not save the Roman Empire, neither politically nor morally. Emperor Constantine abandoned his citadel in Rome after constructing his new citadel of Constantinople, which is now Istanbul, Turkey. Toward the end of the third century, the western part of the empire, which was ruled from Rome, fell into decline and was unable to defend its borders from the Germanic people from the north. The "barbarians" from the north, such as the Visigoths, the Vandals, the Angles, the Saxons, the Franks, the Ostrogoths, and the Lombards, took turns in sacking the helpless Roman Empire, eventually carving out areas in which to settle down. The Angles and Saxons populated the British Isles.

In 476 AD, the last emperor of Western Rome, Flavius Romulus Augustus, was deposed by Odoacer, a German "barbarian" who proclaimed himself king of Italy.

While the western empire of Rome declined, the eastern sector, while not thriving and prosperous, was not declining as the west. Neither were Europeans the only people in the picture. The Chinese and Africans at that time had civilizations that were far more advanced in their culture and technology than the Europeans.

The Moorish Occupation of Europe

If it is ever mentioned that the Moors, who were black and brown from Africa, brought civilization to Europe, most people of western culture would be quite cynical of this claim. Reason is that historical records that do not glorify Europeans are usually suppressed in history books, therefore most people are not aware of these facts. The following information was gleaned from sources such as, but not limited to Wikipedia, National Geographic Magazine, Black History studies, The History Channel, and The New World Encyclopedia.

The ethnicity of the Moors is not clearly established because people of European descent seem to do whatever they could to obliterate any evidence that would point to any fact that black people from Africa had invaded their territory, brought in advanced culture, and were able to live in relative harmony with the people of the land they occupied. The Moorish occupation lasted for over eight hundred years.

The following is an excerpt from the Encyclopedia Britannica that describes the Moors:

> *{Moor, in English usage, a Moroccan or, formerly, a member of the Muslim population of al-Andalus, now Spain and Portugal. Of mixed Arab, Spanish, and Amazigh (Berber) origins, the Moors created the Arab Andalusian civilization and subsequently settled as refugees in the Maghreb (in the region of North Africa) between the 11th and 17th centuries. By extension (corresponding to the Spanish moro), the term occasionally denotes any Muslim in general, as in the case of the "Moors" of Sri Lanka or of the Philippines.*
>
> *The word derives from the Latin term Maurus, first used by the Romans to denote an inhabitant of the Roman province of Mauretania, comprising the western portion of present-day Algeria and the northeastern portion of present-day Morocco.}*

Britannica concluded with the following definition of the Moors:

> *{The term is of little use in describing the ethnic characteristics of any groups, ancient or modern. From the Middle Ages to the 17th century, however, Europeans depicted Moors as being black, "swarthy," or "tawny" in skin colour. (Othello, Shakespeare's Moor of Venice, comes to mind in such a context.) Europeans designated Muslims of any other complexion as "white Moors," despite the fact that the population in most parts of North*

Africa differs little in physical appearance from that of southern Europe (in Morocco, for example, red and blonde hair are relatively common). Today, the term Moor is used to designate the predominant Arab-Amazigh ethnic group in Mauritania (which makes up approximately three-fourths of the country's population) and the small Arab-Amazigh minority in Mali.}

Here is another version of the history and etymology of the word "Moor" by Online Etymology Dictionary:

{North African, Berber, one of the race dwelling in Barbary, late 14c., from Old French More, from Medieval Latin Morus, from Latin Maurus "inhabitant of Mauretania" (Roman northwest Africa, a region now corresponding to northern Algeria and Morocco), from Greek Mauros, perhaps a native name, or else cognate with mauros "black" (but this adjective only appears in late Greek and may as well be from the people's name as the reverse).

Also applied to the Arabic conquerors of Spain. Being a dark people in relation to Europeans, their name in the Middle Ages was a synonym for "Negro". Later (16c. - 17c.); being the nearest Muslims to Western Europe, it was used indiscriminately of Muslims (Persians, Arabs, etc.) but especially those in India. Cognate with Dutch Moor, German Mohr, Danish Maurer, Spanish Moro, Italian Moro. Related: Mooress.}

The following excerpt was adapted from an article entitled "Moors" in the New World Encyclopedia:

> *"The Moors were the medieval Muslim inhabitants of al-Andalus (the Iberian Peninsula including present day Spain and Portugal) as well as the Maghreb and western Africa, whose culture is often called Moorish. The word was also used more generally in Europe to refer to anyone of Arab or African descent, sometimes called Blackamoors. The name Moors derives from the ancient tribe of the Maure and their kingdom Mauretania. Andalusia under Muslim rule produced a society in which culture and science and learning flourished. Muslims, Jews and Christian co-existed in a spirit of mutual tolerance. Much scholarship from this period impacted on European learning, especially via such people as Roger Bacon and Thomas Aquinas. The Fall of Granada in 1492 saw the end of the Muslim presence in Andalusia. This event has had a global impact, giving impetus to the Spanish conquest of the New World inspired by their triumph over the Muslims, which they understood as enjoying God's blessing. What has been described as the Andalusian paradigm suggests that conflict and rivalry is not inevitable for plural societies, that people of different faiths can co-existence and enjoy creative intellectual and cultural exchange".*

To escape a bloody revolution in his homeland Syria, Abd al-Rahman journeyed across North Africa and eventually found himself on the Iberian Peninsula of Europe, which is now

Spain and Portugal. He was the lone survivor of the Umayyad Dynasty after the Abbasids defeated the Umayyad Caliphate in Syria. It was quite a contrast between the Islamic culture he left in Syria, which was culturally more advanced, than the Visigoth population he found on the Iberian Peninsula. Soon Rahman founded the Emirate of Cordoba and sought to emulate the advanced culture he had to leave in Syria. Along with his success in advancing the culture and knowledge in mathematics, medicine, chemistry, physics, philosophy, and astronomy in the Emirate of Cordoba, he greatly expanded his dominion, which was known as Al-Andalus, more recently called Andalusia.

Abd-Al Rahman was ethnically a Barber. This ethnic group is from West and North Africa and is also called Moors. They are generally black and brown people and are of the Muslim faith. Armies from this Moorish region had been employed as mercenaries for Rahman while he was expanding his territory. Eventually, his empire started to flounder and the Moors inserted themselves as rulers of the territory.

The Muslims and the Christians were in fierce competition for control of territory during this era. The Islamic religious ideology had spread out of the Arabian Peninsula as far east as India, into Europe, where it was colliding with the Christian Byzantine Empire; into the Middle East where it was overtaking the ancient Persian Empire, and into North Africa, where it was overtaking the local religions and was largely adopted by the Africans. The occupation of the Iberian peninsula by the Moors began in 711 AD when an African army, under their leader Tariq ibn-Ziyad, crossed the Strait of Gibraltar from northern Africa and invaded the Iberian peninsula, then called Andalus, occupied by the Visigoths.

The Moors, who ruled Spain for 800 years, introduced new scientific techniques to Europe, such as an astrolabe, a device for measuring the position of the stars and planets. Scientific progress in Astronomy, Chemistry, Physics, Mathematics, Geography and Philosophy flourished in Moorish Spain. Basil Davidson, a noted British journalist and historian, wrote that there were no lands at that time (the eighth century) "more admired by its neighbors, or more comfortable to live in, than a rich African civilization which took shape in Spain."

Cordova, one of the more prominent Moorish city was for a long time, the most modern city in Europe. The streets were paved, with raised sidewalks for pedestrians. During the night, ten miles of streets were well illuminated by lamps. This was hundreds of years before there was a paved street in Paris or a street lamp in London. Cordova had 900 public baths. Education in the arts and science was available to all in the Moorish territories which had become a hub of learning for Muslims, Christians, and Jews. All three religious factions worked and studied amicably together. While in Christian Europe ninety-nine percent of the population was illiterate, and even kings could neither read nor write. At that time, all other territories in Europe had only two universities, the Moors had seventeen universities. These were located in Almeria, Cordova, Granada, Juen, Malaga, Seville, and Toledo.

The Great Mosque of Córdoba (La Mezquita) is still one of the architectural wonders of the world in spite of later Spanish disfigurements and adaptation to reflect Christianity. Its low scarlet and gold roof, supported by 1,000 columns of marble, jasper, and porphyry, was lit by thousands of brass and silver lamps which burned perfumed oil. In the tenth and eleventh centuries, public libraries in Europe were non-existent, while

Moorish Spain had more than seventy, of which the one in Cordova housed six hundred thousand manuscripts.

"It is estimated that there are about one thousand Arabic roots, and approximately three thousand derived words, for a total of around four thousand words or 8% of the Spanish dictionary" [*Wikipedia*]. Words beginning with "al," for example, are derived from Arabic. Arabic words such as algebra, alcohol, chemistry, nadir, alkaline, and cipher entered the language. Even words such as checkmate, influenza, typhoon, orange, and cable can be traced back to Arabic origins.

The most significant Moorish musician was known as Ziryab (the Blackbird) who arrived in Spain in 822. The Moors introduced into European culture the earliest versions of several instruments, including the Lute or el oud, the guitar or kithara and the Lyre.

The Moors introduced paper to Europe and Arabic numerals, which replaced the clumsy Roman system. The Moors introduced many new crops including the orange, lemon, peach, apricot, fig, sugar cane, dates, ginger, and pomegranate as well as saffron, cotton, silk and rice which remain some of Spain's main products today.

The Moorish rulers lived in sumptuous palaces, while the monarchs of Germany, France, and England lived in big barns, with no windows and no chimneys, with only a hole in the roof for the exit of smoke. One such Moorish palace "'Alhambra'" (literally "the red one") in Granada is one of Spain's architectural masterpieces. Alhambra was the seat of Muslim rulers from the 13th century to the end of the 15th century. The Alhambra is a UNESCO World Heritage Site.

It was through Africa that the new knowledge of China, India, and Arabia reached Europe. The Moors brought the Compass from China into Europe.

The Moors ruled and occupied Lisbon (named "Lashbuna" by the Moors) and the rest of the country until well into the twelfth century. They were finally defeated and driven out by the forces of King Alfonso Henriques.

The Moorish advanced culture on the Iberian Peninsula was not a unique experience among African and Arab Muslims. After the founding of Islam as a religion in the seventh century, it rapidly spread into Europe, Asia, and Africa. Along with the religious tenets, the Muslims played a pivotal role in the advancement of science, technology, and the arts. These tenets, except for religion, seemed to falter as they devote more and more of their time and energy to religion. It is ironic that in the same era when the Muslims were making great advances in science, mathematics, and the arts, the Christians in Europe were dragging Galileo to inquisition for daring to publish a paper that the Earth orbits the sun.

The Dark Ages of Europe

Europe, the citadel of Christianity, the continent where the pious and passionate teaching and practices of the followers of Jesus Christ were preempted and incorporated into the edict of the Roman Empire, had, by the middle of the fourth century, descended into what is described as the Dark Ages of Europe. As the power and the glory of the Christians increased, so did their militancy and the atrocities they committed.

One of the earlier groups of marauding European killers was the Vikings from Scandinavia. They preceded the rise of the Christian warriors. They traveled in their iconic long boats and raided, plundered, and wantonly killed people along European coastal towns, the British Isles, and even ventured to North America.

European countries have always been at war among themselves and with other states from the dawn of ancient history. Undoubtedly, there were wars among other civilizations, but the focus here is how religion, particularly Christianity, shaped Europe and how the European version of Christianity spread throughout the world. The prevailing opinion of the European society is one of relative peace and civility, but history other than the whitewashed European version says otherwise.

The following are some examples of the situation in Europe after they adopted Christianity. After the disintegration of the Roman Empire, Europe descended into an era of barbarism that lasted for over six hundred years. By the time the peace treaty of Westphalia was signed in 1648 between the warring parties of Europe, it is estimated that about 8 million people were killed because of the various wars in Europe. Given that Europe was much less populated than it is now, that many people killed by war is shocking.

From 1524 until 1648, Europe was plagued by wars of religion. It is important to recognize, however, that religion was not the only reason for these wars. Other reasons included battle for land, money, economic and political power, natural resources, and more.

This is how the article "European History" in Wiki-book.org characterizes a part of the war in Europe:

> *{These wars included the Peasants' War of 1525 in the Holy Roman Empire, the Schmalkaldic War of the 1540s through 1555, an ongoing fight between the Holy Roman Empire and the Turks and the Hussite rebellion.*

> *Religious fighting and warfare spread with Protestantism. The radical new doctrine in Germany brought other simmering social tensions to a boil; peasant revolts flared in 1525, resulting in chaos and bloodshed across Austria, Switzerland, and southern Germany. Wealthy landowners were the target of downtrodden rebels demanding social equality and sharing of wealth in common. Armies loyal to ruling princes suppressed the revolt, and the leaders were executed. Martin Luther, chief initiator of the Reformation, turned against the rebels and defended the authorities' moves to put them down.*

> *The Peace of Augsburg in 1555 declared the Prince's religion to be the official religion of a region or country (cuius regio, eius religio). This resulted in the acceptance of toleration of Lutheranism in Germany by Catholics. When a new ruler of a different religion took power, large groups had to convert religions. Most people found this to be realistic, and the process did not end until 1648.*

In northern Europe (north Germany, Netherlands, and France), the middle class tended to be Protestant, which corresponded with their work ethic and philosophy. Peasants readily converted religions in order to obtain jobs.

With the Treaty of Cateau-Cambrésis in 1559, Spain and France agreed to stop fighting with each other in order to unite against their common Protestant threat, particularly Calvinism, which was considered more of a threat than Lutheranism.

French War of Religion

In France, religious civil war took place from 1562 to 1598 between Catholics and Protestants. The crown usually supported the Catholics but occasionally shifted sides, while the nobility was divided among the two camps. The three leading families in the nation competed for control of France. These families were the Valois family, which was currently in power and was Catholic, the Bourbon family, which consisted of Huguenots (French Protestants), and the Guise family, who was also Catholic. Ultimately, the Bourbon family won the war, but its leader Henry of Navarre was unable to be crowned because the strongly Catholic city of Paris shut itself down. Henry put Paris under a year of siege before finally deciding to convert to Catholicism himself in 1593. The civil war in France was ended by the Edict of Nantes in 1598, which reaffirmed that Catholicism was the official religion in France, but also granted a significant degree of religious and political freedom to Protestants.

Spanish Conflict with the Dutch

In 1566, on the Assumption of the Virgin day, a group of Calvinists in the Netherlands stormed Catholic churches, destroying statues and relics in a town just outside of Antwerp. Dutch Calvinists resented the Catholic religion and their conflicts with the religion, as well as Spanish King Philip II's deep devoutness and close-mindedness toward other religions. The high nobility pleaded with him for more tolerance but some of them were put to death for their insolence. One of the underlying reasons was that Philip wanted to establish an absolute monarchy in the Netherlands and the religious issue gave him a way to put pressure on the parliament. William of Orange escaped to Germany from where he tried to incite a rebellion from 1568 onwards but with little success at first. In 1570 the coastal regions got hit by a weather-related disaster, the All Saints flood that left many regions devastated and the Spanish authorities showed little compassion. William of Orange, then encouraged Sea Beggars, or pirates, to invade the ports of the coast. In 1572 the small town of Brielle was taken by what were no more than outlaws, greeted enthusiastically by the population. The town declared itself for the prince of Orange and this example was followed by a number of other towns in the relatively inaccessible provinces of Holland and Zeeland. Philip sent Spanish troops in response. They took Naarden and Haarlem and inflicted horrible suffering on the population. Other towns proved far harder to take and this caused Philip to run out of money. In what became known as the Spanish Fury, in November of 1576, Philip's unpaid mercenary armies attacked the city of Antwerp killing 7,000 in 11 days. Antwerp was by far the richest city at the time and the influential merchants got the parliament to convene and raise money to pay off the marauding mercenaries. By doing so the parliament basically took over control from the king in far Madrid and this was the last thing the king wanted. He sent more troops with an ultimatum to the parliament to surrender or else and appointed the Duke of Parma as the new governor of the Netherlands. In 1579, the southern ten provinces of the Netherlands, which were Catholic, signed the Union of Arras, expressing loyalty to Philip. During that same year, William of Orange united seven northern states in the Union of Utrecht, which formed the Dutch Republic that openly opposed Philip and Spain. In 1581, the Spanish army was sent to retake the United Provinces of the Netherlands, or the Dutch Republic, who had just declared their independence.

On July 10, 1584, William of Orange was assassinated, and after his death, the Duke of Parma made progress in his reconquest, capturing significant portions of the Dutch Republic. However, England, under the leadership of

Elizabeth I, assisted the Dutch with troops and horses, and as a result Spain was never able to regain control of the north. Spain finally recognized Dutch independence in 1648.}

There were other wars in which up to 10 million people were killed. Some of these included the Napoleonic War, the Thirty-Year War, the Great Northern War, the Nine-Year War, and the Hundred-Year War.

The mother and father of all wars initiated in Europe were World War 1 and World War 2. Over 100 million people perished in these two wars. These wars were fought in the name of God, with chaplains on the battlefields and battle hymns that the soldiers marched to.

If you think there are any deterrence to modern military leaders invoking the name of God, you may be wrong. On August 6, 1945, the United States dropped the first atomic bomb on Japan. A hundred and fifty thousand Japanese died directly as a result, and tens of thousands died from secondary causes, such as cancer and radiation poisoning. In the aftermath of this carnage, President Truman made a statement; the following is an excerpt of that statement: "We pray that he (God) may guide us to use it (the atomic bomb) in his ways and for his purposes." This statement was a sly way of making the case that the use of the atomic bomb by the USA was sanctioned by God and that future use by the USA will be used for God's purpose. This is another example of religion being used to tranquilize the pain of war and to assuage the guilt of those who have any humanity left in them.

Toward the end of the fifteenth century, Europeans hit the pause button on fighting each other and turned their gaze on plundering and pillaging other continents. This was done in the name of Christianity—to "spread the gospel to every corner of the world." The objective of the Europeans was ostensibly to take Christianity to the rest of the world. This was not the Christianity that Jesus Christ and his disciples taught but the perverted version practiced by the Europeans. The culture of this Christianity was the worst form of barbarism and savagery that the world has ever experienced, particularly in the Americas and Africa.

As Christianity was corrupted in Europe, so was the history that was recorded in the various history books written by the European conquerors. Up until a few decades ago, most people of European heritage believed that native people in Africa and the Americas had to be "civilized" and Christianized for their own good. They believed that gold, diamond, and other precious commodities that the "savages" had should be expropriated because "savages" had no use for them. They indoctrinated themselves and those who they influenced that Africans were savages who were "uncultured" and were an inferior class of human beings. The obvious subterfuge was that Africans had to be Christianized and made to worship the European God; otherwise, they cannot go to heaven to live forever with the Almighty. Conversely, if they were not Christianized, they would go to hell to be forever tormented and burned in a cauldron of eternal fire. These natives were relegated to a class of intellectually, culturally, and aesthetically inferior sub-humans.

This belief may not be as pervasive today as it was up until about four or five decades ago, but a watered-down version still persists in the psyche of most people who are influenced by European culture. In fact, no less a person than a president of the United States recently inquired from his advisors, "Why do we still allow people from these shit-hole countries to come into our country?" He failed to understand that the "shit-hole" status of these countries was mainly caused by European and American colonialism and capitalistic exploitation. The wealth and treasures of these countries were expropriated and shipped to Europe, then the natives were expatriated from their homelands and enslaved in foreign countries to enrich the Europeans and Americans. On the back of this colonial exploitation came European and American capitalistic exploitation that sucked trillions of dollars out of these "shit-hole" countries. If the wealth of these "shit-hole" countries were not savagely expropriated by Europe and America, they would not now be in a position to be named "shit-hole" countries by a president of the United States of America. Conversely, it is the expropriated wealth of these "shit-hole" countries that enriched these "first world" countries.

People influenced by European culture need not feel guilty or responsible for what their great-grandparents did. There is no intention here to berate people of European ancestry because most of them are people of conscience with humanitarian principles. I have lived among and worked with people of European ancestry, and I know that most of these people are not infested with the bigotry and the avaricious cravings of their great grandparents' generation. I do know, however, that an uncomfortable amount of them are. I also know that the history that they, along with the rest of us, learn in their formative years was corrupted to glorify Europeans and vilify others. However, it is necessary for all of us to learn and understand the unvarnished history of the world as it actually happened, instead of that which is massaged and manipulated to maintain the air of intellectual, aesthetic, and cultural superiority of Europeans. Only the truth can make us free intellectually. According to Bob Marley, we must "emancipate ourselves from mental slavery. None but ourselves can free our minds."

Ancient Civilized Cultures

While Europe was still in the Dark Ages, civilizations with rich and vibrant cultures abounded in other parts of the world. The Chinese were living in a civilized and well-advanced culture for more than a thousand years before the Common Era (the birth of Jesus Christ). During the Dark Ages in Europe, the Chinese were trading with other civilizations along the Silk Road. Among the things they exported were silk, tea, salt, sugar, porcelain, and spices. Among the things they imported were cotton, ivory, wool, gold, and silver.

The Chinese civilization has been one of the most enduring the world has ever seen. In fact, it is the only civilization that has been in existence over a thousand years before Christ (BC) to the present era without major identity changes. The Chinese civilization has made significant contributions to the human race in the field of science, technology, and culture. Much of the technology that we use today are based on Chinese inventions.

Compare this with the achievements of the Roman Empire, which started in Rome in 753 BC and lasted about 1,200 years. During that time, Rome grew to rule much of Europe, Western Asia, and Northern Africa. Technological and cultural advancement made by the Romans are not impressive. The Romans are credited with inventing the aqueduct and lead pipe to carry water. Remember, though, that these inventions only diverted natural water flow; it could not move water to a higher elevation. The "invention" of Roman concrete was a remarkable, useful, and enduring contribution to society. There are other things listed as inventions by the Romans that I do not consider inventions. For instance, they are credited with inventing air conditioning. What they did was to circulate warm air from a fire through open spaces in the walls of buildings.

The following excerpts summarize some important stages and inventions that characterize the Chinese civilization. These were gleaned from, but not limited to the *World History Encyclopedia, Wikipedia, and System of Knowledge Wiki* [Category:Ancient China | System of knowledge Wiki | Fandom]

> {*The Zhou dynasty*: "Around the year 1046 BCE (Before the Common Era), King Wu, of the province of Zhou, rebelled against King Zhou of Shang and defeated his forces at the Battle of Muye, establishing the Zhou Dynasty (c. 1046-256 BCE). 1046-771 BCE marks the Western Zhou Period while 771-226 BCE marks the Eastern Zhou Period. The Mandate of Heaven was invoked by the Duke of Zhou, King Wu's younger brother, to legitimize the revolt as he felt the Shang were no longer acting in the interests of the people. The Mandate of Heaven was thus defined as the gods' blessing on a just ruler and rule by divine mandate. When the government no longer served the will of the gods, that government would be overthrown." This was justification for social revolution.

Under the Zhou, culture flourished and civilization spread. Writing was codified and iron metallurgy became increasingly sophisticated. The greatest and best-known Chinese philosophers and poets, Confucius, Mencius, Mo Ti (Mot Zu), Lao-Tzu, Tao Chien, and the military strategist Sun-Tzu (if he existed as depicted), all come from the Zhou period in China and the time of the Hundred Schools of Thought.}

{The Yellow Emperor's Canon of Medicine, China's earliest written record on medicine was codified during the Han Dynasty. Gunpowder, which the Chinese had already invented, became more refined. Paper was invented at this time and writing became more sophisticated. Gaozu embraced Confucianism and made it the exclusive philosophy of the government, setting a pattern which would continue on to the present day.

Trade flourished within the empire and, along the Silk Road, with the West. Rome having now fallen, the Byzantine Empire became a prime buyer of Chinese silk. By the time of the rule of Emperor Xuanzong (r. 712-756 CE) China was the largest, most populous, and most prosperous country in the world. Owing to the large population, armies of many thousands of men could be conscripted into service and military campaigns against Turkish nomads or domestic rebels were swift and successful. Art, technology, and science all flourished under the Tang Dynasty (although the high point in the sciences is considered to be the later Sung Dynasty of 960–1234 CE) and some of the most impressive pieces of Chinese sculpture and silverwork come from this period.}

{The Ancient Chinese were famous for their inventions and technology. Many of their inventions had lasting impact on the entire world. Other inventions led to great feats of engineering like the Grand Canal and the Great Wall of China.

Here are some of the notable inventions and discoveries made by the engineers and scientists of Ancient China:

Silk *was a soft and light material much desired by the wealthy throughout the world. It became such a valuable export that the trade route running from Europe to China became known as the Silk Road. The Chinese learned how to make silk from the cocoons of silkworms. They managed to keep the process for making silk a secret for hundreds of years.*

Paper *was invented by the Chinese as well as many interesting uses for paper like paper money and playing cards. The first paper was invented in the 2nd century BC and the manufacture later perfected around AD 105.*

Printing - *Wood block printing was invented in AD 868 and then moveable type around 200 years later. This was actually hundreds of years before the invention of the printing press by Gutenberg in Europe.*

Compass - *The Chinese invented the magnetic compass to help determine the correct direction. They used this in city planning at first, but it became very important to map makers and for the navigation of ships.*

The Diamond Sutra is the world's oldest printed book from the British Library.

Gunpowder *was invented in the 9th century by chemists trying to find the Elixir of Immortality. Not long after, engineers figured out how to use gunpowder for military uses such as bombs, guns, mines, and even rockets. They also invented fireworks and made great beautiful displays of fireworks for celebrations.*

Boat rudder *was invented as a way to steer large ships. This enabled the Chinese to build huge ships as early as AD 200, well before they were ever built in Europe.*

Other inventions include the umbrella, porcelain, wheelbarrow, iron casting, hot air balloons, seismographs to measure earthquakes, kites, matches, stirrups for riding horses, and acupuncture.

Fun Facts -- Gunpowder, paper, printing, and the compass are sometimes called the Four Great

Inventions of Ancient China. Kites were first used as a way for the army to signal warnings. Umbrellas were invented for protection from the sun as well as the rain. Chinese doctors knew about certain herbs to help sick people. They also knew that eating good foods was important to being healthy. Compasses were often used to make sure that homes were built facing the correct direction so they would be in harmony with nature. The Grand Canal in China is the longest manmade canal or river in the world. It is over 1,100 miles long and stretches from Beijing to Hangzhou. They invented the abacus in the 2nd century BC. This was a calculator that used sliding beads to help compute math problems quickly. A clear coating called lacquer was made to protect and enhance certain works of art and furniture. Paper money was first developed and used in China during the Tang Dynasty (7th century)}

In 132 AD, Zhang Heng (78–139 AD) of the Han Dynasty invented the first seismograph called *Houfeng Didong* to measure the movements of the earth and seasonal winds. The seismograph was an urn-like instrument made of copper with a central pendulum.

Chinese developed drilling technology to extract brine from beneath the earth's surface. As deep drilling borehole technology improved, the ancient Chinese were finally able to extract natural gas from the boreholes. The gas was carried by bamboo pipes to its destination and then used as fuel. By the eleventh century, the Chinese were able to drill boreholes over

3,000 feet deep. The same technology was used to drill the first petroleum well in California in the 1860s.

Even though the Chinese were the ones who invented gunpowder and were the ones to make the first firearms, they primarily used gunpowder to make fireworks. The Europeans, however, were the ones to turn this invention into weapons of mass destruction. According to historian Christopher Clarke of the University of Cambridge in the UK, the Chinese empire had banned its citizens, under penalty of death, from invading or subjugating people of other countries.

Not many European are aware that there were ancient civilizations outside of Europe that made any contribution, technically or culturally, to the world. The fact is that while many other civilizations were advancing, Europe was bogged down in the Dark Ages, fighting each other. This glorified view of European superiority was perpetuated by Europeans after they finally caught up with other civilizations. This catching-up and eventual advance in technology was mainly because of ill-begotten gains from colonialism and slavery.

Until a few decades ago, most people influenced by European culture believed that the continent of Africa was this vast primitive jungle where uncivilized, "uncultured" sub-humans live. The early Europeans had become aware of the vast amount of diamond and gold in Africa, so they simply took it away because they had superior war technologies.

There are numerous instances of institutions of higher learning in Africa and elsewhere in the period when Europe was in the Dark Ages. The following is an excerpt from Wikipedia about the University of al-Qarawiyyin:

*{The University of al-Qarawiyyin is a university
located in Fez, Morocco. It is the oldest existing,
continually operating higher educational
institution in the world according to UNESCO
and Guinness World Records and is occasionally
referred to as the oldest university by scholars. It
was founded by Fatima al-Fihri in 859 (note that
this was a Muslim woman, 1161 years ago) with
an associated madrasa, which subsequently became
one of the leading spiritual and educational centers
of the historic Muslim world. It was incorporated
into Morocco's modern state university system
in 1963. The mosque building itself is also a
significant complex of historical Moroccan and
Islamic architecture encompassing elements from
many different periods of Moroccan history.}*

There were also well-developed cultures in Africa when Europe
was still in the Dark Ages. One of UNESCO World Heritage
Sites is an iron mine in Swaziland on the continent of Africa
that UNESCO has deemed the earliest iron mine in the world.
The following is an excerpt from UNESCO World Heritage
List Nomination:

*{Ngwenya Mine is situated on the north-western
border of Swaziland. Its iron ore deposits constitute
one of the oldest geological formations in the world,
and also have the distinction of being the site of the
world's earliest mining activity.*

*Deposits at Ngwenya were worked at least 42,000
years BP (Before Present, year 1 BP would be
approximately 1950 AD) for the extraction of red*

haematite and specularite (sparkling ores). The peoples concerned belonged to the Middle Stone Age, which flourished in southern Africa for about 100,000 years, until almost 20,000 years ago. The red ochre was also used by later peoples. The ancestors of the present San (Bushman) peoples for their rock paintings, of which there are many in Swaziland. The Swazi names of these pigments "libovu" (red ochre) and "ludumane" (sparkling ochre) indicate that exploitation of these minerals extended into historical times.

By about AD 400, other Bantu-speaking peoples had arrived from north of the Limpopo River. They were agro-pastoralists who also smelted iron ore. They extracted the ore by using extremely heavy iron hammers and traded the iron widely throughout the region.

There is modem open cast mine which was opened in 1964 to mine iron ore. The open cast mine was a catalyst to industrial and economic development for Swaziland. The railway line and the electricity reticulation lines were established because of the open cast mining. The Matsapha Industrial Site area was developed as a direct result of the needs and proceeds of the open cast mining.

On the same site there is a sacred pool that is widely used by the local community. The community believe that the waters form this pool can heal different illness and misfortunes.

Justification of Outstanding Universal Value:

This mine is known to be one of the oldest mine in the world. In 1964 charcoal nodules from the site were sent for radio carbon dating and a date of 43,000 BC was obtained making this one of the oldest known mining operation in the world. However the mine can be older than this date. It is thought this ores were mined until 23,000 BC. Ancient mining tools found in the site were more specialised and foreign to those that were found on Stone Age sites. These were choppers picks and hammers made of dolerite and were identified as mining tools. They produced evidence of early iron ore mining and mining of red ochre that was widely wed in cultural activities and in rock paintings. C14 dates obtained beforehand place the beginning of iron ore mining at about AD 400. This mine constitutes of two mines. The red ochre and haematite mine which date to 43,000 BC and the iron ore mine which date back to AD 400.

This mine is not only important to the Swazi people but it contains history of early industrial development for the Southern African Region. Iron Ore was also mined and supplied to other parts of the region. This iron ore mining eventually led to the gradual change of tools in the region from stone tools to iron tools.

Criteria (iii): The mining technology dating back to 43,000 BC is representative of a period in the development of ancient traditional industries in Southern Africa. This is distinctly demonstrated in these mines as it starts with the mining of cosmetics (red ochre and specularite).

The mines bear a testimony of a cultural tradition of mining that has disappeared. The country therefore celebrates a group of people and technology, although disappeared but was able to influence the whole subregion as it lead to the gradual change from stone tools to iron tools as well as the wide use of these minerals (red ochre) in rock art.}

The following information on the great empire of Mali in West Africa, along with other civilization colonized by Europeans, were gleaned from sources such as, but not limited to, BBC Radio 4, "In Our Time," Wikipedia, *Encyclopedia Britannica*, Face2Face Africa, and BlackPost.org.

The Empire of Mali flourished when Europe was in its Dark and Middle Ages, lasting from 1235 CE to 1670 CE. The Empire of Mali was located in Western Africa. It grew up along the Niger River and eventually spread across 1,200 miles from the city of Gao to the Atlantic Ocean. Its northern border was just south of the Sahara Desert. It covered regions of the modern-day African countries of Mali, Niger, Senegal, Mauritania, Guinea, and The Gambia.

Mali was a rich empire with the richest gold mines in the world. They had a rule of law that was comparable to the Magna Carta in England. The wealth and generosity of its most famous leader, Mansa Musa, was world renowned, and he is said to have been the richest person of all times. On a pilgrimage to Mecca, it is said that he gave away so much gold that it caused a depression in the price of gold for several decades. Of course, Mansa Musa having so much gold meant that the citizens of his empire were being shortchanged, which was not a good thing, but the point demonstrated here is that Africa was awash in gold and diamond before the Europeans started their feeding frenzy in Africa and have subsequently expropriated most of these precious minerals. The capital of Mali was Niani, but the empire included other cities like Timbuktu. One of Mansa Musa's great accomplishments was his commission of some of the greatest buildings of Timbuktu. In 1327, the Great Mosque in Timbuktu was constructed, and Timbuktu would later become a very influential center of learning.

Towards the end of Mansa Musa's reign he built and funded the Sankore Madrasah, which subsequently became one of the greatest centers of learning in the Islamic world and the greatest library in Africa at that time. The Sankore Madrasah is estimated to have housed between 250,000 and 700,000 manuscripts, making it the largest library in Africa since the Great Library of Alexandria.

Timbuktu had been a centuries-old, significant city in West Africa. In the fourteenth century, it became the commercial, religious, and cultural center of West Africa. With its population of traders, merchants, and scholars, Timbuktu was known throughout Western Africa, its fame extended to Europe and Asia. Timbuktu is best known for its famous Djinguereber Mosque and prestigious Sankore University, both of which were established in the early 1300s under the reign of Mali's renowned ruler, Mansa Musa.

After a period of decline of the Mali Empire, in 1894, French colonial forces seized Timbuktu. French control of the city continued until September 20, 1960, when Timbuktu became part of the newly independent Republic of Mali.

Another famous center of learning in ancient Africa was the Great Library of Alexandria, Egypt. It was one of the largest and most significant libraries of the ancient world. The library was part of a larger research institution called the Mouseion (Museum of Alexandria). The library acquired a large amount of papyrus scrolls largely because of the Ptolemaic kings' aggressive and well-funded policies for procuring texts. It is unknown precisely how many such scrolls were housed at any given time, but estimates range from forty thousand to four hundred thousand at its height.

Colonial Atrocities

Colonialism, in the sense of one country invading and controlling another, has been a factor in the human experience from ancient times, but the occurrence of European colonialism appears to be more brutal and inhumane. The era of European colonialism started when Portugal invaded Ceuta, Morocco, in 1415. Possession of Ceuta would indirectly lead to further Portuguese expansion. The main area of Portuguese expansion, at this time, was the coast of Morocco, where there were grain, cattle, sugar, and textiles, as well as fish, hides, wax, honey, and the vast quantity of African gold.

So how did the Europeans come to dominate the rest of the world? They were not any more intelligent than any other group of *Homo sapiens* because historical data show that other cultures at that time were more advanced culturally and intellectually than Europeans, even though most modern Europeans are quite convinced that Europeans were more intelligent than other ethnic groups. They were not even an ethnically homogeneous group of people, so they could not claim any genetic trait of superior intelligence. They fought and conquered one another all the way from the Ural Mountains to the Rock of Gibraltar. I was convincingly told by an Englishman many years ago that he was "pretty sure that God is an Englishman." Those were the days when "the sun never sets on the British Empire," when we, as children, sang our hearts out in school, "Rule Britannia, Britannia rules the waves . . ."

The Europeans were successful colonizers for the following reasons:

1. The constant conflicts among themselves had desensitized their sense of humanity and sharpened their skills in warfare.
2. Their passion for aggression was intense, as we shall see when we look at atrocities committed in places that they colonized.
3. The firearms (guns, artillery, cannons, rifles, and muskets), which were invented in China but never used wantonly as weapons by the Chinese, were turned into efficient weapons of mass destruction by Europeans.
4. The Portuguese and the Spaniards, who initiated colonialism, developed the caravel—the nimble ship that was faster and more maneuverable than most others at that time—gave them great seafaring advantage.

5. Their model of colonialism actually transferred thousands of tons of gold, silver, diamond, and other precious minerals from other continents to Europe. The European "rebirth of learning" or Renaissance was made possible by ill-begotten treasures and profits from Africa and the Americas.

6. Religion was used as an elixir to motivate the warriors and pacify the vanquished. This was clearly evident in South America and most of Africa.

It is a logical estimation that if the value of all the commodities, including gold, diamond, silver, rubber, and agricultural products, that Europeans have expropriated from Africa and the Americas to European countries were to be valued in today's US dollars, and the amount of profit made from that amount accrued to the original amount expropriated, it would add up to several times the total gross domestic product of all the European countries put together. We are talking about tens of trillions of dollars.

If you ever visited London, England, you probably have seen and wondered in disbelief at the unimaginable worth of the crown jewels in the Tower of London. These treasures of gold and diamond were not mined in England or purchased from anywhere else; they were simply expropriated from what England called its colonial territories.

Europeans believed that they were on a mission from God. They believed that God had given them the mandate to Christianize, colonize, kill, and plunder; also, they can keep the spoils of the plunder as the Christians in the Crusades did. Nothing seems to motivate and impassion people than greed driven by religious fervor.

Although the Portuguese and the Spaniards initiated colonialism and the transatlantic slave trade, it was not long before the British, French, Dutch, Belgians, and Germans joined in. Not all European countries participated in colonialism, but you know what people say, "A rising tide floats all boats."

The Christian Church operating from Rome in the fifteenth century was as complicit in the Transatlantic slave trade as were the slave masters and slave traders who wreaked havoc on the vulnerable population of Africa and the Americas. Church leaders argued that slavery served as a natural deterrent and was a Christianizing influence to "barbarous" behavior among pagans. Using this logic, the Pope gave a concession to the Portuguese king, Alfonso V, permitting him to invade, search out, capture, vanquish, and subdue all Saracens and pagans. This is what Pope Nicholas V wrote in his infamous bull (decree) of 1452, which was a reiteration of previous papal decrees,

> *{The Roman pontiff, successor of the key-bearer of the heavenly kingdom and vicar of Jesus Christ, contemplating with a father's mind all the several climes of the world and the characteristics of all the nations dwelling in them and seeking and desiring the salvation of all, wholesomely ordains and disposes upon careful deliberation those things which he sees will be agreeable to the Divine Majesty …}*

Having introduced himself with this air of a divine hypocrite, Pope Nicholas V continued,

> *{… since we had formerly by other letters of ours granted among other things free and ample faculty to the aforesaid King Alfonso – to*

invade, search out, capture, vanquish, and subdue all Saracens and pagans whatsoever, and other enemies of Christ wheresoever placed, and the kingdoms, dukedoms, principalities, dominions, possessions, and all movable and immovable goods whatsoever held and possessed by them and to reduce their persons to perpetual slavery, and to apply and appropriate to himself and his successors the kingdoms, dukedoms, counties, principalities, dominions, possessions, and goods, and to convert them to his and their use and profit ...}

As the 1455 bull indicates, at first the Church officially limited African slave trading to Alfonso of Portugal. Regardless, other European groups soon followed. During the late fifteenth and sixteenth centuries, French and English mariners occasionally attempted to raid or trade with Portuguese settlements and autonomous African communities.

The Encyclopedia Britannica also has an article citing how Pope Nicholas V legitimize the slave trade.

> *{Although he did much to bring about ecclesiastical and political peace, his diplomacy is not without criticism. In 1452 Pope Nicholas V issued a papal bull entitled Dum Diversas, which authorized Afonso V of Portugal to conquer "Saracens (Muslims) and pagans" in a disputed territory in Africa and consign them to "perpetual servitude." It has been argued that this and the subsequent bull (Romanus Pontifex), issued by Nicholas in 1455, gave the Portuguese the rights to acquire slaves along the African coast by force or trade. The edicts are thus seen as having facilitated the Portuguese slave trade from West Africa and as*

*having legitimized the European colonization of
the African continent}*

Here we have pope Nicholas V in a decree given to the
Europeans to expropriate the possessions of all Muslims and
all other "pagans", and to reduce the persons of these "pagans"
to perpetual slavery, while at the same time declaring himself to
be "the key-bearer of the heavenly kingdom and vicar of Jesus
Christ." This was beyond hypocrisy; it was the reflection of an
entire culture that had lost its moral scruples. Instead of being
horrified by this papal bull, the European population readily
embraced the decree of the pope, freeing their conscience to
execute this atrocity. Capturing, enslaving, and dehumanizing
Africans and Native Americans were not considered sinful or
inhumane by Europeans in general; however, it took a decree
from the pope to give the moral and religious legitimacy to these
inhuman acts.

Sir John Hawkins, the revered British sailor, was the first English
slave ship captain to bring African slaves to the Americas. His
ship, ironically called *The Good Ship Jesus*, left the shores of his
native England for Africa in October 1562. He was ostensibly a
religious man who insisted that his crew "serve God daily" and
"love one another." Our colonial heritage in the West Indies
taught us that John Hawkins was one of England's great heroes.
Sir John Hawkins was knighted by the British monarchy. He
was a pioneering English naval commander and administrator.
He was also a privateer and an early promoter of English
involvement in the Atlantic slave trade.

Various passages from the Bible were often used to justify
atrocities of slavery and colonialism.

In August 1492, Christopher Columbus and his crew set sail from Spain, hoping to reach India by sailing west. On October 12, the ships made landfall, not in the East Indies, as Columbus assumed, but on one of the Bahamian islands. After four voyages to the Americas, he died thinking that he had reached some island off the coast of India, so he named this chain of islands West Indies.

The atrocities that Christopher Columbus and the Spanish conquistadors committed in the New World was really mind-boggling. All this was done in the name of Christianity and a mandate from the pope, to colonize and enslave people of other countries and spread the gospel to the "uncivilized." What a travesty!

The two most infamous conquistadors were Hernan Cortes, who "conquered" the Aztec Empire, and Francisco Pizarro, who led the conquest of the Incan Empire. The atrocities these scoundrels and their men committed is best told by Bartolome de Las Casas, who was a sixteenth-century Spanish landowner, friar, priest, and bishop, famed as a historian and social reformer. For his advocacy of the natives, he was called the Apostle of the Indians. He arrived in Hispaniola as a layman then became a Dominican friar and priest. He was a strong advocate for the natives as he witnessed the brutality that they suffered at the hands of the Spaniards.

In his book *Devastation of the Indies*, Bartolome de Las Casas wrote about conquistadors training dogs to attack natives:

> {*The Spaniards train their fierce dogs to attack, kill and tear to pieces the Indians . . . The Spaniards keep alive their dogs' appetite for human beings in*

this way. They have Indians brought to them in chains, then unleash the dogs. The Indians come meekly down the roads and are killed. And the Spaniards have butcher shops where the corpses of Indians are hung up, on display, and someone will come in and say, more or less, "Give me a quarter of that rascal hanging there, to feed my dogs until I can kill another one for them."}

Bartholomew de Las Casas further commented, *"I saw here cruelty on a scale no living being has ever seen or expects to see."* He chronicled many more atrocities committed by the Spaniards. Here is another excerpt from Bartholomew de Las Casas book:

{The Spaniards with their horses, their spears and lances, began to commit murders, and strange cruelties: they entered into towns, burroughs, and villages, sparing neither children nor old men, neither women with child, neither them that lay in, but that they ripped their bellies, and cut them in pieces, as if they had been opening of lambs shut up in their fold. They laid wagers with such as with one thrust of a sword would paunch or bowel a man in the midst, or with one blow of a sword would most readily and most deliverly cut off his head, or that would best pierce his entrails at one stroak. They took the little souls by the heels, ramping them from the mother's dugges, and crushed their heads against the cliffs. Others they cast into the rivers laughing and mocking, and when they tumbled into the water, they said, now shift for yourself such a one's corpse. They put others, together with their mothers, and all that

they met, to the edge of the sword. They made certain Gibbets long and low, in such sort, that the feet of the hanged one, touched in a manner the ground, every one enough for thirteen, in honor and worship of our Savior and his twelve Apostles (as they used to speak) and setting to fire, burned them all quick that were fastened. Unto all others, whom they used to take and reserve alive, cutting off their two hands as near as might be, and so letting them hang, they said; Get you with these letters, to carry tidings to those which are fled by the mountains. They murdered commonly the Lords and Nobility on this fashion: They made certain grates of pearches laid on pitchforks, and made a little fire underneath, to the intent, that by little and little yelling and despairing in these torments, they might give up the Ghost.

One time I saw four or five of the principal lords roasted and broiled upon these gridirons. Also I think that there were two or three of these gridirons, garnished with the like furniture, and for that they cried out pitifully, which thing troubled the Captain that he could not then sleep: he commanded to strangle them. The Sergeant, which was worse than the hangman that burned them (I know his name and friends in Seville would not have them strangled, but himself putting bullets in their mouths, to the end that they should not cry, put to the fire, until they were softly roasted after his desire. I have seen all the aforesaid things and others infinite. And forasmuch as all

*the people which could flee, hid themselves in the
mountains, and mounted on the tops of them,
fled from the men so without all manhood, empty
of all pity, behaving them as savage beasts, the
slaughterers and deadly enemies of mankind: they
taught their Hounds, fierce Dogs, to tear them in
pieces at the first view, and in the space that one
may say a Credo, assailed and devoured an Indian
as if it had been a swine. These dogs wrought
great destructions and slaughters. And forasmuch
as sometimes, although seldom, when the Indians
put to death some Spaniards upon good right and
Law of due justice: they made a Law between
them, that for one Spaniard they had to slay a
hundred Indians.*

*One time the Indians came to meet us, and to
receive us with victuals, and delicate cheer, and
with all entertainment ten leagues off a great city,
and being come at the place, they presented us
with a great quantity of fish, and of bread, and
other meat, together with all that they could doe
for us to the uttermost. See incontinent the Devil,
which put himself into the Spaniards, to put them
all to the edge of the sword in my presence, without
any cause whatsoever, more than three thousand
souls, which were set before us, men, women, and
children. I saw there so great cruelties, that never
any man living either have or shall see the like.*

*Another time, but a few days after the premises, I
sent messengers unto all the lords of the province
of Havana, assuring them, that they should not*

*need to fear (for they had heard of my credit) and
that without withdrawing themselves, they should
come to receive us, and that there should be done
unto them no displeasure: for all the country was
afraid, by reason of the mischiefs and murderings
passed, and this did I by the advice of the Captain
himself. After that we were come into the province,
one and twenty lords and caciques came to receive
us, whom the Captain apprehended incontinently,
breaking the safe conduct which I had made them,
and intending the day next following to burn them
alive, saying that it was expedient so to do, for
that otherwise those lords one day, would do us
a shrewd turn. I found myself in a great deal of
trouble to save them from the fire; howbeit in the
end they escaped.}*

The native population was wiped out by the wanton cruelty of
the Spaniards. The Spaniards gave the natives quotas of gold
that they should bring back to them. If they missed their quota,
they simply cut off their hands. It is often said that the natives'
population died off from European disease for which they had
no immunity, but we do know that because of what is called
herd immunity, an epidemic does not kill more than about
50 percent of a population. Second, why did not the natives'
disease kill off the Europeans? Why did not the natives fight
back? They were probably armed with bows and arrows, while
the Europeans had cannons, muskets, and other firearms. They
may have been terrified and mesmerized by these weapons.
Christopher Columbus wrote in his log that when he landed
in Jamaica, the natives came out with bows and arrows. His
men fired off a few volleys at them (probably killing dozens of

them), and the natives scattered. The next day they came back bearing gifts.

One has to wonder where God was in all this. The Spaniards supposedly came to the Americas to Christianize the natives, but the mission they accomplished was plunder and carnage. They did force their religion down the natives' throats, but what they succeeded mostly in doing was brutalizing then robbing them of their gold and committing genocide on a grand scale of the people they came to Christianize.

Did God approve of what the Spaniards were doing? If not, why didn't he stop it? The popular answer is that God allows humans to have free will. But it was not the free will of the natives to be slaughtered, burned alive, and be torn to pieces by dogs. It is illogical that anyone can believe two things at the same time that are diametrically opposed—that God is omnipotent, loving, and caring and at the same time stood by and allowed the carnage that the Spaniards inflicted on the Native Americans. The denialism that infects our culture has inhibited us from having a logical dialogue with ourselves. As a matter of logic, can both of these things be true? The follow-up question is, could all these attributes of omnipotence, loving, and caring that we ascribe to God be just a figment of our imagination and cannot be demonstrated in any logical way?

Countless other people are killed in regional wars and genocide around the world, in the near genocide of the North American natives, in the slavery and Jim Crow era; yet God allowed it to continue without abatement. There is no evidence that he/she/it/they lifted a finger to stop it. These atrocities went on for generations after generations. Millions of people died at the hands of evildoers.

From all the foregoing unresponsiveness of God to human suffering, it is logical to conclude that the entity we call God just does not sense or respond to the physical or emotional sensibilities of human beings. If he did so in biblical times as it is recorded in the Bible, it certainly does not happen in modern times, according to the records of factual data.

During the few years of the reign of the Third Reich in Germany, 6 million Jews were exterminated from the continent of Europe, mostly in gas chambers to accomplish mass killing. These Jews were not combatants fighting to control territory; they were humble people who were mostly interested in being left alone to take care of their business and practice their religion. Did God defend them in their time of needs as he was purported to have done when Daniel was thrown in the den of hungry lions? How God delivered Daniel has been quoted ad infinitum in prayers and songs before the dawn of the Christian era, yet there has never been any instance of God delivering any group of human beings when they are at the mercy of people who commit unmitigated atrocities.

Adolf Hitler, who orchestrated the Jewish Holocaust, was born to a practicing Catholic mother and was baptized in the Roman Catholic Church; his father was a freethinker and skeptical of the Catholic Church but was, nevertheless, a Christian. In 1904, Hitler was confirmed at the Roman Catholic cathedral in Linz, Austria. He was a Christian by any measure that was used to judge Christianity. In reality, he was a monster who attempted to annihilate several ethnic groups of people and promote his "master race." He initiated World War 2, in which more than 75 million people were killed. Yet so many people believe that our loving God could stop this carnage of monstrous proportions but just stood by and did nothing because he (God) gave humans free will to do whatever they want to do.

Any opposition of German Christians to Adolf Hitler and his Nazi takeover of their country was tentative, even after he eliminated the Seventh-Day Adventists, the Jehovah's Witnesses, the Bahai Faith, the Salvation Army, and was in the process of eradicating Judaism by the genocide of the Jewish people. He banned trade unions, he banned others political parties, opponents were rounded up and jailed, yet the churches, Catholic and Protestant, cozied up to Hitler and his despicable Nazi regime.

In his essay titled "Evangelicals for Adolf: Christians in Hitler's Germany," Ralph Allen Smith wrote in his opening paragraph,

> *{Christian compromise with Nazi Germany's political leadership is well documented in painful detail. There was resistance, but it was the exception rather than the rule. German Christianity was terribly timid. Leadership lacked spiritual strength because of serious Biblical ignorance and unbelief. But it was not just the leaders. Christians in Germany—Protestants even more than Catholics—not only cooperated with the Third Reich, a large percentage even celebrated it.}*

This gives us an insight into the practice of Christianity in general. It is mainly an organization that will sacrifice any core belief in any moral law for short-term material gain. Another example of this travesty of Christian principles was Pope Nicolas

V issuing a series of papal bulls (decrees) that unleashed the Europeans to start the enslavement of Africans.

If we analyze the natural disasters and the atrocities that humans have inflicted on their fellow humans -- the disasters of the bubonic plague (The Black Death), Covid-19, malaria, the sickle cell anemia, and other plagues that have inflicted mankind for thousands of years, how can we still claim that God is protecting us? If God were protecting us, wouldn't we all die naturally and peacefully? Are we not like the youthful ball player to conveniently forget or ignore natural disasters such as the tsunamis in Japan and Indonesia (to name only these two recent ones), that killed hundreds of thousands of people? We also conveniently forget the hundreds of millions of people who died from man-made warfare. Are we not changing the narrative like the childhood baseball player who changed his narrative when it is not politically correct to accept reality?

If we have a logical thought process, how can we believe that God is omnipotent (can make anything and everything happen or prevent it from happening), that he is loving, kind, and is our protector and, at the same time, he can stand by and allow these human and natural disasters to cause all this pain, suffering, and death? Is this not diametrically opposed and diametrically contradicting?

Is it not blatantly illogical to believe at one and the same time the cliche that God gives humans free will to commit whatever atrocity he chooses and that everything that happens is the will of God?

Most of us cannot even entertain the probability that maybe things happen as a consequence of natural physical processes.

In the minds of most of us, God exists as the kind, loving protector, but it is evident from empirical data that he does not determine natural, biological, or physical processes; neither does he determine the actions of humans.

In the Bible, Daniel 3, the story is told of three Hebrew men, Shadrach, Meshach, and Abednego, who were thrown into a fiery furnace by Nebuchadnezzar, king of Babylon, when they refused to bow down to the king's image. The three were prevented from being harmed by the power of God. According to the story, they were seen unperturbed and unharmed in the furnace, joined by another person who appeared to be the Son of God.

Why did God not protect the 6 million Jews from Hitler or the tens of millions of Africans who were enslaved and brutalized by Europeans? For that matter, why has God not stopped all the injustice that is happening all over the world? We know the hollow excuse that God gives human free will, that those who suffer will reap their reward in heaven, or that God will punish evildoers in "his own time." Do not hold your breath, though, outside of current or ancient folklore, there is no material evidence that this is not just another imaginary concept.

In the two world wars, over a hundred million people were killed. God did not stop the carnage. The combatants were comparably armed, so if there is any excuse that could be made why God did not intervene, that could be it; but in the case of the slaughter of the Native Americans, the invaders came from thousands of miles away to massacre them. The natives were armed with mere bows and arrows against the power of the European cannons, muskets, and rifles. Did God not see the injustice, or perhaps God just does not sense or respond to the physical or emotional sensibilities of human beings?

It is not believed to be expedient to question what we perceive as the actions of God, but if we do not, our knowledge will never get better. If humans had abandoned the inquiring spirit of Galileo and continue to believe that Earth is the center of the universe, we would still be living in the Dark Ages.

The Greed for Africa's Treasures

Until a few decades ago, at least half of all the gold ever mined on planet Earth was mined in South Africa.

This is how *Encyclopedia Britannica* introduced its article on the gold bonanza in South Africa:

> {*South Africa experienced a transformation between 1870, when the diamond rush to Kimberley began, and 1902, when the South African War ended. Midway between these dates, in 1886, the world's largest goldfields were discovered on the Witwatersrand.*}

The article continues,

> {*Gold was discovered in the area known as Witwatersrand, triggering what would become the Witwatersrand Gold Rush of 1886. Like the diamond discoveries before, the gold rush caused thousands of foreign expatriates to flock to the region. This heightened political tensions in the*

area ultimately contributing to the Second Boer War in 1899. Ownership of the diamond and gold mines became concentrated in the hands of a few entrepreneurs, largely of European origin, known as the Randlords. South Africa's and the world's biggest diamond miner, De Beers, was funded by baron Nathaniel Mayer Rothschild in 1887, and Cecil Rhodes became the Founding Chairman of the board of directors in 1888. Cecil Rhodes' place was later taken by sir Ernest Oppenheimer, co-founder of the Anglo-American Corporation with J. P. Morgan.}

Except for Russia, Australia, and Canada, almost all of the rest of the world's diamonds were and are still being produced in African countries (Botswana, Angola, Congo, South Africa, Sierra Leone, Lesotho, and Namibia). [Source: geology.com.]

Africa is abundantly rich in gold, diamond, and other precious minerals. Thousands of Europeans have lost their lives fighting one another and fighting the natives in Africa. They were not fighting to admire the lions, tigers, and elephants. They were not fighting to Christianize and civilize the "hapless black natives". They were fighting to expropriate the wealth of Africa and transfer it to Europe.

The Boer-British War was fought between the Dutch settlers (called Boers or Afrikaans) and the British for possession of gold and diamond producing territories in Southern Africa. The irony here is that two European countries were fighting and killing each other thousands of miles from their own shores for territories and commodities that did not belong to them.

In January 1879, British troops invaded the Zulu Kingdom in Southern Africa. The pattern here is that the Europeans would stop at nothing to gain possession of the vast gold and diamond deposits in Africa. The Zulus fought valiantly, even though their weapons were a limited amount of old secondhand firearms and spares. The British were equipped with all the modern weapons of warfare. The Zulus managed to defeat the British decisively in the first battle but were defeated in the end. As a young man, I remember watching the horribly despicable movie called *Shaka Zulu*. It was a degrading portrayal of the Zulu people and their king that was produced by the media for mass brainwashing, otherwise known as the moving-picture industry, otherwise known as Hollywood. This portrayal was taking place while gold and diamond were being hauled from Africa by the shiploads.

The following are excerpts from the *Encyclopedia Britannica*:

> *{The 1867 discovery of diamonds in the Cape Colony, South Africa, radically modified not only the world's supply of diamonds but also the conception of them. As annual world diamond production increased more than tenfold in the following 10 years, a once extremely rare material became accessible to Western society with its growing wealth. Today South Africa maintains its position as a major diamond producer.*

> *As the predominantly agrarian societies of European South Africa began to urbanize and industrialize, the region evolved into a major supplier of precious minerals to the world economy; gold especially was urgently needed to*

back national currencies and ensure the continued
flow of expanding international trade. British
colonies, Boer republics, and African kingdoms
all came under British control. These dramatic
changes were propelled by two linked forces: the
development of a capitalist mining industry and a
sequence of imperialist interventions by Britain . . .

A chance find in 1867 had drawn several thousand
fortune seekers to alluvial diamond diggings along
the Orange, Vaal, and Harts rivers. Richer finds
in "dry diggings" in 1870 led to a large-scale rush.
By the end of 1871 nearly 50,000 people lived in
a sprawling polyglot mining camp that was later
named Kimberley.

Initially, individual diggers, black and white,
worked small claims by hand. As production
rapidly centralized and mechanized, however,
ownership and labour patterns were divided
more starkly along racial lines. A new class of
mining capitalists oversaw the transition from
diamond digging to mining industry as joint-stock
companies bought out diggers. The industry became
a monopoly by 1889 when De Beers Consolidated
Mines (controlled by Cecil Rhodes) became the sole
producer. Although some white diggers continued
to work as overseers or skilled labourers, from the
mid-1880s the workforce consisted mainly of black
migrant workers housed in closed compounds by
the companies (a method that had previously been
used in Brazil).}

In gold and diamond mines in South Africa and other African countries controlled by Europeans, miners were x-rayed to reveal any jewels they may try to hide in any part of their bodies. Imagine the cancer rate that this practice caused.

The story of African diamonds has been a source of intrigue ever since the first nugget was discovered by Europeans. The movie *Blood Diamond* did a good job of capturing the greed for African diamonds.

"The town of Kolmanskop in Namibia was once one of the wealthiest in the world—its hospital had the first Xray unit in the southern hemisphere. Now it is buried in the desert," so stated an article by the BBC (*British Broadcasting Corporation*) in January 2017 captioned *"The ghost town that was abandoned when the diamonds ran out."*

Kolmanskop was a town in the Namib Desert that became important when it was discovered that diamonds abounded in the sand, and you could literally pick up many nuggets that your feet may have dislodged while walking in the sand. Overnight, Kolmanskop became one of the richest towns in the world. Unfortunately, though, these riches did not accrue to the people of Kolmanskop. In September 1908, the German colonial government proclaimed a large expanse of this territory that contained the diamond-bearing sand "forbidden land," forbidden to everyone but the German authority or anyone authorized by that authority. It is like they created the land, the desert, the sand, and the diamond, and the Native Africans were the trespassers.

The German colonial authority awarded sole mining rights to a German diamond company. By 1912, a town had sprung up, producing a million carats of diamond each year.

By the onset of World War 1, more than 5 million carats of diamonds had been processed in the region. The desert floor was systematically scraped clean when new machinery was introduced to recover the precious stones. Giant electric shovels allowed the sand to be shifted a truckload at a time.

Lifestyle was lavish and life was good for the Europeans. Although the population of the town at its prime, which excluded the Native Africans, was just a couple hundred diamond searchers and their families, the town had amenities such as an ice factory, electricity in most of the houses, a modern hospital, swimming pools, a private school, a ballroom, a casino, a theatre, a sports hall, and even a tram line. Only the Europeans enjoyed these facilities; the Native Africans had to settle for apartheid-style working condition outside the city limit. In addition to the subhuman working and living conditions, they were x-rayed each time they were leaving the diamond-processing facilities for diamonds they may be hiding in their body cavities. Imagine how many deaths and suffering from cancer these daily x-rays caused.

By the 1930s, the town's riches were largely depleted and diamond deposits were found 168 miles to the south, close to Namibia's border with South Africa, where many of Kolmanskop's miners moved on to. The town and its luxuries were abandoned for more lucrative diamond-mining territories, and the desert once again claimed Kolmanskop. Millions of carats of diamond were expropriated by the Germans; nothing accrued to the Native Africans.

The Feeding Frenzy for Africa

The information for the colonial feeding frenzy for Africa was gleaned from, but not limited to sources such as Encyclopedia Britannica, Wikipedia, the PBS series: Africa's Great Civilization, and South African History Online.

In order to bring some form of civility to the feeding frenzy that the colonial powers were engaged in to colonize and pillage the continent of Africa, fourteen European countries and the United States convened a conference in Berlin, Germany, in November,1884. The objective of the conference was to discuss how to amicably divide the resources of Africa, and supposedly, to bring civilization to Africa in the form of Christianity and trade. Of these fourteen nations at the Berlin Conference, France, Germany, Great Britain, and Portugal were the major players. Notably missing were any representatives from Africa.

There was already a lot of conflict between the powers of Europe about how to share the spoils of Africa. Britain and the Dutch had already fought multiple wars over the gold and diamond in Southern Africa and were still spoiling for more conflict. The audacity of these leaders was their premise that they were meeting to bring civilization and Christianity to those people who the Europeans considered the uncivilized natives of Africa. They looked straight past the carnage and suffering they were inflicting on the land and people of Africa and hypocritically talked about Christianity and civilization. Of course, they were convinced that God was on their side and that God had sanctioned their actions because they were taking the doctrine of the Christian faith to "the savages"; besides, "those savages" had no use for the gold, diamond, ivory, and other valuable commodities. Indeed, the pope, who represented God on this planet, had already sanctioned and sanctified these colonialist and capitalistic atrocities.

The Berlin Conference would last 104 days, ending on February 26, 1885. The conference has come to represent the European pillaging and partitioning of the continent. The Berlin Conference did not begin the scramble, that was well under way; it only allowed the rapacious occupiers to devise a common strategy to expropriate the vast riches of Africa without fighting each other. At the time of the conference, 80 percent of Africa remained under traditional and local control. The Europeans only had influence on the coast. Following it, they started grabbing chunks of land inland, ultimately creating a hodgepodge of arbitrary boundaries that was superimposed over indigenous cultures and regions of Africa.

King Leopold II of Belgium was able to get the group of pillagers to concede the entire area which had come to be known as the Belgian Congo to him as his personal property (not a colony of Belgium). This is over a million square miles of African territory in the Congo River basin in Central Africa, vastly rich in natural resources, more than 84 times the size of Belgium, the country of which he was king.

While the mindless plundering of land for natural resources caused vast environmental degradation to the continent of Africa, there is a larger story of corruption and inhumanity. The argument Leopold used to convince his colleagues to concede over a million square miles of African lands to him was a commitment that he would bring Christianity and civilization to the Africans. What he diligently worked to achieve was personal gain at the expense of the Congolese people, using them as slave labor to extract natural resources. If production waned or targets were not met, they risked severe punishments ranging from the severing of a hand to death.

The truth about these atrocities was finally revealed. Photographic evidence gathered by English Missionary Alice Seeley Harris was taken and widely distributed through anti-slavery publications, eventually shaming the Belgian Government, and forcing Leopold to relinquish personal control of the colony. But by the time this happened in 1908, it was estimated that 10 million people—half of Congo's population—perished during Leopold's inhumane rule.

Atrocities committed by King Leopold II of Belgium in the Congo were on par with that committed by the Spaniards in the Americas. Yet these Europeans were proud Christians, doing God's work.

The role of the Christians was to convince the natives they colonized that if they accepted their inhumane treatment with humility, when they die, they would go to heaven but those who disobeyed would go to hell, unless they repented. The colonizers usually lived in their ill-begotten opulence for the rest of their lives. Occasionally, for a little added insurance, just in case that there was a judgment to face after their death, they would sometimes "repent" on their deathbed. Religion played a big part in pacifying people to accept slavery and brutality. The colonizers also cultivated an air of superiority among themselves and a sense of inferiority toward the people they colonized, all this to justify their inhumane treatment toward the people they controlled.

It is doubtful if the atrocities committed by these oppressive regimes could have succeeded without religion. If enemies invade your homeland, you can fight them until you physically lose the battle. If that enemy has superior weaponry and is killing your people, and at the same time telling you that they also have a superior God who is aiding them, it will not take much more than that to completely demoralize and mesmerize you into submission.

There is a photograph circulating on the Internet, captioned, "Is this a photograph of a 'Human Zoo' at the 1958 World's Fair?" which features a little African girl about three or four years old in a stockade being viewed by a crowd obviously in wonderment of what they convinced themselves was an inferior subspecies of the human race. The story continues, "Expo '58 in Brussels featured a reconstructed African village populated by real people shipped over from the Belgian Congo." This photograph has been circulating now for several years; chances are that you will be able to view it on the Internet.

The atrocities that King Leopold committed in the Congo was not an anomaly; this was the typical treatment by Europeans of the people that were subjugated by them, whether by enslavement or subhuman labor practices.

Why did God allow King Leopold II to brutally massacre 10 million Congolese? Why is God so impotent when all these atrocities are committed so frequently across the globe? Why is God so impotent when millions of people were, and are still suffering and dying at the hands of greedy and unethical people who wield power? Other than unsubstantiated assertions, where is the real proof of the omnipotent and endearing goodness of God? Is it all in our unquestioning belief and unquestioning imagination?

When Mother Theresa gave all she had in terms of service in the harsh streets of Calcutta, India, and still saw no abatement in the suffering of the people, she confessed that she had lost faith in God. This was reported by several news agencies in August of 2007. The following is how Reuters news agency reported the news at that time:

> {*A book of letters written by Mother Teresa of Calcutta reveals for the first time that she was deeply tormented about her faith and suffered periods of doubt about God.*
>
> *"Jesus has a very special love for you. As for me, the silence and the emptiness is so great that I look and do not see, listen and do not hear," she wrote the Rev. Michael van der Peet in September 1979.}*

It has to be recognized that there were enlightened people in Europe and the United States who were opposed to the practice of slavery and rapacious colonialism, even among the ruling class; William Wilberforce of England and Bartholomew de Las Casas of Spain come to mind.

The Transatlantic Slave Trade

The Portuguese, in the sixteenth century, were the first to engage in the Atlantic slave trade. In 1526, they completed the first transatlantic slave voyage to Brazil. Then the British, the Spanish, the French, the Dutch, and the Danes followed. Initially, slaves were captured by the Europeans raiding villages. This method was mainly practiced by the Portuguese. Later the Europeans were able to exchange slaves with African village leaders for goods that the Africans needed from Europe, such as guns, gunpowder (it is unlikely that the guns they bartered were working properly), mirrors, knives, cloth, and beads brought by boat from Europe. The African chiefs who swapped slaves for European goods were as complicit in the slave trade as the Europeans; however, they could not have known the brutality that the slaves were subjected to, from the time they were placed on the slave ships to the rest of their lives in servitude.

The instance of the transatlantic slave trade was not the first or only practice of slavery. Other kingdoms and principalities had practiced slavery since the time of prerecorded history. The difference, though, is that slavery practiced by non-Europeans were generally not dehumanizing and brutalizing, nor was race or color a factor. This cannot be said about the European transatlantic slavery.

In the Bible, Joseph, who was a Hebrew man, was sold into slavery by his brothers to the Egyptians. He rose in status to become a governor in Egypt. This could never have happened in the context of Europeans enslaving Africans or people from the Americas.

The Muslims who predated the Europeans in enslaving Africans seemed not to be as brutal and dehumanizing as the Europeans. Besides, there was no one to come back from the Americas and the Caribbean to tell their kinsmen the story of the brutality.

The following is an excerpt from the Wikipedia article "History of Slavery in the Muslim world," describing the tasks of slaves captured in Africa:

{Slaves were widely employed in irrigation, mining, and animal husbandry, but the most common uses were as soldiers, guards, domestic workers, and concubines. Many rulers relied on military slaves, often in huge standing armies, and slaves in administration to such a degree that the slaves were sometimes in a position to seize power. Among black slaves, there were roughly two females to every one male.}

The following is also an excerpt from a Wikipedia article titled "Slavery in Antiquity.":

{In Ancient Egypt, slaves were mainly obtained through prisoners of war. Other ways people could become slaves was by inheriting the status from their parents. One could also become a slave on account of his inability to pay his debts. Slavery was the direct result of poverty. People also sold themselves into slavery because they were poor peasants and needed food and shelter. The lives of slaves were normally better than that of peasants. Slaves only attempted escape when their treatment was unusually harsh. For many, being a slave in Egypt made them better off than a freeman elsewhere. Young slaves could not be put to hard work, and had to be brought up by the mistress of the household. Not all slaves went to houses. Some also sold themselves to temples, or were assigned to temples by the king. Slave trading was not very popular until later in Ancient Egypt. Afterwards, slave trades sprang up all over Egypt.}

Many of us will remember the book *Roots* by Alex Haley and the TV mini-series that was made from this book. Haley traced his ancestral roots from a slave whose real African name was Kunta Kinte, back to a village in Gambia where young Kunta was captured and taken to America as a slave. Haley traveled to the village in Gambia to familiarize himself with the culture where his ancestor came from. Even though the movie was a sanitized version of slavery in America, it was heart-wrenching enough to cause widespread distress to those who watched it. As widely watched as this movie was, I do not recall it being shown again on television.

The book dramatized conversations that Kunta would have had with his father. They were reenactment of what Haley learned about the life and culture in Gambia when Kunta Kinte was kidnapped. One of these conversations was about slaves. His father told Kunta that slavery was practiced, and slaves were well respected in his culture. The rights of slaves were guaranteed by the laws of their forefathers. People became slaves in their culture in different ways: people who were captured in wars, people who had committed crimes and slavery was their sentence, and people who were destitute because of events like famine and had voluntarily asked to be put in slavery. All masters had to provide slaves with basic amenities, such as food, clothing, shelter, and a plot of land to farm on. Half of what was produced was shared with their masters. Masters could not beat their slaves, except those who became slaves because of crimes they had committed. Slaves could buy their freedom or gain freedom by marrying into his master's family.

There are at least two lessons to be learned from Kunta Kinte's culture: First, their treatment of slaves was humane, whereas the European treatment of slaves was brutal; not bad for people

Europeans called uncultured savages. Second, Africans who captured and sold villagers to Europeans had no clue how uncivilized these Europeans were in the treatment of their slaves.

In the first segment of the transatlantic triangular slave trade, goods such as firearms, textiles, and wine were shipped from Europe to Africa; these goods were bartered for slaves captured and warehoused by African chiefs and European slave traders. In some cases, the Europeans ventured onto the interior and captured natives themselves. In the second part of the triangular trade called the middle passage, the human cargo of slaves was crammed into slave ships in very inhumane conditions. Slaves were laid out in rows in the holds of ships where they were not enough head room even to sit up properly. They were chained in position in the dark belly of the ship, in their own vomit, excrement, blood, and unimaginable stench. They were beaten mercilessly into submission. A large percentage of these hapless souls died from the conditions on the ship before they reached their destination in the "New World."

When the slave traders completed this middle passage and arrived in the Americas and the Caribbean, they sold their slaves, mostly by auction to the highest bidder. They then bought goods, such as sugar and coffee, which were produced by enforced slave labor. They then sailed back to Europe on the third leg of their slave triangle, where they sold the goods that they picked up in the Americas and the Caribbean.

The middle passage of the slave trade triangle transported over 12 million Africans across the Atlantic Ocean to the Americas and Caribbean into a life of enslavement, from the sixteenth to the nineteenth century.

The ethics of the European culture leading up to the end of the twentieth century was that black people were a subspecies somewhere between apes and humans (humans meaning Europeans). In fact, they generally believed that all other ethnic groups that did not look like them were intellectually and aesthetically inferior to Europeans. The Belgians could not have believed that the Congolese were humans when they mutilated and slaughtered them to provide more gold and rubber. The Portuguese and Spaniards could not have believed that the native people of the Americas were humans when they were slaughtering the natives to feed their dogs. The Englishmen who committed heinous atrocities in Africa and almost committed genocide to expropriate land from the Native Americans could not have believed that these natives were humans.

Prior to the end of the twentieth century, Europeans had concocted the fallacy that black people were the result of a curse that Noah had placed on the descendants of his son Ham *[Bible: Genesis 9]*. According to the Bible, Noah was drunk and naked in his house because he had too much wine to drink. His son Ham went into the house, saw his father's "nakedness," went and told his brothers. Noah was so upset with Ham that he put a curse on the descendants of Ham that they should forever be slaves to their brothers' descendants. Some theologians and their followers over the years have interpreted this Bible passage to mean that black people are the descendants of Ham (Hamites), and their enslavement is the curse of Noah; therefore, it was sanctioned by God. A contrived narrative was finally found in the Bible to legitimize slavery and racism.

Science has shown that the dark color of a person's skin has more to do with a pigment in the skin called melanin that prevents skin cancer when our skin is exposed to ultraviolet rays from the sun, rather than the adaptation of a story in the Bible that people with black skin are the recipient of a curse from Noah on the descendants of his son Ham. This story was actually preached from church pulpits in the USA. This pigmentation is in the skin of black and white people, only less abundant in white people.

In more recent decades, the perception of superiority by people influenced by European culture appears to be softening into a more benign perspective. This may be the result of more exposure to scientific knowledge. There is a slow and reluctant acceptance of the reality that the color of a person's skin does not make them superior or inferior in any objective sense of the word, even though superiority in wealth and the derivatives of wealth may have caused one race of people with a particular skin color to become superior in some materialistic ways. This holier-than-thou attitude can be compared to what used to be said of the British Commonwealth: "All countries of the British Commonwealth are equal, but Britain is more equal than the others."

Present-day Europeans and people of European descent need not feel guilty for the atrocities that their great-grandparents committed, but they should at least be aware of these atrocities in a factually accurate way, without the misinformation and bias in favor of a European narrative. One has the right to be as biased and prejudiced in one's own opinion as one wants to be, but one does not have the right to deny other people the basic human rights that should be equally available to everyone in the society. These rights include, without prejudice, equal access and facilities for education from kindergarten to college, equal opportunity for employment, equal opportunity to live where he or she chooses, and equal protection and enforcement of the laws of the land.

Slavery in America

The following information about slavery and Jim Crow in America was gleaned from, but not limited to, the following sources: *Roots* by Alex Haley, *Peculiar Institution: Slavery in the Ante-Bellum South* by Kenneth M. Stampp, Wikipedia, *History.com, HistoryNet.com, Encyclopedia Britannica, PBS, and WesternCivilization.com.*

Slavery in the United States is generally accepted to have started in 1619, when an English privateer ship sailed into Point Comfort in Virginia and offered "20 and odd Negroes" for sale. These Negroes were bought by the governor of Virginia. Other historians, however, saw this event only as an inflection point where slavery started to become the driving force in the commercial life of America's antebellum South.

Slavery was not confined to the United States; it was also rampant and brutal in the Caribbean and South America. The rapid expansion of the cotton industry in the Deep South after the invention of the cotton gin greatly increased demand for slave labor. The United States became polarized over the issue of slavery and other autonomy in governance that the Southern states were demanding, causing a split into slave states and free states. The Southern states, which would later become the Confederate States, became quite wealthy from agricultural products, such as cotton, tobacco, sugarcane, corn, and wheat, produced by slave labor. For these crops, they needed a vast number of slaves. They also resented paying taxes to the federal government. All these tensions were partly responsible for the civil war of 1861.

Africans were easier for the Europeans to enslave mainly because of two reasons: First, the color of their skin made it impossible to blend into any other ethnic group without easy detection. Second, they were thousands of miles and the Atlantic Ocean away from their homeland, they could not escape back to their homeland and their native culture. Attempts were made to enslave the Native American and Caribbean people, but these attempts were generally not as successful as enslaving Africans because these natives were in familiar territory and escaping was much easier.

In 1993, historian Clarence J. Munford estimated the value of the labor performed by black slaves in the United States between 1619 and 1865, compounded with 6 percent interest, to be US$97.1 trillion. In today's dollars, without further compound interest added, that would be US$172 trillion.

A slave had no rights as a human being in the Southern United States during what is known as the antebellum (prewar) period; a slave was the property of "the master," and the authority of the master was almost absolute. Short of wantonly killing a slave, the state did not interfere with what the master wanted to do with his property, the slave. Even after wanton killings, it would be very unlikely that there would be any justice for the slave. A slave could not testify in court against a white person; therefore, if a white person killed a slave for the fun of it, unless another white person was willing to attest to the crime, nothing would come of it. Even if a white person testified to such crime, it was rare that there would be any justice in favor of the slave, or any black person for that matter. If a slave owner (the master) wanted to have sexual intercourse with a slave, the slave had no right to object. What right should the property of the master have to object to the will of the master?

Slaves typically worked sixteen hours per day and six days per week for their master. On large plantations, they were generally managed by an overseer. Punishment was swift and brutal for misbehavior or failure to meet the production quota. Whipping was the more frequent form of punishment, but castration and other forms of mutilation were also used. Some masters paid the public jail to incarcerate and punish their slaves for violation of the master's rules, but punishment by overseers and other people authorized by the master was more common. Punishment was sometimes administered by the master himself. Slaves were also punished by placing them on torture devices, such as stocks and pillories. Ball and chain were also used to restrain the slaves, and branding them with hot iron as a means of identification was also a common practice. Trying to escape usually attracted the worst punishment. If a slave was not docile enough, the master usually increased the level of punishment to "break in" the slave and make him or her more submissive, or the master may send the slave to a professional "slave breaker" to do the job.

There are situations where the state overrode the authority of the slave owners if the state considered such actions expedient. For instance, slaves were not permitted by state law to be off their owner premises without a written pass from the master. This privilege was only given to docile slaves who could be trusted not to attempt to escape. Needless to say, if a black person were seen off a plantation, he would be immediately challenged by any white person because rewards were offered for bringing in escaped slaves. It was a state crime for anyone to teach a slave to read or to write. It was a crime for a slave to attempt to learn to read or write.

Marriages between enslaved men and women had no legal status, but many did marry and raise large families; most slave owners encouraged this practice. The children of slaves automatically became the property of the owner of the child's mother. The father had no role, except to sire the child. Breeding of the female slave was encouraged since this could be very profitable to the owner, especially after the ban on the transatlantic slave trade, when slaves became more expensive. Family units did exist on slavery plantations, even though most of the slave owners had no qualms in breaking up the family to sell one or more family member. As the property of the slave masters, slaves were often used as collateral for loans. Slaves were often willed from master to his children as one would do household properties. Slaves were leased out to farmers as a company would lease out a tractor. The interesting thing is that if the lessee caused any damage to a slave, the owner of the slave had the right to, and usually did, take the lessee to court to recover damages. The slave owner could do almost any damage to the slave if he so chose, and he could sue for damages done by others; but the slave had no say in what damages were done to him or her by the master. Many masters took sexual liberties with enslaved women and rewarded obedient behavior with favors, while rebellious enslaved people were brutally punished. A strict hierarchy among the enslaved (from privileged house workers and skilled artisans down to lowly field hands) helped keep them divided and less likely to organize against their masters.

The transatlantic slave trade was technically abolished in the USA in 1808. This, however, did not stop slave importation since the federal government did not have the resources, or in some cases the desire, to patrol the coastal waters, and the Southern states did not have the conscience to comply. What this ban did was to drive up the price of slaves. Driven by labor demands from new cotton plantations in the Deep South, the Upper South sold over a million slaves to the Deep South after 1808. The total slave population in the South eventually reached 4 million.

Not all slave owners were cruel and inhumane. Some of them, especially those with smaller number of slaves, treated their slaves as other human beings. The humane ones tried to keep families together. They did not brutalize and torture their slaves to wring the last ounce of labor out of them. They would also give the slave family a small plot of land they could farm in their spare time, the product of which they shared with the master (sharecropping). This made a lot of sense; it gave the slave some degree of self-worth, whereby he or she had the perception of feeding his or her family, rather than depending on the meager daily ration of slave food. It also gave them a small degree of autonomy to decide for themselves what they ate. They also usually had enough food left over to sell to the master. The master also benefited from this arrangement since it meant less slave food that he had to provide. These benevolent slave owners occasionally allowed some slaves to buy their freedom with money they saved from their sharecrop enterprise. This practice was generally discouraged by the state. Slave owners sometimes bequeathed freedom in their will for slaves so that when the master died, the slave became free.

Religion played a pivotal role in the lives of the slaves. Initially, some slave owners were wary of allowing the slaves to be exposed to Christianity. They argued that slaves may start to question their status as slaves and start to aspire to freedom.

The slave owners were pleasantly surprised, however, that the message of the mainstream preachers facilitated their cause. The mainstream Christian churches made sure that the slaves only heard a concocted version of the Bible and of the Christian gospel.

An excerpt from the book *The Peculiar Institution - Slavery in the Anti-Bellum South* reads as follows:

> *{Church leaders addressed themselves to this problem and prepared special catechisms and sermons for bondsmen and special instructions for those concerned with their religious indoctrination.}*

There was a well-established protocol among Southern clergymen to preach to slaves that their role as slaves was sanctioned by the Bible. The Bible passage "And that servant who knew his master's will and did not prepare himself or do according to his will, shall be beaten with many stripes" [Luke 12:47] was a mantra that Southern clergies never failed to instill in the slaves. To buttress this mantra, the slaves were assured that if they accepted their situation with humility, they would go to heaven when they die and enjoy all the amenities that the Heavenly Father has at his disposal. (Sounds much like the exhortation that was given to the marauding Christian Crusaders that plundered Jerusalem and massacred its residents.) When those poor slaves were burdened down with their problems, it is not hard to understand why they were singing, "Swing low, sweet chariot, coming for to carry me home."

Another justification that the slave owners and their Christian enablers used was that they were actually doing the Africans a favor by enslaving them.

This is how HistoryNet.com describes the audacity:

> *{By the 1830s, many Southerners had shifted from, "Slavery is a necessary evil," to "Slavery is a positive good." The institution existed because it was "God's will," a Christian duty to lift the African out of barbarism while still exerting control over his "animal passions."}*

That was the extent of the moral depravity that the Christians and the capitalists had. That was the extent to which they used Christianity and capitalism as tools to control the destiny of others.

Another edict practiced by the mainstream Southern clergy was never to entertain any complaint by slaves about ill-treatment by the master or overseers. The slaves' mission was to obey their master so that when they died, they would go to heaven. Seeing that the church could use religion to pacify the slaves, the slave masters changed from their skepticism to become totally tolerant to the teaching of religion to their slaves. They now embraced and encouraged the teaching of this bastardized Christianity. As long as there was a white minister in the church, slaves could go to church on their one day off on Sundays. Some of the larger plantations even constructed churches on their properties to facilitate the indoctrination. The slave so much needed spiritual upliftment in their troubled lives that they gladly accepted this situation.

The Thirteenth Amendment to the Constitution of the United States declared on December 18, 1865, abolished slavery in the United States, at least in name only. During the Reconstruction Era, farmers in Southern states found ways to "hire" black workers under terms that were slavery in all but name, even pursuing anyone who tried to escape, just as they had in the days of the Underground Railroad.

During the civil war, the slaves were promised forty acres of land and a mule for each family, but President Andrew Jackson annulled the proclamation, and the ex-slaves got nothing. They had to go back to work for their ex-masters or starve to death. This new paradigm was hardly any better than slavery since the ex-slave owners only paid enough to keep the ex-slaves indebted to them under the same slavery conditions.

It is evident that in the case of the slavery experience in the Americas and the Caribbean, mainstream Christianity was subservient to the cause of rapacious capitalism rather than the cause that the founders of Christianity, Jesus Christ, and his apostles, had intended.

Whereas the bastardized teaching of the holy scripture was the norm in the Southern states, emerging was a new movement, the abolitionist movement, that embodied what the teaching of Christianity ought to be. The abolitionists were an international group of people of conscience who believed that the brutal and inhumane slavery practiced by Europeans and Americans was unconscionable and ungodly. They did not just have that belief; they did whatever they could to fight that injustice.

Abolitionists in England were fighting mainly for the abolition of slavery in the British colonies. William Wilberforce, who was a Member of Parliament in England, was the driving force behind this movement. After the formation of the Committee for the Abolition of the Slave Trade in 1787, William Wilberforce led the cause of abolition through parliamentary campaigns. The

British Parliament finally abolished the slave trade in the British Empire with the Slave Trade Act 1807. Wilberforce continued to campaign for the abolition of slavery in the British Empire, which he lived to see in the Slavery Abolition Act 1833.

Europeans and Africans worked for the abolition of the slave trade and slavery. Well-known abolitionists in Britain included James Ramsay, William Roscoe, Granville Sharp, Thomas Clarkson, and Josiah Wedgwood.

Efforts to end slavery in the American colonies had been present since the colonial era, when Quakers were the primary torchbearers of the movement. They were successful in outlawing the practice above the Mason-Dixon line by the first decade of the nineteenth century. The abolitionists movement had never achieved anything greater than a minority status, probably no greater than a nuisance status in terms of popularity, but its members were tenacious and proactive.

The abolitionist movement, in its early years, was directed at people in the Northern states, convincing them, by providing speakers and documentation, that slaves, frequently if not always, were horribly mistreated in the South. People from the Northern states got to see firsthand that blacks, some of whom were eloquent, well educated, and good Christians, were not inferior human beings. The abolitionists succeeded in greatly raising Northern support for the abolition of slavery. Only then was there political support for ending slavery nationwide.

Abolitionists initially began by advocating a gradual form of emancipation in the 1820s, whereby slaves would be purchased from their owners and sent back, or recolonized, to their African "homeland." The concept, pushed by the American

Colonization Society, was always hampered by the lack of funds and the opposition of many blacks, who rightly viewed America, not Africa, as their native country.

A prominent member of the antislavery movement was William Lloyd Garrison who was a journalist and publisher from Massachusetts. He was best known for his widely-read antislavery newspaper, *Liberator*, which he founded in 1831 and published in Boston. Because of frustration in the progress of reforms regarding slavery, he founded the American Anti-Slavery Society in 1830, which called for immediate and universal emancipation of slavery, using the *Liberator* as his medium of advocacy.

Roman Catholic statements against slavery also grew increasingly vocal during this era. In 1815, Pope Pius VII demanded the Congress of Vienna to suppress the slave trade. In the Bull of Canonization of Peter Claver, Pope Pius IX branded the "supreme villainy" of the slave traders. Pope Gregory XVI and Pope Leo XIII also condemned slavery in their official manifestos. However, what is written in a papal manifesto does not necessarily translate to what was happening on the plantations of the Southern American states, or the sermons delivered on Sundays in the local churches, or what the clergies were preaching to the slaves.

The main weapons of the abolitionists were pamphlets and other publications decrying the evils of slavery. These publications argued that slavery was a social and moral evil and often used examples of African American writings and other achievements to demonstrate that Africans and their descendants were as capable of learning as well as Europeans and their descendants in America, given the freedom to do so. To prove their case that one person owning another was morally wrong, they first had to convince many, in all sections of the country, that Africans were human, with the same mental attributes as Europeans. Yet even many people among the abolitionists did not believe the two races were equal.

It took the Thirteenth Amendment of the United States Constitution in 1865 to finally end involuntary servitude. Again, the end of the institution of slavery in the United States did not constitute a purge in the evil intents of the majority of its people. The Jim Crow era that followed was as evil and ungodly as the era that preceded it.

Other well-known Americans who fought for the abolition of slavery are

> **Frederick Douglass**, who was born a slave but lived to become an American social reformer, abolitionist, orator, writer, and statesman. While being a slave, the wife of his master taught him to read and write, although this was forbidden by law. After escaping from slavery, he further educated himself and became a national leader of the abolitionist movement working from Massachusetts and New York. He became famous for his oratory and incisive antislavery writings. Accordingly, he was described by abolitionists in his time as a living counterexample to slaveholders' arguments that slaves lacked the intellectual capacity to function as independent American citizens. Northerners at the time found it hard to believe that such a great orator had once been a slave.

Sojourner Truth was born into slavery in New York and became an important voice in the fight for racial and gender equality. Truth escaped slavery in 1827 and may be best known for her speech "Ain't I a Woman?" delivered at the Ohio Women's Rights Convention in 1851.

John Brown was a radical abolitionist who organized various raids and uprisings, including an infamous raid on the federal armory at Harpers Ferry, Virginia. He advocated that speeches, sermons, and petitions were accomplishing nothing, that moral persuasions were hopeless, and saw violence as unfortunately necessary if slavery in the United States were to be eliminated.

Harriet Tubman was a fugitive slave and abolitionist who was known for helping escaped slaves reach the North via the Underground Railroad network. Tubman risked her life to lead hundreds of family members and other slaves from the plantation system to freedom on this elaborate secret network of safe houses. A leading abolitionist before the American Civil War, Tubman also helped the Union Army during the war, working as a spy, among other roles.

Not all Christians of European ancestry agreed with the dehumanization and cruelty meted out to the slaves by their slave owning colleges and the state legislatures that protect them. During this era of conflict, between Christians who were facilitating the brutality of slavery and those Christians who saw slavery as ungodly and inhumane, whose side was God on? The only gospel the slaves heard preached to them was that which pacified them by telling them that the only way they can go to heaven was to obey and show reverence to their masters. The slave masters probably never heard a word of admonition from the clergies about the atrocities meted out to the slaves. God did not even make the clergies preach his authentic words. Why?

If God could send down plagues to change the mind of the pharaoh to free the Egyptian slaves, as the Bible said he did, why could he not do something to free the people the European enslaved? Or is that story just another myth? Did God just allow this to happen for hundreds of years while our pee-pee-cluck-cluck mentality continues to tell us how loving and kind God is to us?

Jim Crow in America

The following is an introductory passage from a PBS article about Jim Crow in the United States of America:

> *{The segregation and disenfranchisement laws known as "Jim Crow" represented a formal, codified system of racial apartheid that dominated the American South for three quarters of a century beginning in the 1890s. The laws affected almost every aspect of daily life, mandating segregation of schools, parks, libraries, drinking fountains, restrooms, buses, trains, and restaurants. "Whites Only" and "Colored" signs were constant reminders of the enforced racial order.}*

Legally and in theory, blacks were supposed to be treated separately but equally. This has rarely ever happened. Facilities for black people were always inferior to that of white people if they existed at all. Blacks were systematically denied the right to vote in most parts of the Southern States by the use of contrived tests, intimidation, and other draconian means.

The mentality that was pervasive in the Southern states, and to a lesser extent in the North, was that black people were inferior and that it was degrading for white people to coexist with them, that the only useful function of black people was to serve as slaves to enrich the European population. Blacks were to be treated much like you would treat mules. You have to "break in" black people as you would break in a mule to make it compliant to the master's command because Negroes were not any more intelligent than the mules.

Nineteenth-century Europeans and Americans, and still many who live today, were brainwashed by skewed information about European superiority and grandeur. This misinformation was also filtered down to all of us who are influenced by European culture. They did not know that there were universities and other institutions of higher learning in Africa at the time when Europeans were in the Dark Ages, slaughtering one another in endless wars. They did not know that when Africans were studying physics, mathematics, medicine, astronomy, and the arts, Europeans were imprisoning scientists for daring to say that Earth is not the center of the universe. They did not know that the riches and opulence of Europe is derived from tons of gold, diamonds, and other resources expropriated from Africa. There are many estimates that put the value of this looting and expropriation of gold, diamond, and other African commodities at tens of trillions of US dollars, after the necessary appreciation in value and accrued interest is applied. They did not know that the weaponization of a Chinese invention, the gun powder, and the weaponization of Christianity, coupled with their passion for wars and conquests, gave them a distinct advantage in the conquests of other civilizations. They did not know that the science, arts, and hygiene that they eventually embraced had its origin in Africa and were taken to Europe by the Moors who were black people from Africa. They did not know that the dark color of a person's skin is a pigmentation that prevents skin cancer.

The following article is an excerpt from a publication by the Library of Congress titled: "Jim Crow and Segregation". The article is from a collection prepared to assist teachers in classrooms.

> {With the Compromise of 1877, political power was returned to Southern whites in nearly every state of the former Confederacy. The federal government abandoned attempts to enforce the 14th and 15th amendments in many parts of the country. By 1890, when Mississippi added a disfranchisement provision to its state constitution, the legalization of Jim Crow had begun.
>
> Jim Crow was not enacted as a universal, written law of the land. Instead, a patchwork of state and local laws, codes, and agreements enforced segregation to different degrees and in different ways across the nation. In many towns and cities, ordinances designated white and black neighborhoods, while in others covenants and unwritten agreements among real estate

interests maintained residential segregation. African Americans were denied the right to vote by onerous poll taxes, unfairly applied tests, and other unjust barriers. The signs we associate today with Jim Crow—"Whites Only," "Colored"— appeared at bus stations, water fountains and rest rooms, as well as at the entrances and exits to public buildings. Hotels, movie theaters, arenas, night clubs, restaurants, churches, hospitals, and schools were segregated, and interracial marriages outlawed. Segregation was not limited to African Americans, but often applied to other non-white Americans.

Segregation was often maintained by uniformed law enforcement. In other instances, it was enforced by armed white mobs and violent attacks by anonymous vigilantes. African Americans resisted these pervasive restrictions using many different strategies, from public advocacy and political activism to individual self-defense and attempts to escape to a better life. In the century following the end of Reconstruction, millions of African Americans moved away from the South in what became known as the Great Migration, only to discover that they faced discrimination in the northern states.

In the middle of the twentieth century, generations of resistance to segregation culminated in the Civil Rights movement, in which African Americans launched widespread demonstrations and other public protests to demand the rights and protections

provided by the Constitution. As a result, a series
of landmark court cases and new legislation in
the 1950s and 60s, including the Civil Rights
Act of 1964 and the Voting Rights Act of 1965,
relegated many of the Jim Crow laws and practices
of the previous century to the dustbin of history.
The impact of a century of segregation can still be
felt today, and, although the specific segregation
policies of the 19th and 20th centuries have been
discredited, voices calling for equal rights for all
can still be heard today.}

(In June of 2013 the Supreme Court effectively struck down
the heart of the Voting Right Act of 1965, freeing nine states,
mostly in the South, to change their election laws without
advanced federal approval. Since then, there has been a frenzy
of laws passed and proposed by various states to make it more
difficult for black people to vote).

Jim Crow was more than a series of rigid anti-black laws. It
was a way of life. Under Jim Crow, African Americans were
relegated to the status of second class citizens. Jim Crow was the
legitimization of anti-black racism. It was enforced vigorously
by law enforcement officers and vigilante groups. In addition, it
was upheld and endorsed by the majority of the white citizenry.
Many Christian ministers and theologians taught that whites
were God's chosen people and blacks were cursed to be servants.
They taught that God supported racial segregation. Educators
at every level in the academic systems promoted the belief that
blacks were innately, intellectually, and culturally inferior to
whites. Pro-segregation politicians gave eloquent speeches on
the great danger of integration which would mongrelize the
white race. Newspaper and magazine writers routinely referred

to blacks as niggers, coons, and darkies. Their articles routinely reinforced anti-black stereotypes.

The saddest part of the Jim Crow era was the vitriol with which it was implemented. Hate and inhumanity was pervasive among the white population toward the black population. As recently as in the 1990s, graffiti dehumanizing and abusing black people were frequently encountered in public places, such as restrooms, were offensive and sickening. There was no discernable rational reason why this hatred should exist. Africans were brought to America involuntarily and in chains against their will by Europeans. They spent their lives creating wealth for the European diaspora in the New World, tens of trillions of dollars in today's USA dollars. Why there was so much hatred is unfathomable.

When Jim Crow is examined in the context of religion, it becomes even more perplexing. How could people who practiced devout Christianity, who sang with such passion,

> *"All things bright and beautiful, All creatures great and small, All things wise and wonderful, The Lord God made them all,"*

were so filled with hatred, unleashing such a level of cruelty on other creatures, even if in their mind, these creatures were not human? They used religion to rationalize their behavior. We have seen where the biblical story of Ham was used to create the narrative that black people are cursed by God and condemned to be slaves. We have seen several examples where religion was used to motivate people to do ungodly things or to pacify people into hopeless servitude. The Africans had adopted the bastardized Christianity that was preached to them. They sang about looking over Jordan and seeing a holy band of angels "coming for to carry me home." Alas! That band of angels never came. A more ethereal ploy was also employed, one which the slaves had to accept by faith (that is, they had to believe it without any material evidence) that "if you obey your master unconditionally, when you die, you will go to heaven and live with the Holy Father in eternal paradise." In spite of their supplications, the Holy Father never came to their rescue. All the material and physical evidence pointed to the indifference of God to their suffering and despair, yet they were being asked to accept by faith (no evidence) that if they meekly obeyed their masters, the Heavenly Father would provide for them a place in this mystical heaven. Is it that God is indifferent, or is it that God is not the loving, merciful, protective, and benevolent entity that we make him out to be, but an inanimate, impassionate entity? About 13 million slaves were kidnapped from Africa and forced into involuntary servitude and brutality, and God did not raise a finger to stop the injustice.

"Black Codes" were strict local and state laws that detailed when, where, and how formerly enslaved people could work and for how much compensation. The codes appeared throughout the South as a legal way to keep black citizens in an inferior and second class status, to take voting rights away, and to control where they lived and how they traveled.

State laws and local ordinances ensured that the legal system was stacked against black citizens, with former Confederate soldiers working as police and judges, making it difficult for African Americans to win court cases. One of the most ruthless organizations of the Jim Crow era was the Ku Klux Klan (KKK). It was founded in 1865 in Pulaski, Tennessee, as a private club for Confederate veterans. The KKK grew into a secret society terrorizing black communities and permeating the white Southern culture with its members at the highest levels of government and in the lowest echelons of criminal back alleys.

Laws forbade African Americans from living in white neighborhoods. Segregation was enforced for public pools, phone booths, hospitals, asylums, jails, and residential homes for the elderly and handicapped. The North was not immune to Jim Crow-like laws. Some states required black people to own property before they could vote, a catch-22 situation since preventing black people from owning property was another objective of the Jim Crow policy. Schools and neighborhoods were segregated, and businesses displayed "Whites Only" signs. Jim Crow laws were not designed just to segregate blacks from white, but it also ensured that blacks were dehumanized and continued to live in poverty. It also created the falsehood that blacks were less intelligent and less able to acquire "culture" than white people.

Given that law enforcement officers were complicit with the hate groups that terrorized blacks, most of the atrocities against black people were not prosecuted. One of the terror tactics used by these uncivilized whites was lynching, where for simple infractions or misdemeanors, black men or women would be strung up on trees, hanged, their bodies mutilated, and the corpse left for public viewing for days. A white audience would be invited to enjoy the spectacle. Even children were invited to watch. Most of these same people would be in church next Sunday, worshipping God.

Lynching in America

A black person growing up in the Southern States in the 19th and 20th century lived their lives in fear of the terror tactics called lynching. It was the major tool of a society where the law of the land was to maintain white supremacy and keep black people in a state of subservience and powerlessness, where killing a black person wantonly was met with glee and acclamation by the majority of the white population. Lynching, an act of terror meant to spread fear among blacks, served the broad social purpose of maintaining white supremacy in the economic, social and political spheres.

Lynchings were frequently committed in an atmosphere of celebration like executions by guillotine in medieval times; lynchings were often advertised in newspapers and drew large crowds of white families. They were a kind of vigilantism where Southern white men saw themselves as protectors of their way of life and their white women. By the early 20th century, the writer Mark Twain had a name for it: the United States of Lyncherdom.

Lynching gained momentum during Reconstruction, when viable black towns sprang up across the South and African Americans began to make political and economic inroads by registering to vote, establishing businesses, and running for public office. Consequently, the majority of the white citizenry felt threatened by this rise in black prominence. Foremost on their minds was a fear of sex between the races. Some whites espoused the idea that black men were sexual predators and wanted integration in order to be with white women.

Lynchings were covered in local newspapers with headlines spelling out the horrific details. Photos of victims, with exultant white observers posed next to them, were taken for distribution in newspapers or on postcards. Body parts, including genitalia, were sometimes distributed to spectators, or put on public display. Most infractions were for petty crimes, like theft, but the biggest one of all was looking at or associating with white women. Many victims were black businessmen, or black men who refused to back down from a fight. Headlines such as the following were common:

"Five White Men Take Negro Into Woods; Kill Him: Had Been Charged with Associating with White Women" went over The Associated Press wires about a lynching in Shreveport, Louisiana.

"Negro Is Slain By Texas Posse: Victim's Heart Removed After His Capture By Armed Men" was published in The New York World Telegram on December 8, 1933.

"Negro and White Scuffle; Negro Is Jailed, Lynched" was published in the Atlanta Constitution on July 6, 1933.

Newspapers even printed that prominent white citizens in local towns attended lynchings, and often published victory pictures—smiling crowds, many with children in tow—standing next to the corpse.

Although rape is often cited as a rationale, statistics now show that only about one-fourth of lynchings from 1880 to 1930 were prompted by an accusation of rape. In fact, most victims of lynching were political activists, labor organizers or black men and women who failed to behave as the white establishment expected of them. They were deemed "uppity" or "insolent." Though most victims were black men, women were by no means exempt.

According to black journalist and editor Ida B. Wells, who launched a fierce anti-lynching campaign in the 1890s, the lynching of successful black people was a means of subordinating potential black economic competitors. She also argued that consensual sex between black men and white women, while forbidden, was widespread. Thus lynching was also a means of imposing order on white women's sexuality. Wells, who would later help found the National Association for the Advancement of Colored People, was forced to flee Memphis after her offices were torched.

At the National Memorial for Peace and Justice, in Montgomery, Alabama., there is an area with 805 hanging steel rectangles, the size and shape of coffins. These steel plates represent each of the counties (and their states) where a documented lynching took place in the United States.

More than 4,075 documented lynching of African Americans took place between 1877 and 1950, concentrated in twelve Southern states, as compiled in the Equal Justice Initiative (EJI) study, *Lynching in America: Confronting the Legacy of Racial Terror.*

The number of African Americans killed by white supremacists as recorded in this museum is horrifying, but even more so are the circumstances of individual lynching, some described in brief summaries along the walk:

""Parks Banks, lynched in Mississippi in 1922 for carrying a photograph of a white woman";

"Caleb Gladly, hanged in Kentucky in 1894 for walking behind the wife of his white employer;"

"Mary Turner, who after denouncing her husband's lynching by a rampaging white mob, was hung upside down, burned and then sliced open so that her unborn child fell to the ground."

This was the state of the Christianity practiced in America. The same people who lynched a black man for walking behind a white woman, and those who hung the woman upside down for denouncing her husband's lynching, set her on fire, and then disemboweled her so that the unborn baby in her womb fell out of her gut to the ground; these same people, more than likely put on their Sunday best on Sunday morning and went to church to praise God for the privilege and satisfaction to kill other human beings without consequence, and the supreme authority he gave to them to do so. This is what they must have convinced themselves.

What of the loving and merciful God we serve? The people who committed or condoned these wanton atrocities considered themselves Christians and were convinced that they were such because they suffered no consequence for their evil deeds. It is inevitable that they had concluded that if they were doing something wrong, God would have punished them. They must have believed that their atrocities were in the ambit of God's moral law; otherwise, how come they were still so prosperous and "superior" to black people, whereas God had done nothing to protect other races of people?

With lynching as a violent backdrop in the South, Jim Crow as the law of the land, and the poverty of the sharecropper system, blacks had no recourse. This triage of repression ensured blacks would remain impoverished, endangered, and without rights or hope. White people could accuse blacks at will and have them lynched, rarely was a white person punished for a crime committed against a black person. Even for those whites who were opposed to lynching and Jim Crow in general, there was not much they could do to ensure justice. If there was an investigation, white citizens closed ranks to protect their own and rarely were mob leaders identified.

The desire to keep African Americans as second-class citizens was not only on an individual level but was also on a community scale. Whole communities were destroyed, usually by fire, if it were perceived by the white vigilantes and their enablers that the community was prospering. One community that suffered such unfortunate fate was Greenwood, Tulsa, Oklahoma, USA.

According to a *New York Times* article published on June 20, 2020,

> {*On May 30, 1921, the Greenwood district of Tulsa, Oklahoma, was a thriving black community: a rarity in an era of lynchings, segregation and a rapidly growing Ku Klux Klan. By sunrise on June 2, Greenwood lay in ruins: burned to the ground by a mob of white people, aided and abetted by the National Guard, in one of the worst acts of racial violence in American history.*}

The Greenwood massacre has been called the single worst incident of racial violence in American history. The white residents were deputized and given arms by city officials. The attack, carried out on the ground and from private aircraft dropping incendiary bombs, destroyed more than thirty-five square blocks of the district, at that time the wealthiest black community in the United States, known as Black Wall Street.

It is estimated that over three hundred people were killed and several hundred injured. About ten thousand black people were left homeless, and property damage amounted to more than $1.5 million in real estate and $750,000 in personal property (equivalent to $32.25 million in 2019).

The destruction and massacre were triggered by an easily-resolvable issue, which goes to show that the white marauders were just spoiling for a fight, an excuse to burn Greenwood. A white female reported that a black man assaulted her. The black man was jailed and was scheduled to be lynched. A group of black men from Greenwood went to the jailhouse where the black man was held, to plead his case with the court officers. The court officers assured the men that they would do what they could to stop the lynching. When the group of black men were leaving the courthouse, they were attacked by a group of marauders and a fight ensued. This led to the destruction of Greenwood.

Greenwood was not the only prosperous African American community to be torched and destroyed by white mobs.

In the summer of 1917, dubbed Red Summer, white mobs attacked the residents of East St. Louis, Illinois. The city was burned to the ground. The carnage raged for three days and nights, leaving as many as thirty-nine black people and nine white people dead. The East St. Louis massacre launched a reign of racial terror throughout the United States that historians say stretched from 1917 to 1923, when the all-black town of Rosewood, Florida, was destroyed. During that period, at least ninety-seven lynching were recorded, thousands of black people were killed, and thousands of black-owned homes and businesses were burned to the ground. Fire and fury fueled massacres in at least twenty-six cities, including Washington, DC; Chicago, Illinois; Omaha, Nebraska; Elaine, Arkansas; Charleston, South Carolina; Columbia, Tennessee; Houston, Texas; and Tulsa, Oklahoma.

In spite of the Fourteenth and Fifteenth Amendments to the Constitution of the United States and civil rights laws passed in the '60s, Jim Crow practices were still pervasive in the USA, especially in the Southern states. This promoted a series of civil rights activities and court actions by African Americans and white sympathizers of black civil rights movement.

Spearheaded by the National Association for the Advancement of Colored People (NAACP), the growing civil rights movement initiated lawsuits to undermine the legal foundation of Jim Crow segregation in the South. The landmark *Brown versus Board of Education of Topeka* ruling held that separate facilities were inherently unequal and, thereby, declared segregation in public education to be unconstitutional. There was massive and acrimonious opposition to this ruling. In 1963, Gov. George Wallace of Alabama was to be seen blocking the door of the University of Alabama, proclaiming, "Segregation today ... Segregation tomorrow ... Segregation forever." The occasion was a vehement opposition to two black students who were scheduled to start attending that university. Authorities in the South actively resisted federal court orders to desegregate;

therefore, some leaders of the civil rights movement turned to direct action and nonviolent civil disobedience.

To protest the inhumane treatment and inferior public facilities for blacks, civil rights leaders led by Dr. Martin Luther King Jr. organized a bus boycott in Montgomery, Alabama. Civil rights activists launched the Montgomery Bus boycott in 1955 after Rosa Parks, an African American woman, refused to vacate her seat on a bus for a white person. Dr. Martin Luther King, Jr. emerged as a leader of the boycott. It was the first mass direct action of the civil rights movement and provided a template for activists across the country. The boycott took place from December 5, 1955, to December 20, 1956, and is regarded as the first large-scale U.S. demonstration against segregation.

Approximately forty thousand black bus riders, the majority of the city's bus riders, boycotted the system. They met to form the Montgomery Improvement Association (MIA). The group elected Martin Luther King, Jr., the twenty-six-year-old pastor of Montgomery's Dexter Avenue Baptist Church, as its president and decided to continue the boycott until the city met its demands.

Although African Americans represented at least 75 percent of Montgomery's bus ridership, the city resisted complying with the protesters' demands. To ensure the boycott could be sustained, black leaders organized carpools, and the city's African American taxi drivers charged only 10 cents, the same price as bus fare, for African American riders. Many black residents chose simply to walk to work or other destinations. Black leaders organized regular mass meetings to keep African American residents mobilized around the boycott.

Freedom riders took on the task of desegregating public transportation services and facilities. Images of freedom riders being beaten and hospitalized for daring to ride into Southern states in the "white only" section of interstate busses shocked the nation. Busses that they were riding in were burned. The riders were mercilessly beaten by angry white mobs while the police and other law enforcement conveniently absented themselves. This was happening even after federal laws were passed in 1960 that declared segregated facilities for interstate passengers illegal.

Marches were a potent tool used by the civil rights movement to expose the inhumane conditions that African Americans were subjected to. The most significant of these was the march on Washington, which was a massive protest march that occurred in August 1963. About 250,000 people gathered in front of the Lincoln Memorial in Washington, DC. The aim of this event was to draw attention to continuing obstacles and inequalities faced by African Americans a century after emancipation. It was also the occasion of Martin Luther King, Jr.'s now-iconic "I Have a Dream" speech.

There were other notable marches staged by African Americans to highlight the struggle to gain a modicum of equality and respect in the United States of America. In each case, they were beaten and brutalized by law enforcement and thugs.

On March 7, 1965, the then twenty-five-year-old activist John Lewis attempted to lead over six hundred marchers across the Edmund Pettus Bridge in Selma, Alabama. The marchers came under brutal attacks by state troopers and local law enforcement. Batons, dogs, and water jets from high-pressure fire hoses were used on the marchers. John Lewis, who organized the march and who lived to become a United States congressman, was savagely beaten and managed to survive a fractured skull. Footage of the violence collectively shocked the nation and galvanized the fight against racial injustice.

It would be remiss not to mention the part played by white people of conscience in this struggle. White civil rights activists joined blacks, not only in marches, but also as "freedom riders" and volunteers to register people to vote. They were beaten and bludgeoned as much as the African Americans. A typical example of this was the brutal murder of three civil rights workers in Neshoba County in Mississippi. Two of them were white men from New York, Michael Schwerner and Andrew Goodman, working with the Congress of Racial Equality (CORE). The third was James Chaney, a local CORE worker.

On June 21, 1964, the three men went to investigate the burning of a church in Neshoba, Mississippi. That was the last time they were seen alive by their comrades. As court documents revealed, the three men were apprehended on their way back from the investigation by a deputy county sheriff who was also a ringleader of the Ku Klux Klan. They were taken to jail, released, then recaptured by the same sheriff deputy, this time with a posse of other KKK members. They took the civil rights workers to an earthen dam where they killed them and buried their bodies in a shallow grave.

This case would have been just another case of "three men missing," were it now for the relentless effort of the FBI. State and local law enforcement did very little to apprehend the perpetrators of this crime. On October 27, 1967, seven of those indicted by the FBI, including the deputy sheriff, were found guilty.

After someone becomes aware of all these wanton cases of injustice, murder and oppression spanning hundreds of years and causing millions of deaths and dehumanization of innocent people, how can anyone still hold on to the conviction that there is a loving and caring God protecting us? The doctrine of the secular humanist does not have to straddle this dilemma.

Bigotry, personal and institutional, still pervades the American society. Most of it is subtle and exists as unconscious bias. It is expressed in the vast disparity in the average wealth between black and white households.

The following is an excerpt from an article posted by the Brookings Institute in February 2020 titled "Examining the Black-White Wealth Gap":

> {A close examination of wealth in the U.S. finds evidence of staggering racial disparities. At $171,000, the net worth of a typical white family is nearly ten times greater than that of a Black family ($17,150) in 2016. Gaps in wealth between Black and white households reveal the effects of accumulated inequality and discrimination, as well as differences in power and opportunity that can be traced back to this nation's inception.}

This disparity has its origin in the Jim Crow system. As we have seen that in the past, black communities that attempted to become prosperous were simply burned down. A system called redlining was practiced in the USA from the federal government down to the lowest level of real estate agents. For decades, many banks in the United States disproportionately denied mortgages loans to people living in black neighborhoods compared to loans given to people in white neighborhoods. The banks, along with realtors, actively screened people of color to prevent them from owning property in white neighborhoods, thus corralling people of color into depressed neighborhoods. In addition, people in black neighborhoods found it much harder to get loans from the banks even if they have the same collateral as a person in a white neighborhood. The US government once backed this policy that started in the 1930s and took place across the country. This included many of the nation's largest cities, such as Atlanta, Chicago, Detroit, Tampa, and others with large minority populations.

In these neighborhoods, job opportunities are scarce, wages are low, morale and self-esteem are low. Since schools are funded from local resources, facilities that promote better education in schools are always inferior to schools in white neighborhoods. Therein lies this vicious cycle of poverty and low self-esteem that plague the black neighborhoods. There are people who pull themselves up by the bootstraps, but in most cases, there are neither boots nor straps to make this happen.

During the Bill Clinton presidency, legislations were enacted to outlaw redlining to bring about some equality in the financial sector, but the banking community saw this as an opportunity to capitalize on these legislations. They saw this as a bonanza to rake in money. They reacted in a very bizarre way that led to one of the worst financial catastrophes in the history of the USA. They abandoned the principle of carefully vetting borrowers and gave mortgage loans to people who asked and those who did not ask for loans. They gave loans to people who had little or no collateral and very little means of paying off the loan. These people got unsolicited letters in their mail, inviting them to apply for mortgages or home equity loans. This is not unusual, except that those who were not qualified also got loans. The bankers packaged these so-called subprime loans into discrete bundles, then they came up with some fraudulent equation to beguile investors that they were making genuine investment when they bought these subprime loan packages. It was not long before the house of cards came tumbling down. Most of these properties purchased with little or no collateral went onto foreclosure. Home equity loans with weak collateral suffered the same fate. This racketeering scheme resulted in one of the worst financial catastrophes in the history of the world.

CHAPTER 4

BIAS, BIGOTRY, AND RELIGION

Activism for Good or Evil

The struggle against racial injustice was not only in the United States. Mahatma Gandhi and his followers encountered a similar struggle in South Africa and India. In South Africa, the apartheid regime inflicted incalculable economic and inhumane suffering on the Native Africans. Nelson Mandela was a legendary freedom fighter against Apartheid in South Africa.

African Americans were not the only ethnic group to suffer from the atrocities of European in the United States of America. A partial genocide was inflicted on the Native Americans. When the Pilgrim Fathers landed at Plymouth Harbor, Massachusetts, in 1620, the natives welcomed them, helped them to survive and to establish their colony. This provoked two questions: If the natives could have foreseen the brutality in the hearts of these newcomers, wouldn't they have slaughtered them there and then instead of welcoming and helping them? Conversely, if a boatload of Native Americans made their way to any port in Europe in 1620 and declared that they were there to establish a colony, wouldn't they be slaughtered immediately? The answer to these questions exposes the innate nature of these two cultures.

The following is an excerpt from the History Channel:

> {North American colonists' warfare against Native Americans often was horrifyingly brutal. But one method they appear to have used—perhaps just once— shocks even more than all the bloody slaughter: The gifting of blankets and linens contaminated with smallpox. The virus causes a disease that can inflict disfiguring scars, blindness, and death.}

There are numerous credible historical accounts that European settlers gave blankets intentionally contaminated with smallpox to the Native Americans. This action was in effect a primitive form of biological warfare.

Before the European Americans started to expand into the central plains, there were more than 500 million buffalos roaming the great planes. These buffalos were the lifeblood of the Native Americans. They depended on these animals completely. Every part of the buffalo was used to supply the needs of the Native Americans. Buffalo skins were used to make tepees, clothes, moccasins, bedding, bags, baskets, saddle covers, and water bags. Dried buffalo dung provided fuel for fires. Buffalo horns and hooves were made into cups.

The European Americans were aware of this dependency. They systematically exterminated the buffalos by whatever means necessary, poison and mass shootings being the main method. In a few decades, the 500 million buffalos were exterminated, except for a few hundreds. This was the beginning of the complete subjugation of the Native Americans. The dehumanization of Native Americans and the expropriation of their land continued without abating to the extent that most of them now live on substandard reservations.

During the 1980s, I lived in Chicago for a number of years. For some time, I had to travel each weekday from the South Side of Chicago to the North Side using the L train or the city bus as my mode of transportation. On my way each day, I had to pass by a rundown community with decrepit buildings and all the other signs of decadence of mind and material assets.

As the weeks went by, I noticed that demolition equipment was brought in, and the decrepit old buildings were being cleared out. It was not long before elegant new middle and lower-income housing units started to grace the skyline. The edifice of a church was also erected to grace the skyline. I found out later that a church community had initiated this project. With the help of the city government, they had undertaken the urban renewal of several rundown city blocks and transformed it into a proud community with residents of high self-esteem. Flowers and food gardens were springing up everywhere. If I had the opportunity to meet the residents of that community, I am sure their story would have been that of revitalization and spiritual renewal. I am sure they would tell me that their children were doing better academically and in their social environment at home.

This church group was demonstrating the potential of a religious organization to be a source of inspiration and progress in a community. By virtue of being a church organization, they had the passion and the energy that made things happen, and it was much easier for them to organize and concentrate that energy into endeavors that benefited the community.

Many existential changes in history were initiated by religious groups. Religious leaders like Dr. Martin Luther King Jr. and Mahatma Gandhi are examples of these visionary leaders. You also have religious leaders who squander these opportunities while they build mega-churches and fly around the world in Learjets. The influence of religion can also be pernicious. Religion has done a lot to facilitate the transatlantic slave trade, to brutalize the slaves, and perpetuate the carnage of the Native American and Native Caribbean people. Remember the travesty of King Leopard going to the Congo to "Christianize" the Congolese people but ended up slaughtering 10 million of them and pillaged the resources of the Congo? Leopold was not the only villain; the British, Spaniards, Portuguese, French, and Germans committed gruesome atrocities in their so-called colonies with the blessing and in the name of their religion.

The god gene of the Europeans and Americans seems to be expressed in the brutality and exploitation of people of other cultures. Jesus Christ was transformed by Europeans from a pious Palestinian preacher, who believed in feeding the poor and loving your neighbor, to a blue-eyed Caucasian, whose followers sided with slavery, genocide, and brutality. Christianity was bastardized from what Jesus Christ and his disciples intended, to serve the cause of rapacious capitalism, colonialism, brutality, and dehumanization of people of other cultures.

Did God allow or cause people of European ancestry to dehumanize and brutalize people of African ancestry? We recognize that this form of oppression happens among other cultures, but the scope of this book is not wide enough to cover the whole spectrum of man's inhumanity to man, so we have to concentrate on the atrocity that is affecting or has affected us directly.

Religion has been the arbiter that has defined our perception of everything in the universe ever since humans acquired the ability to think. This was necessarily so because our ability to prove, or at least to logically rationalize what we imagined, was still infantile. Science was not in existence at that time. Our primordial minds imagined that everything happened because a god commanded it to happen, and that the gods had the mental and physical attributes of human beings, but were infinitely more powerful. Then science gradually made its way into the human experience and found that there is a natural law that governs the existence of everything. The only problem is that this natural law is completely neutral to human sensibilities, it does not respond to what humans wish or pray for.

This primordial mindset is static, it does not change as new knowledge is acquired. Because of this mindset, the Roman Catholic Church, which was the de facto ruler of what used to be the Roman Empire, convicted Galileo Galilei and sentenced him to house arrest for the rest of his life for daring to write that the Earth is not the center of the universe. This same mindset is denying Darwinian evolution and is impeding research into the mutation and treatment of pathogens. This same mindset is denying that human activities are increasing the average temperature of the earth which is causing devastating climate changes. This mindset is generally anti-science because the proponents are generally pro-religion.

To contemplate what role God plays in this scheme of things, one will first have to define his or her concept of God. Some people believe that God is an anthropomorphic being, that is, God has human attributes, even though these attributes are infinitely more powerful than the human attributes. It is believed that he can listen to and empathize with our prayers and other individual emotional situations. It is believed that he can punish us for doing something wrong or reward us for doing something right. Bear in mind that "right and wrong" is an arbitrary concept. What is right in one culture may not be right in another culture. This mindset empowers some group of people to fight and kill in the name of religion, and to believe that it is justifiable to commit atrocities and claim that they are doing it in the name of God.

It is scary for anyone to be subservient to the doctrine of a deity that can only be experienced by blind faith in what an ancient guru postulated, or an ancient Pope decreed; where people believe something even though it is totally illogical, just because an old guru or an old pope said so; where the only backup one has to determine what is true from what is fake is his or her own imperfect mind. It is obvious to any free thinker that this failure to logically evaluate situations makes it easier for despots, cult leaders, and conspiracy theorists to control our lives.

On the other hand, there are those who believe strongly that God (or whatever you name your divine deity) is one and the same as Mother Nature, that there are natural, physical, not supernatural, forces that cause rain to fall or flowers to bloom, lightning to flash and thunder to blast, that cause people to get sick and die or recover from illness. They may believe strongly that these forces are the forces that dictate the laws of physics and chemistry. They know that they are yet to learn what these mysterious forces are. They know that they are yet to understand what caused life to happen, but they also know that to imagine how it happened and then assume that what they imagine is reality, is borderline insanity. They believe that love and hate, bigotry and tolerance, passion and passivity, anger and happiness are the consequences of their actions, their culture, and their genetics, not a curse or blessing from God.

People Are Not Born with Bigotry

There was a time in Jamaica's colonial history when the British colonial masters tried to "whiten" the population. Leading up to the emancipation of slavery in 1834, the white colonial masters were wary that the black population had outnumbered whites by a considerable margin, and if there were a general revolution, they would be at great disadvantage.

By 1850, the black Jamaican population outnumbered the white population by a ratio of twenty to one. Enslaved Jamaicans mounted over a dozen major uprisings during the eighteenth century. The colonial government was afraid, so they decided to solve this problem by "whitening" the population of the country. The colonial government gave Europeans very generous incentives to settle in Jamaica. Land and money were given to Europeans who wanted to settle on the island. As a result of this policy of the colonial government, if you visited Seaford Town in Westmoreland, Jamaica, in the early and mid-1900s, you would think that you were in a village in Germany. The houses and churches were German architecture. The inhabitants were mostly white Catholic Germans. These white villagers in the middle of an island consisting of mostly black people lived in peace and harmony without fear of persecution. Because of interracial marriage and migration, this ethnic community is no more as unique in Jamaica as it used to be.

In addition to these groups who were given special treatment, there were also other Europeans, Chinese, and Indian indentured servants. Another significant group that came to Jamaica in the post-slavery era were refugees seeking refuge from political and religious persecution in Europe. When Jews were refused entry into the USA and other countries, they were welcomed in Jamaica. Because of this experience, Jamaica evolved into a multiracial community where you will not find much racial bigotry as I have experienced in the USA, for example.

I grew up in a community in Jamaica where a minority of white people had settled from about the middle 1800s. They were mostly Jews, English, Irish, or Scottish. There were even more who were light-skinned mixed race also called mulattos. This group of white people lost their ethnic identity a few generations before my time. Some of them had eyes as blue as old blue-eyed Frank Sinatra and skin probably whiter than his. If you asked them their ethnicity, they would say, "Jamaican." The fact that their ancestors were of a different culture was a vague and distant concept to them. They have no other identity but Jamaican.

The following story will illustrate this situation. A multibillion aluminum ore-processing plant was built in Jamaica in the late 1960s by Kaiser Aluminum Co. This plant processed bauxite, the ore from which aluminum is produced. Local people and foreign expatriates were employed at this plant. One day at the cafeteria, a white American man bought his lunch and shared a table with another white man. The American was new and was anxious to make acquaintance with more seasoned workers. He started a conversation by asking his table companion, "Say, how long have you been in Jamaica?"

His table companion replied, "A ya me baan ah grow sah."

The American was somewhat confused, and after a few moments of ponderous thoughts because he did not understand the lingo, he asked, "Could you say that again?"

The other man repeated, "A ya me baan ah grow sah."

This other man was a white Jamaican who felt more comfortable responding in his Native Jamaican dialect. He understood, but was not fluent in speaking American English. The translation of his reply to the American was "I was born and grown up here."

Needless to say, this white American was surprised to find a white Jamaican whose lineage was Jamaican all the way back to his great grandparents.

Our community was rural; therefore, there was not much intermingling of our people with people in urban communities; therefore, the culture remained undiluted for a long time. Even though the community was rural, there were institutions, such as schools, churches, post offices, police stations, and other government agencies that provided health care, agricultural extension services, and other amenities. Local professionals, such as carpenters, masons, shoemakers, tailors, and seamstresses, saw their role as providing service to the community rather than trying to enrich themselves.

The people in our community, black and white, were poor. They were poor in terms of traditional Western standards but rich in human values. Back then, in our community, a person's value in life was not measured in terms of material possessions but how caring they were to other people and the honesty and other humanitarian values they practiced.

The white people in our community did not know about white privilege and did not expect any privilege because of their color. Neither black nor white exhibited any color prejudice, superiority complex nor inferiority complex with regard to the way they interacted with their neighbors of a different color. The young men and not-so-young men, black and white, sat together on bar stools, sipping White Rum, or playing dominos; sometimes sitting by the roadside commiserating. Blacks and whites participated in "morning sport," where people got together as a group and performed tasks, such as planting a field or doing construction work on their neighbor's house, all as community work for one another—without pay.

There were no homeless people in the community. A house owned by the family was the home for all the family members. When someone came of age, the parents would give him or her a plot of land at least big enough to build a house and to farm on. Renting was very rare. On the rare occasion when someone would leave home outside of the usual practice of marriage or cohabitation, friends or relatives would shelter him or her until he or she could acquire somewhere to live.

Enough food was never a problem; everyone planted enough food to feed his or her family and to offer some to anyone who ran short or to sell. Selling was the last option. The food we planted were yams of various varieties, sweet potato, Irish potato, cassava, banana, dasheen, badoo, coco, corn, gungo peas, red peas, green peas, black eye peas, various varieties of beans, and others that I cannot recall. The following animals were also raised to be sold or be eaten: cattle, goats, sheep, and poultry. Many members of the community were fishermen since a fishing village was nearby. Food supply was therefore, nearly 100 percent locally produced. Clothes were made by local tailors and dressmakers. Shoes were made by local shoemakers.

Fruits were various and abundant year round. There were mangoes, scores of different varieties. There were citrus fruits: oranges, tangerines, mandarins, grapefruits, sour oranges, limes, lemons, and ortaniques. There were otaheite apples, American apples, star apples, custard apples, rose apples, hog apples, sweetsops and soursops. There were jackfruits, bread fruits, passion fruits, guineps, and avocado pears. There were June plums, hog plums, red plums, yellow plums, cocoa nuts, cashew nuts, peanuts, papayas, pineapples, guavas, cherries, bird cherries, naseberries, strawberries, hog berries, stinking toes, tamarinds, grapes, and wild grapes. As for vegetables, we planted cabbage, cauliflower, turnip, carrot, cucumber, callaloo, okra, tomato, beet, and eggplant. Also grown for local consumption and for sale outside the community were coffee and pimento. Livestock, food, fruits, or vegetables not consumed within the community were sold outside.

People in our community generally observed the moral law which should be the hallmark of every religious experience. The Golden Rule which Jesus Christ espoused was generally practiced in our community. The story of the good Samaritan was well known and practiced often. Service to the communities was more important than selfishness and the accumulation of material wealth. Religion itself did not play a dominant role in ours or neighboring communities, even though there were many Christian denominations; namely, Presbyterian, Church of God, Roman Catholic, Moravian, Baptist, Seventh Day Adventist, Anglican, Jehovah's Witness, Rastafarian, and Pocomania. Even though many of the early immigrants into our community were Jews, Judaism was not a practiced religion there. This was probably because the early Jewish immigrants kept a low profile because they were butting up against the same religious group of people who were persecuting them in Europe. One hint of this scenario is the names of people on the headstones of an old Jewish cemetery in south Manchester, Jamaica. On most of these headstones you will find the names of people whose first names were Jewish, such as Abraham and Sarah, while their last (adopted) names were Spanish or Portuguese. If the people who eviscerated Africa, enslaved its people, and committed horrible atrocities in the Americas and the Caribbean had the kind of religious experience practiced in our community, what a wonderful world this could have been!

In summary, we were just a big happy family. There were no racial tensions, prejudices, or bigotry because our people were not born with it, did not inherit it, and did not learn it from anyone. Racial prejudice is not in one's DNA that is passed down from generation to regeneration. You learn it from the culture that nurtures you. One can also unlearn it by educating oneself and rejecting the misinformation and bigoted habits that have been acquired since infancy.

END

Another book by
Wilberforce Reid

My
Jamaican
Experience

My Personal Experience of the
Good Old Days, the Days of Wrath
and a Look at Our Future Challenges

by Wilberforce Reid

In this book, Wilberforce wrote about the natural beauty
of Jamaica, the warm culture of the Jamaican people, and
Jamaica's unique place in the history of international sports
and commerce. The book also tells the story of the era when
Jamaica was ground zero in the cold war between the CIA of
the United States and the KGB of the Soviet Union.

Lightning Source UK Ltd.
Milton Keynes UK
UKHW011832130921
390533UK00006B/349/J